Beyond The Widow's Peak

ASHLEY MCCONNELL

For those afraid of the dark, this won't help.

Beyond The Widow's Peak

CHAPTER 1

IVING IN THE MOUNTAINS OF NORTH CAROLINA YOUR entire life, you grow up hearing all the local folklore. There was Moth Man. Big Foot. The Moon-Eyed People. Even the Brown Mountain Lights. But none scared me more than the unknown of what lurked in the mountains under the cloak of darkness. When you live in the Appalachian Mountains, you're raised to close the blinds at night. Even if you hear something calling for help, no, you didn't, and you never went outside after sundown. On a cold winter evening twenty years ago, my elementary school best friend, Kendra, told me a story that *still* haunts me, today.

Harper Cooper moved from bustling New York City to the quaint North Carolina mountains in the mid-nineties with her parents and younger brother. Leaving her friends and way of living behind, she never felt settled. She always felt like she was being watched, even when no one was in sight. For the first few months, whenever she brought it up to her parents, they dismissed her concerns, telling her that she was getting used to a slower-paced lifestyle and that the feeling would go away. A year later, she still felt uneasy about the town but was making friends, so she ignored the gnawing feeling… until she couldn't anymore.

One Friday night, after a long week in high school, Harper and her friends wanted nothing more than to sit outside, enjoy a bonfire, and decompress. That was one perk of moving, Harper did enjoy. Living in the mountains, the nights were chilly, so she and her friends could enjoy bonfires year-round.

While walking towards the house, they heard a haunting noise that sounded like someone crying for help. Harper's instincts kicked in and she started running towards the cries in the woods, but before she could get to the tree line, her friends caught up and stopped her. They all returned to her house before the sun dipped below the trees and explained the Appalachian folklore of The Beast while sitting around the fire.

The story goes on to tell us on that very night, she felt more uneasy than usual and disregarded what her friends had previously told her. Harper opened her blinds to allow some of the spring-time moonlight in the pitch-black room to brighten it up. Laying there, she heard a woman wailing outside and immediately shut her eyes, afraid of what she might see if she peered over the windowsill and into the thickly wooded backyard.

The following day, while walking to school, the air felt unnaturally still, so Harper quickened her pace, nearly running into the building. The familiar routine of her day was disrupted as she made her way home by an unexpected sighting. In the woods, at the corner of her eyes, she caught a glimpse of a strange creature gazing at her with unfamiliar eyes. She sprinted home to tell her parents, recounting it was a giant being, about eight feet tall, with black skin, thick fur, hanging arms with long nails and white eyes. Her parents brushed it off, telling her it was most likely a bear or large wolf, and to stay inside.

The next day, Harper never made it to school. She left the

house at seven, and the school called her parents by ten, asking if she would be in. Visibly shaken, her parents told the school she had left at her usual time and should be there.

They filed a missing person's case immediately, and the search for Harper began. Unfortunately, we all know this story doesn't have a happy ending. Four long and emotionally draining days later, the search party found Harper's small frame, wholly mauled. Her parents and authorities attributed it to a large wild animal, but her friends knew better...

It was The Beast.

The story played back in my head as I sat in the sterile, cold police station, answering questions about a murder in which I was not involved. Fidgeting with an empty paper cup in front of me, desperate to escape the suffocating atmosphere. As sad as it is, people always go missing in the mountains. When novice hikers attempt these old mountains, they get lost and are never found.

What's not common, was Luke Anderson's disappearance and murder. He was found in the woods by the cabin, his body almost unrecognizable.

CHAPTER 2

Ten days ago

I'VE LOST COUNT OF THE NUMBER OF TIMES I'VE BEEN TOLD I shouldn't own a rental property. When I purchased a cabin in the North Carolina mountains two years ago, everyone in my family, and my friends thought I was crazy, but if I'm honest, most had valid concerns.

"*That place is run down. When will you have the time to renovate it?*"

"*You don't even know how to renovate homes; how will you do this?*"

"*That's going to be expensive, you know.*"

"*Cora, you have a job. Why do you need another source of income?*"

"*You don't know what kind of person might stay there. How can you ensure you're not inviting a serial killer to your home?*" That was my mom's primary concern.

I let everyone's thoughts cloud my mind at first, swirling until I had firmly decided against buying the home. A week went by, but I realized this would be a project that pushed me physically, mentally, and emotionally.

When I signed on the dotted line that fateful, warm August day, I knew I was embarking on my biggest project to date. I knew this was going to be much larger than any home renovation I had tackled before. Despite my previous experiences of redecorating rooms in my house, I was well aware of the cabin's massive renovation would require a completely different skill set. I work full-time from home as the Marketing Director for Alliteration, a large book publisher, so my days are filled with networking, strategizing ways to grow our customer reach, chatting with authors, and setting up book tours. I do more, but those are the aspects I enjoy the most; clearly, plumbing and electricity are *not* on the list.

Once the keys were in my hand, my adventure began. The first time I opened the door to the cabin, a rat ran out. At that moment, I wondered if I was in over my head.

I was thirty, single, and didn't exactly understand what a miter saw was, but I knew I needed to learn quickly. The cabin had been sitting empty for about a year when I purchased it, so, in addition to the horrible musty smell, the previous owner left absolutely everything. The rooms were filled with old furniture covered in spiderwebs, and there was rotting food in the unplugged-for-a-year refrigerator. I took inventory of everything in the house, deciding if there was anything worth salvaging. I saved one coffee table that was still in good shape, but everything else needed to go.

I took two weeks off to start the decluttering process and got to work. I rented a dumpster, and with the help of my friend, Isaac, we slowly emptied everything from the cabin. I swore he was in love with me because no one else would have spent their precious time, especially on weekends, helping me remove all the crap in that place.

Once I had a blank slate, I realized how in over my head I was. The windows weren't sealed, the floors creaked, the outlet in the spare bedroom sparked whenever anything was plugged in, and one of the toilets didn't flush.

To a trained home renovator, this would've been a breeze. For me, I was climbing Mount Everest.

It took two years of relying on Isaac and YouTube videos, but the cabin finally has functioning plumbing, electricity and looks brand new. I sanded and re-stained all the wood paneling in the house, giving it a modern cabin feel, and decorated it with the same vibe. I wanted this cabin to be where people could create unforgettable memories, celebrate personal victories, and, disconnect and relax. The musty smell was long gone, and it was finally available for someone's romantic weekend getaway.

I posted the listing on Airbnb's website, shared the link on my social media accounts, and waited patiently. With the project out of the way, I was focusing entirely on work again. I felt less stressed and participated more at virtual team happy hour celebrations. The highlight of my day was being present at weekly family dinners and even started to flirt with Isaac for fun.

Isaac and I had been friends for over ten years, and I had always contemplated the possibility of a romantic relationship but never thought about pursuing it. I would rather have him as my friend forever than date him and shatter our friendship if it didn't work out. I kept the flirting to a minimum and extraordinarily playful—so much so that he was unaware of my intentions. The shame of the matter came when he asked me out but I politely turned him down. Ever since, he's ghosted me—exactly what I was hoping to avoid.

Having this house finally done had a positive impact on both my mental and physical well-being, and I was ready for people to enjoy the fruits of my labor.

CHAPTER 3

Nine days ago

I STARED AT THE COMPUTER SCREEN, SORTING THROUGH my work emails, and accepting meeting invitations for the next three weeks. I looked at the clock and sighed, it was an exhausting day and barely eleven. I tucked a strand of my limp black hair behind my ear, ready to start my weekend. Friday mornings drag on because I have a call with my boss's boss I always dread. She's excellent, but incredibly intimidating. I'm done after I get off that call.

Glancing up from my computer, I see eighty-year-old Mrs. Bethel walking down the street to the coffee shop on time. Every morning she walks by at exactly 11:02, and walks back around 11:30. I've lived in my house for four years, and this woman follows the same schedule every day except if it's too cold, snowy, or rainy.

I flipped my phone over to pause the audiobook and noticed I had a new notification from Airbnb. I received my first booking, after waiting for more than a month. Elated doesn't even correctly depict how excited I am. I had poured my literal blood, sweat, and tears into the place, and it was finally going to be appreciated by someone other than me. I clicked on the reservation for more details of the stay. It looked like it was booked for three people for a two-night stay this weekend and were arriving tomorrow mid-day.

I thought it would be a challenge renting a cabin with zero reviews, but it happened much quicker than I anticipated. I mean, yeah, I was hopeful. It would take some time, though.

Everything I wanted to do, like pull together a visitor's handbook, needed to be done within twenty-four hours. I sorted through the rest of my cluttered inbox trying to make heads and tails of it all to plan my to-do list for next week. I had put in some extra hours earlier this week to implement a new email system and logged off by three to take care of the cabin before the guests arrived.

I headed into my kitchen to grab a sweet iced tea and returned to my desk to get started on the visitor's guide. My goal with this was to list the best places to eat and shop, the most picturesque waterfalls that were must-sees, and the phone numbers for the local police department and fire station. As more people visited, I would make improvements to the guide. Using my sub-par graphic design skills, I pulled together something that resembled a booklet one would pick up at a rest stop in the middle of nowhere, but it would do just fine for now.

My home was only half an hour away, so I printed two copies of the guide and planned to bring it to the cabin. I hopped in the car and drove over, admiring the beautiful autumnal leaves that began to change color. The Fall in the Appalachian Mountains was a beautiful sight; the leaves transformed into beautiful deep reds and oranges and peppered the sidewalks, and the sun poked through the almost barren trees.

Driving up the winding road felt like five miles but in reality it was barely one. As I turned the last corner, the cabin came into view. It sat perched atop a hill and overlooked some smaller mountains, so the sunsets were breathtaking. I pulled up the long and steep driveway, admiring the cabin on the way up. When I say cabin, don't think of a small one in the woods. This was a larger space than I had anticipated purchasing, but I couldn't pass up the view and price. The bottom half of the house was beautiful stonework. The top half was a medium-brown stained wood siding.

Walking up the large staircase to the dark wood front door, I admired all the work I had done to restore the original piece. When the lock clicked, I opened the door to the beautiful mountain retreat, inhaling the woodsy smell that had long replaced the mustiness. I stepped inside and admired the amount of natural light the massive windows overlooking the vast mountains allowed in. Opening the sliding door and stepping out onto the wraparound balcony, I took a deep breath. The smell of decaying leaves and burning wood tickled my nose. Before heading back inside, I walked around, checking everything was in order. I placed one of the visitor's guides on the table in the entryway and the other on the kitchen counter, along with a basket of snacks. I wanted to ensure that my guests felt welcomed and comfortable.

I walked through the rest of the house, and everything was in place. Each room was checked. I admired the house with a fresh perspective, the once creaky floorboards now fixed, the new toilets flushed without causing any flooding, and all outlets posed no fire risk. When I purchased this house it would test my limits, but I didn't realize it would help me grow as a person. Now, two years later, I am pretty self-sufficient in my home; the only time I needed to call someone to help me was when my air conditioner went out. As I locked the door one final time before my guests arrived, I felt a sense of pride. I had taken on a massive undertaking and, with a lot of help, made it a beautiful place for people to stay.

When I pulled back into my driveway, I sent a message to the guest who had booked the cabin. I sat on my screened-in back patio, turned on the outdoor fireplace, cuddled up with a blanket and book, and typed out a message while watching the sun dip below the trees.

Hi, Luke! I'm Cora, the owner of The Widow's Peak! I just wanted to formally thank you for booking and entrusting us with your weekend.

What time are you planning on arriving tomorrow? An hour before you check in, I will send over the code to get into the lockbox with the guest key.

A little bit about this little slice of paradise:

I purchased the house two years ago looking for a project, and boy, did I find one. I've spent countless hours making The Peak feel like a home away from home, so if you feel like anything is missing, please don't hesitate to let me know—it will only help improve others' stays!

I read the message one more time, ensuring that it didn't come across too forward before pressing send. I read for a bit before the crisp November air made its way into my space, signaling it was time to go inside and make dinner. I turned off the fireplace and collected my blanket, having no intentions of going back outside tonight. Making my way to the kitchen, I opened the refrigerator, poked my head around, and hoped that something delicious magically appeared overnight. I hadn't been to the grocery store in a few days and barely had enough to make a salad. By "barely enough," I mean I had three pieces of romaine lettuce and a handful of squishy cherry tomatoes I could probably salvage.

It's known that genes skip generations. That's more than evident in my family. My mom was an award-winning chef in New York City; meanwhile, I could barely boil water without burning myself. I did my best to have some healthy meals, but between work and the cabin keeping me busy, I fell off the wagon and relied on my good old friends McDonald's, Cook-Out, and Sonic to make me dinner a few nights per week.

There was no chance of me finding anything in my pantry

either, so I grabbed my phone, opened the Door Dash app, and ordered from Sonic for the second time this week.

As it was a Friday, delivery would be a while, so I put on a true crime documentary that showed how the store security cameras have helped solve missing person cases. It's fascinating, but damn, it leaves me on edge.

I've lived alone since I was seventeen. After watching the first episode about a girl disappearing in a Target parking lot, I didn't go there for at least a month. There was something about watching these shows made me aware of my surroundings because this shit happens every day.

I was sitting on the edge of my seat, when the bell rang. I jumped out of my skin, forgetting I had ordered food. I went to the door to find an exhausted eighteen-year-old delivery kid shivering, with my bag of Sonic in his hand.

"Are you Cora?" he asked, lips chattering. It had just dipped below fifty degrees. He should be wearing a jacket. When did I turn into my grandma?

"Yes, I am." I reached out my hand to grab the bag. "There was supposed to be a drink with this, right?"

His mouth opened, but no words came out. His eyes got big and darted down to his feet.

"No, ma'am, it wasn't there with the rest of your food. I can go right back and pick it up for you. I'll be back in under fifteen minutes. I'm so—"

I cut him off before he could apologize, "It's Kevin, right?" I vaguely remembered seeing his name on my app earlier. He nodded.

"Kevin, it's not a problem; please don't worry about it. I didn't need a large Coke anyways. I need to up my water intake." I smiled at him, trying to ease his concerns.

His eyes met mine again, "Are you sure?"

"Absolutely. It's getting cold out there; why don't you get back in the car? Have a great night!"

"Thank you, ma'am! You as well!"

I closed the door and turned off the porch light. I needed to stop my love affair with Coca-Cola and start drinking more water. My once-clear skin was paying for my sins and is now peppered with breakouts along my chin. I settled back on the couch, resuming my show until I had made myself so paranoid I had to get up to check every window and door. It's times like these I wish I had a dog or a boyfriend. If we're honest, I would lean towards the dog. I had thought about adopting a dog a few times, but I travel a bit for work, so it wouldn't be fair for it to go to a kennel once or twice per month.

After watching a few episodes of *The Office*, I checked the doors and windows, and turned off the lights before heading to bed.

CHAPTER 4

Eight days ago...

ONCE MY HEAD HIT THE PILLOW, I REMEMBER NOTHING. At seven-thirty, I woke up gasping and clutching my chest. Like clockwork, once per week, I have an awful nightmare of being framed for a murder I didn't commit. Without fail, I wake up drenched in sweat from the same dream.

It starts innocently enough. I'm alone, walking through a lush forest, looking for something. I walk for a while, finding a shoe in the exact location every time, then come across a man's body lying there, covered in blood.

I run back into the town, barreling into the police station, telling them everything I saw, but when I look down, I'm covered in blood. A minute later, I have handcuffs shackled around my thin wrists, and I cannot talk.

I tried to calm myself, so I laid back, removed the covers from my body, and reached for my phone. I rubbed the sleep from my eyes, scrolled through my notifications, and clicked on the new message in the Airbnb app.

Luke had responded.

Hi, Cora! It's nice to meet you. From the pictures, The Widow's Peak looks like a fantastic spot, and you did a great job renovating it! I plan to be there around 2 P.M; please let me know if that works for you.

My iPhone camera took decent photos because I took them all myself. I had already invested enough money into this place, and figured my phone would do just fine, at least at first.

Hi, Luke! That works perfectly. I will message you the code around 1 P.M.

In a massive shift in my mood, I felt a twinge of excitement in my stomach. Today was the first time someone other than a friend or family member would enter The Widow's Peak.

Many thought naming the house was crazy, but I felt calling it something would help set it apart from the others on the rental site. The balcony around the house reminded me of a widow's walk, a rooftop platform found in coastal homes, where mariners' wives would stand out and wait for their spouses' return. I took the "widow's", from that and the "peak", from a mountain peak, and there we have it.

The Widow's Peak.

After experiencing this nightmare regularly for the past several months, I discovered a solution. I take a shower, put on my clothes, and go to Mrs. Bethel's preferred coffee shop.

I threw on my favorite pair of stretchy jeans, an oversized sweatshirt, and my boots and stepped out into the brisk air, locking up behind me. As I walked down the street, I happened to bump into the one and only Mable Bethel.

"Cora Grace Lincoln! How are you this morning?" approaching quicker than you'd expect from an eighty-year-old, she waved a bony hand in my direction. She was also the only person in my life that has ever called me Cora Grace. I'd always gone by Cora. When I met Mable and asked my name, she wanted my full name.

"Mable! I'm doing well, how are you? You're out earlier than normal."

"I was up before the sun this morning; I couldn't sleep. I wanted to get a head start on my day. Did I tell you my grandson, Griffin, will be in town next week? I'd love for you to meet him!"

"You mentioned it a few months ago. I'd love to meet him. You name the day and time, and I'll be over there, okay?" I smiled warmly at her. She had been trying to set me up with Griffin since I moved in. I met him once in passing, and he was cute, but we were never formally introduced.

"I'll give you a call if that works?"

"Absolutely. It's chilly out here; head back home. I'll stop by early next week for tea."

"Be careful, and I'll see you then!"

Mable walked back down the road toward her house, and I finished the uphill walk to The Higher Ground. The early morning sun made the coffee shop look even cozier than usual, inviting me in to spend more money than I should on caffeine. I ordered my hot caramel latte and found a seat by the window to watch the out-of-town visitors gawk at the stores and the beautiful sights. While the cabin was at the top of a mountain, my house was at the bottom, close to civilization. I stared out the window at the falling leaves when Miranda, the head barista, and my best friend, sauntered to me with my drink.

"Another nightmare, Cora?" She extended out her arm, handing the large paper cup over.

I nodded, not wanting to make eye contact. Miranda was the only person I told, about my nightmares. I knew others would judge me. They would all insinuate all the true crime I absorb has led to the night terrors. Get rid of the podcasts, shows, and books; the nightmares will disappear.

Unfortunately, I think it's a deeper-rooted issue.

"You know you should talk to someone about that. It's been

going on for a while now, and I don't feel like that's normal." I knew she meant no malice. She's my best friend and only wanted what was best for me.

"It's on my list of things to do, trust me. I can manage it better now, so we're fine."

Miranda nodded, tucking a piece of her blonde hair behind her ear. "If you need a recommendation, I'd be happy to share my psychiatrist's contact information. If we went to the same one, we'd share even more in common."

I laughed in response. She could tell I wasn't in the mood to talk about this again, so she patted my shoulder and walked away. I snuggled further into the armchair, watching the world go by. By the time my coffee was almost gone, the nightmare was long forgotten.

I looked at my phone and weighed my options: I could go home and nap or head to the grocery store and pick up the food I desperately needed.

I sighed, sinking lower into the chair. Sometimes, I hated being an adult. I didn't take advantage of my early twenties nearly enough because I was so focused on getting my dream job—a big regret I had in life. As I walked back to my house, I decided to do the adult thing and get groceries; it was still early, so it wouldn't be too busy. I hopped in the car, drove the fifteen minutes to the store, was in and out within a half hour, and was on my way home. I glanced at the clock as I pulled back into my driveway.

It was just after noon.

I unpacked all the groceries and sent Luke the lock box code a little early, just in case he got to the cabin sooner than he expected. I went about my day and listened to an audiobook while I did a deep clean on the house, keeping my phone handy just in case Luke had any questions or problems. I lost track of time and pulled myself out of cleaning mode around five.

I checked my phone, and there were no messages from Luke,

so either the group made it there without problems or they were running late. I checked the security camera I installed by the cabin's front door, and no one had shown up, yet. I would have thought maybe they would have reached out, but this was my first time working with tenants, so I was trying not to be a complete control freak.

Doing a deep clean in the Fall made the house feel like a new beginning was upon us, so I leaned into that and made a tomato bisque soup. While it wasn't as good as the restaurant-grade one my mom makes when she comes to visit, it filled the void and gave my body the sustenance it craved and my wallet a much-needed reprieve.

Around seven, there was still no sign of life at the cabin, so I sent another message to Luke, checking to see if the group was all right, but again, there was no response. I was headed out to Miranda's house for a bonfire with our friends. I fixed my hair, put on a cute top with a sherpa-lined flannel jacket, a pair of brown boots, and was ready to head out. Miranda lived just down the street, so I walked on over with a bottle of my favorite red wine in hand.

As I walked up to the red brick front steps she threw open the front door. It's like she had sonar hearing.

"Cora!" The warm air from inside her house hit my face. "Come inside; you're the first one here."

The inside of her house always smelled like a bakery; I don't know if it's the candles she burns or an air freshener, but I have never seen Miranda bake.

"Who's coming tonight?" I asked, dipping a chip in some homemade salsa.

"The usual crew, plus the new guy Aria is dating," she answered, handing me a plate of chicken wings to put on the kitchen table. The usual crew consisted of my three best friends—Aria, Lucy, and Miranda, and their respective spouses.

We've known each other since our first year of high school, and our friendship still hasn't wavered after all these years. I situated everything on the table while we mindlessly chattered, wondering if we would like Aria's new beau.

"Hey, Miranda?" I called out from my spot on the living room couch while she flittered around the house, picking up a few dog toys on the floor.

"Is someone here?" her voice came from down the hallway in her bedroom.

"No, but I need to run something by you. Can you come here?"

"Be right there!" I heard the sound of plush dog toys hitting the woven basket and her heavy footsteps sulk down the hallway. She sat next to me.

"Okay, spill. What's going on?"

"The guy that rented the cabin. He never showed up. I've sent a few messages, but he's not responded. Is that weird?"

"I mean, it's a little weird, but shit happens, right? They could have gotten into an accident and are running late. Did you give them the code already?"

"Yeah, I sent it earlier this afternoon."

She shrugged, plates of sliced fruits and vegetables in her hands. "I wouldn't overthink it. I'm sure people are no-shows all the time."

"You're probably right; I just wanted this to go well. What if they leave a bad review?"

"Cora, they're not going to leave a bad review if they haven't even stayed in the place. Please relax. It'll all be okay, I promise. Between your new true crime obsession and these nightmares, you're a ball of anxiety lately."

As I opened my mouth to respond, the doorbell rang, and the group funneled in. We enjoyed a beautiful night outside until our bottles of wine were empty and laughed until our stomachs hurt. It was nights like tonight that made me so incredibly happy my job allowed me to be remote most of the time. It meant I could stay in the town I loved with my nearest and dearest friends… and the family I merely tolerated.

While everyone took an Uber, I walked home around midnight, ready to fall into my bed and sleep for as long as my body would allow.

CHAPTER 5

Seven days ago...

I SLEPT IN THIS MORNING, FULLY PREPARED TO HAVE A message or two from Luke letting me know where they were.

I was concerned at this point something had happened to them—what if they were in an accident on their way to the cabin?

Should I go over there and check the area?

I had done everything I needed yesterday, so my day was wide open, if I needed to go to the cabin, I could.

Making my way to the kitchen, I made a salad for lunch when my phone chimed.

A new message from Luke.

Hi Cora, I apologize for the late response, but we had something come up last minute, and we won't be able to make it this weekend. Please, go ahead and keep the money; we won't cancel. I will also leave a five-star review to help you get more business.

I read the message no less than five times. Was this guy serious?

Don't get me wrong, this isn't a bad situation for me, but this just feels fake. No one is *that* nice in today's world.

I needed to go to the cabin to ensure no one was there, but I also wanted to take advantage of the perfect reading spot. It's a brisk fifty-three degrees today, so I bundled up, grabbed a book off my shelf, and drove to the cabin.

Pulling up the winding road, I expected to see an empty driveway, but there was a red SUV parked by the garage. My pulse quickened. No one should be here. I parked next to the car and got out with my keys in between my fingers.

A tall woman with curly brown hair stood by the front door, staring right at me as I walked up to her.

"Hello, may I help you?" My voice shook.

"Hi, I'm Cathleen. I was looking for my husband." She outstretched her hand, and I glanced at it before reaching mine.

"I'm Cora, and I own the cabin. Who is your husband?"

"Luke Anderson, he and two of his friends booked this place for two nights."

I nodded, putting the pieces together. "That's why I'm here; they never checked in."

I watched as the color drained from her face. "They didn't?"

"No, I'm sorry. Have you spoken to Luke?"

"Yeah, he said he was here with his friends. He didn't think I would talk to his friends' wives because they were all home. I don't know why I'm here. I guess I had a hunch that he was being unfaithful."

"I'm sorry to hear that. Unfortunately, I think this might be a dead end here; he messaged me earlier and told me he couldn't make it."

"He did?" Cathleen's eyebrow shot up.

"Yup," I nodded, not wanting to get involved with their marital issues.

She looked defeated, "It appears this is a dead end. I'm sorry for the intrusion." Her tone was flat, and she spun on her heel walking back to her car. "Hey Cora," she said while opening the door, "If you hear from him again, will you let me know?"

"Of course." Cathleen wrote her number down on a sticky note and handed it over before she drove away like a bat out of hell.

I unlocked the front door and went inside. Everything was exactly as it was left. The travel guides were still untouched. No one had been there. I went upstairs to the loft area and sat on the window seat that looked out over the mountains. This was the most peaceful room in the house, with a cozy chair and a huge bay window.

I thought about how weird the encounter with Cathleen was. Did Cathleen think Luke had taken his mistress to my cabin?

That's what she said, but it's weird she just showed up. Was she going to confront him?

That could have been bad for them and terrible publicity for my little cabin.

I pushed it to the back of my brain; there was no reason to think about it anymore. No one was at the house, and their lives had no impact on mine.

I opened my book and read for a few hours, immersing myself in the world of a lighthearted romance. I took a step back from thrillers for the time being since I was already so on edge with all the true crime podcasts, I listen to and shows I watch.

Unaware of the passing hours, I looked up just in time to see the sun dipping below the mountain peaks, shading the sky with yellows and deep pinks. Two years of sunsets, in the house, but none of them took my breath away like this one. Admiring the pillowy clouds and waited until the sky turned a dark blue, I soaked in the beautiful late-Fall sunset.

Once I double-checked that all doors and windows were locked, I headed home eager to tackle a new but hectic week ahead. The first half of the week was packed with meetings and deliverables, as I prepared for a work trip from Wednesday through Friday.

As a storm brewed outside, I attempted to make some dinner and settled in because I was cozy inside and had no reason to go out.

Though I knew I should have been focusing on work for the week, this weekend was a whirlwind of emotions. I was so excited about sharing the cabin I loved with others, but the wife had caught me off guard. No matter how hard I tried, I couldn't hide the strange feeling at the way she had held her hands on her hips and observed the cabin closely. I understood why she was there and if I were in her shoes, suspecting my husband of infidelity, I would have done the same.

CHAPTER 6

Four days ago…

IME FLIES WHEN YOU'RE WORKING ALMOST FIFTEEN hours per day. I love my job and the people I work with, but damn, these long hours are catching up with my thirty-two-year-old self. I packed my suitcase, and it was filled to the brim with the perfect attire for Fall in New York City. I made it to the airport in record time, my wheels coming to a screeching halt in the parking garage; I was once again almost late for boarding my plane, a trait I had picked up from my dad. While I was always on time for work meetings and the occasional friend get-together, I had no sense of time in any other aspect of my life.

Thankfully it was mid-day on a Wednesday, and there was no line at security, so I could move right on through and proceed to sprint towards my gate. I was wheezing when I got there, just as my boarding group was called. I made my way to my First-Class seat, a perk of flying for work so often, and settled in with my iPad; I had downloaded some shows I wanted to catch up on, so I was set. The flight to New York was just over three hours, so by hour two, I had finished my shows and reached for the newest book I had picked up at the airport when I traveled a few weeks ago. It was a thriller about an abandoned house, and I was immediately immersed in the world and couldn't flip the pages quickly enough. As the plane's landing gear touched down on the runway, I hit the biggest plot twist and audibly gasped, thankful that the older man sitting next to me had his headphones on and was also lost in a book.

We disembarked the plane, and I was hit with the familiar sound of the thick New York accent that I had grown to love. I alternated between traveling to New York and Los Angeles for work but always felt more comfortable amongst New Yorkers. They were no bullshit, get-to-the-point people, which I respected; plus, they had the best pizza and sandwiches. I ordered an Uber and an hour later was in my hotel room, eating the best slice of pizza and reading the rest of the book. That book messed with my mind, and now I was alone in a hotel room, nowhere near home. Usually, books don't bother me, but this one hit just close enough to home that I was spiraling quickly. I reached for my phone to text Miranda.

> **Cora: SOS**
>
> **Miranda: You ok?**
>
> **Cora: Yeah, I just read a thriller, and now I'm on edge.**
>
> **Miranda: Are you at the hotel already?**
>
> **Cora: Yes**
>
> **Miranda: Want to call?**

I took that as a green light to call her. The phone rang twice before she picked up.

"What did I tell you about reading thrillers and watching all that true crime shit?" There was no hello; she knew precisely why I was calling; after all, she was the only person I told about my nightmares.

"I know I'm being silly about this; I just don't know what's up with me the last few days."

"I think you need to take a step back from everything you've been reading and watching. I know it's Fall, and you want to embrace the spooky, but at what point are you going to call it? You're not built for all the scary crap you've been inundating your pretty brain with; you read romance novels and swoon over all your book boyfriends."

I chewed my lip, knowing damn well that Miranda was right. "You're right. This weekend was just a little strange, and I'm letting that carry over into the week."

"What happened this weekend?" Miranda questioned.

I remembered I hadn't told her about Cathleen's arrival at the cabin. "You know the guy that was supposed to stay in the cabin— the one who booked it?" I didn't wait for a response; she knew whom I was talking about. "His wife showed up at the cabin on Sunday. I had decided to go over and check that everything was still in place, and when I pulled up the driveway, a woman was standing there, staring up at the cabin."

"What the actual fuck?"

"Exactly my thoughts."

"Who was it? What happened? I can't believe you didn't call me!"

"It was the guest's wife. He told her he was going on a guy's trip, and she didn't believe him; she thought he was cheating on her. I think she went to the cabin to catch him in the act."

"Holy shit, that's intense! So how did it end up?"

"I told her he had messaged me that he couldn't make it and would let her know if I heard from him again. She gave me her number and left just a few minutes after I had arrived."

"That's so uncomfortable. I mean, it was probably nothing.

What are you going to do?" Miranda was eating this up; the woman loved drama.

"Leave it alone, which I figured you would say."

"Do you judge me for wanting some gossip in our boring lives? We live in the town where we grew up, your job provides nothing exciting to talk about, and mine just brings in unhappy customers."

A laugh escaped my mouth; she was right; we lived dull lives. "That's fair. Thanks for letting me get it all out there."

"That's what friends are for. I'm here to be your shoulder to cry on, but sometimes I have to tough love this shit."

"I appreciate you more than you know! I'm in a hotel room; entertain me; what's happening with you?"

Miranda spilled all the details about her co-worker and how she was leaving her husband. When you live in a small town, nothing is a secret. We chatted for a while, and after a long day of travel, I crawled into bed and fell asleep.

CHAPTER 7

Three days ago…

MY ALARM BLARED BRIGHT AND EARLY THIS MORNING. I was due in the office to meet with the Marketing new hires at nine. I needed to get ready and look like a proper, functioning human being today instead of the disheveled mess I usually am, so coffee was a must.

Quickly, I got ready, was out the door with my tote bag swung over my shoulder. I stopped at Starbucks since it was on the way to the office and ordered my ever-so-controversial pumpkin spice latte.

Back home, people gasp and clutch their chests when you even mention the latte that shall not be named. *And* I'm the dramatic one.

I made it to the office with some time to spare, making my rounds, saying hello to all my co-workers, and found the conference room where the new hire orientation was being held. I was there to greet them, introduce myself, and welcome them to the team. The rest of their day was filled with onboarding activities.

I found a quiet office, determined to get some work done and not spend my time here chit-chatting (like I did last time).

My stomach growled, signaling lunch. We usually have a big team lunch the first day I'm in New York, but my team's calendars were booked today and couldn't find a time that accommodated our schedules, so I was off to the local pizza place. I ordered a slice of pepperoni with one cheese and sat in Central Park to eat. There was a chill in the air, but I loved inhaling all of New York's smells. Something was alluring about the aroma of street cart hot dogs, exhausts, the different colognes and perfumes walking by every few minutes.

I had some time to kill before my next meeting, so I took advantage of the brisk weather and walked around the park, listening to my book. My book was paused, when Miranda's face lit up my phone screen.

"Cora!" Miranda sounded panicked on the other end of the phone.

I gave her a second to elaborate, but she didn't, "Miranda!?"

"Cora, this isn't funny. I'm being serious. What was the name of the guy that was supposed to be renting your cabin?"

I paused, "Luke, why?"

"Luke, what?"

"Um…" I raked my brain, trying to visualize the last name on the piece of paper Cathleen had given me. "Anderson, I believe."

There was silence on the other end of the phone. "Miranda?"

She sighed, "His body was just found in the woods."

I stopped mid-step, my breath caught in my throat. "What?! Where?"

"A few miles away from The Widow's Peak."

I was silent. Why was he found there? "But…he told me he wasn't coming. Why was he there?"

"I'm not sure. Not many details have been released yet, but I think you're next on their list to talk with."

"Was there a cause of death?"

"Not an official one. He was found mauled to death, or so they said. They're not sure by what. They just found him this morning, so you'll probably need to go in for questioning."

"I'm in New York right now, I—I can't come home." My heart hammered in my chest, and I fidgeted with the button on my jacket.

"The news mentioned that the police were going to contact you. I would be ready to come home if they call."

My index finger picked at the skin on my thumb, my anxiety building.

"Cora, you still there?" Miranda's voice was low.

"Yeah, sorry. I'm heading back to the office now; I'll let you know if they call me."

"Sounds good, be safe up there."

"I'm in New York, not the jungle."

I pulled my headphones out of my ears, fully aware of my surroundings. I walked the three blocks back to the office and went back to my floor, doing my best to think of a logical situation as to WHY Luke would tell me they weren't coming, but his body was found near the cabin.

I finished the workday and returned to the hotel. Our team was going out for dinner and drinks tonight, so we ended our day early and went to the bar down the street for some much-needed cocktails. It was a stress-free night which makes spending time with my co-workers always lovely. We're not your typical marketing team. We're an eccentric bunch as we work so well together.

As I downed another glass of wine, everything happening at the cabin drifted to the back of my mind. The wine only shifted my thoughts briefly because it was all I could think about when I returned to my hotel room. I showered and lay in bed, turned on the television mindlessly staring at it.

Hours went by, and all I could think about was Harper from all those years ago.

CHAPTER 8

Two days ago…

DESPITE NOT SLEEPING AT ALL LAST NIGHT, I WAS UP bright and early, to treat my team. I stopped at the local deli with the best bagels, and went to Starbucks for a box of coffee. I found an available conference room near all the desks and set everything up. My team was so grateful for the early morning life-giving sustenance and devoured everything I had brought.

Our day was half over before we knew it. I returned to my office and checked my phone which I left on my desk. I saw three missed calls from an unknown number. I headed to an empty conference room and listened to the message.

It was from a detective in Byglass County, North Carolina.

"You've got Detective Ambrose," his southern drawl echoed over the phone.

"Hi, you've got Cora Lincoln."

"Yeah, Miss Cora." His southern twang emphasized the -a. "We were callin' about a Luke Anderson that was missin' and was just found in the woods near your cabin. Would you be able to come in this weekend?"

My heart raced. "I'm in New York for the rest of today, but I fly home tonight. I can come in first thing tomorrow."

"There's no rush, if I'm honest. We're still waiting on the Medical Examiner, so take your time. Why don't ya take tomorrow to relax and come on Sunday morning?" The soul in his voice was like a warm blanket, reminding me of home amongst the harsh New York accent I'd been surrounded by the last few days.

"Sounds good. I'll be in first thing Sunday." I exhaled, my heart rate returning to normal.

"Safe travels, Miss Lincoln."

We hung up, and I sat down. How do I always end up involved in these situations? I took a minute for myself, breathing deeply. I took one last deep breath and was out the door with a plastered smile, going about the rest of my day. I made my rounds and said goodbye to the team before grabbing my suitcase and ordering an Uber, making it to the airport, two hours before my flight, a stark contrast from my flight to New York.

I checked my watch, it was just after three thirty, and I had skipped lunch, so I made my way to the Mexican restaurant, ordered chips and guacamole, a burrito, and a giant margarita—sure to sleep through the flight. I bought a bottle of water, a bag of chips, a new rom-com and sat at the gate for an hour and a half before boarding.

I had a window seat in first class on this plane, but it didn't matter because my eyelids were heavy thanks to that margarita, and the long days in New York. I was asleep before the wheels left the runway.

My eyes fluttered open just before they touched down in North Carolina.

CHAPTER 9

One Day Ago...

WAKING UP THIS MORNING IN MY BED ONCE AGAIN FELT wonderful. Don't get me wrong, the hotel I stayed in while in New York City was posh, but that's the exact opposite of my style. I opt for more of a chic cabin look—warm, soothing colors, plush rugs, and versatile pieces. I'm not one for stark whites and places that appear sterile.

The morning started like any other: I got ready for the day, went to get coffee and breakfast, and returned home before the mid-day thunderstorm rolled in. I looked out the window, debating if I should head to the cabin, maybe something would stand out to me. I tossed on my heavy coat with a hood and was out the door. The cabin came into view, and the clouds snuggled against the second-floor windows. I didn't see anything suspicious but getting out of the car left me feeling a different way.

Inside, it felt more ominous, and a shiver ran down my spine. There was a chill in the air, more than the dropping temperature outside. I walked around the house, but nothing was out of place. I grabbed a water bottle out of the fridge, poured myself a small glass of bourbon with a large ice cube, and made my way to the couch, overlooking some trees with a clear view of the afternoon sun and a walking trail about 200 feet below.

Snuggling in the brown leather couch with a blanket, reaching for the book I started Tuesday night before bed, I took a long sip of the chilled bourbon.

I read for a while, never feeling settled.

Around two o'clock, a feeling crept in me as if I was being watched. I made my way over to the big window, and there was no one on the road or walking trail. I stood there and looked, hoping that I would see something, but having no other option but to ignore my feeling, I sit down.

The clouds got thicker and darker. My view disappeared, much like my sanity. A loud clap of thunder pulled me from my book once more. I looked down and could see my heart racing in my chest through my sweatshirt.

"Calm down, Cora! Everything is fine. You're just on edge with everything going on." I spoke the words out loud, hoping that hearing my voice would help, but instead, my voice shook and sounded less confident than I felt. I reached for my glass of bourbon, only to be met with the giant ice cube hitting me in the nose. My drink was long empty.

The chill in the air hadn't gone away, something I had hoped the alcohol and heat would fix. But there I was, staring at the thermostat stating it was seventy-three degrees in the cabin. Typically, I leave it at seventy, and it's comfortable. There was a lot of rain, and I know the outside temperature dropped.

I poured myself another drink, refilled my water bottle, and moved back to the couch. From the corner of my eye, through the slats of the blinds, I saw something on the deck. I stopped dead in my tracks.

Another shiver involuntarily ran down my spine. The logical

part of my brain knew nothing was out there. I separated the blinds and peeked through—sure enough, there was nothing there.

I picked at my cuticles when I got to the couch, giving myself more to think about. If Luke had messaged me and told me he wasn't coming:

Why was his body found just down the road?

What if someone took his phone and sent that?

What if someone intercepted him on his way up here?

I chewed on the inside of my mouth, descending into the depths of my thoughts when a large bolt of lightning illuminated the dark sky. The crack of it was loud enough to shake the cabin.

Pulled out of my thoughts, my focus was solely on the feeling I wasn't alone a feeling that wasn't there earlier.

I grabbed a knife out of the block in the kitchen, held it firmly at my side, and walked the house, checking all the windows and doors to ensure they were locked, inspecting the rooms to make sure I didn't have an unexpected visitor. The place was clear. I returned to the living room, ready to sit, but a fire caught my eye outside the window.

It was near the woods where hikers had found Luke's body. It was suspicious. I tried to be reasonable, but there was a lot of lightning, so that must have been it.

I debated calling the local fire department, but the fire started to dwindle, the rain extinguishing it within minutes.

I pulled my knees up to my chest and turned on the television, hoping for a distraction. Every fiber of my being wanted to lock up, bolt to the car and go back to my house, but the storm would make it impossible to see on my way down the mountain. I sipped my drink while watching a home renovation show on HGTV to help ease the unsettledness. The windows rattled as the wind blew, and the house creaked. I kept thinking something ran by the window but shook it off.

Coming to the cabin, might make me a little bit jumpy, but I didn't think it would be that bad. I placed my untouched second bourbon on a coaster. The alcohol was making me distort reality, and there was nothing out there.

After all, I had motion sensor lights on the deck, which never went on. I took some large deep breaths and started to calm down. The storm had slowed, and the clouds were dissipating.

As soon as the rain stopped completely, I would head home. In the quiet house, my phone rang. It scared the shit out of me. *Damn it, Miranda.* "Hello?" I tried to level my voice.

"What's up with you? You sound like you just saw a ghost." Miranda laughed. I hadn't told her I was going to the cabin. I forced a laugh out, not saying anything. "You're back in town, right? Did you want to grab some dinner?"

Dinner would be good. It would get me back to my day-to-day setting and out of this house that was creeping me out. "Sure, I should be home in an hour or so."

"Did you go to Target without me?" she feigned sadness.

"No, I'm at the cabin. I wanted to see if there was anything I could share with the police tomorrow when I talk with them."

"I wish you would have called. I would have kept you company. I imagine it's weird up there right now?"

I swallowed hard. "Yeah, a little bit. The thunderstorm didn't help." There was a loud rapping at the door. "Hey, can I call you right back? Someone is knocking on the door."

"Of course." There was one final gust of wind, then, the line went dead. The television paused. The Wi-Fi must have dropped. I walked over to the front door, expecting to see a neighbor or police officer, but instead, there was no one there.

My heart hammered in my chest. I was positive someone was knocking at the door. I quickly returned to the living room to check the security camera footage on my phone, but the Wi-Fi was still down.

The rain stopped.

I took this as my opportunity to get out of there. I turned off the television, washed my glass, and was out. I locked up and bolted to my car, checking the backseat before getting in.

I drove slowly down the mountain on the twisting road, feeling increasingly unsettled as I went by the barren trees.

Halfway down, a large tree branch was blocking the road. To my dismay I had to move it. I took a deep breath, pulled on my hood to shield me from stray raindrops, and moved the branch near the edge of the woods.

Walking back to my car, not even a minute later, I heard what I could best describe as a shriek. A loud rustling amongst the leaves. Then, I caught a glimpse of a tall, black figure with white eyes in the brush.

I stood there, paralyzed with fear, while making eye contact with the creature. Snapping out of my trance, I threw myself into the car, and drove as quickly as possible. I kept my eyes on the road and refused to look at the tree line, as tears cascaded down my face when I pulled into my driveway. I sat trying to understand what I had encountered. I can't tell anyone about that because no one would believe me. I'm terrified.

It was The Beast. Exactly like the drawings in folklore. The Beast that killed Harper.

Whatever I saw, I never wanted to see it again. I freshened up before driving to Miranda's house because after today's events, I felt safer driving over than walking alone.

We went to our favorite Italian restaurant, Amici's, for dinner. Even though I tried my hardest to put everything in the back of my mind and be present, I was failing miserably. Mindlessly, I swirled my spaghetti around my spoon before Miranda pulled me out of my daze. "What's up with you? You're off tonight."

Her brows pulled together, concern washing over her face.

"You're going to think I'm crazy…." I trailed off, knowing exactly how it was going to sound.

"Try me." I had some faith that our friendship, which had spanned half of our lives, would help Miranda not think I had completely lost my mind.

"Do you remember the story of Harper Cooper?" I wiped my palms on my jeans.

"Vaguely. Is that the one with the missing girl who was found mauled?"

I nodded. "I feel like there might be parallels between Luke and Harper…."

I waited for Miranda to laugh in my face. However, much to my shock, she didn't. Instead, she placed her fork down, took a sip of water, and met my eyes. "Surely you don't think that it—"

I cut her off, "—I've probably just gone off on a tangent, but this situation isn't sitting right with me. First, he didn't show up. Then, he told me he wasn't coming. Then, his body was found a few days later near the cabin. Does that not throw up red flags?"

"That was just old folklore, Cora. I'm sure there was a reasonable explanation for why Luke bailed. He might have been on his way and decided to turn back."

"But what about the message? The timing of everything just seems off."

"I'm sure there's a rationalization for it. You've been swamped with work, then had to travel, and returned to a dead guy on your property. You're traumatized! I would be if I were you. This isn't like one of your true crime podcasts, this is real life. You need to stay away and let the professionals do their jobs."

I knew Miranda was probably right. I had been working more than usual and was out of my element for a few days, so I was likely still on edge.

"There's one more thing," I added, a final plea to have her believe me.

Miranda raised an eyebrow questioningly, so I continued.

"I think I saw something on my way home. I had gotten out

to move a branch in the road, and I heard a shriek, then some rustling, and then I saw something."

She coughed, clearly taken aback by the bomb I had just dropped. "Excuse me?! You saw what exactly?"

"A figure? A creature? I'm not sure what to call it. It was tall, had black skin, and glowing white eyes. The unsettled feeling I had in the cabin was amplified when I saw whatever it was. I jumped back in the car and didn't look back. I didn't know what I was going to see."

Her jaw was slack, and her eyes were bulging. "Are you going to tell the police? Or, is it just best to leave it alone?"

"I might just leave it alone and let them do their investigation." I needed to devise a plan before arriving at the station tomorrow.

"That's the best course of action." She shook her head in disbelief, and I could see the fear in her eyes.

"I just want to put it out of my mind. I don't even want to go back tomorrow for the questioning."

She inhaled sharply, "I can't even imagine. We can change the subject if you'd like." But how do you change the subject when I could have seen what we thought was a creature in folklore?

We changed topics and started talking about work, which helped successfully push everything out of my mind, and we enjoyed the rest of our dinner before parting ways.

Walking back into my house felt like a warm hug after the coolness in the cabin; whatever it was, I wanted no part of it. I showered and got ready for bed, knowing I had an early morning meeting at the police station. I opened my laptop while in bed and responded to a few urgent work emails. It felt like the Google Chrome icon was beaconing me in and clicked it—down the rabbit hole, investigating Harper Cooper.

Despite knowing better, I couldn't resist delving into the thirty-year-old case, and now it's nearly midnight. I've checked the doors twice, and all the lights in the house are on. I know my neighbors are still awake and I'm expecting them to have some questions for me tomorrow.

I found more parallels between Harper's case and Luke's, as well as other instances of people disappearing and being discovered mauled in the Appalachian Mountains. Any survivors have undergone years of therapy and have since shared their terrifying, near-death encounters with The Beast.

CHAPTER 10

Present

I DON'T THINK I SLEPT MUCH LAST NIGHT. THE LAST time I looked at the clock, it was already past six. The sun would soon be rising, and only then did I finally feel at ease enough to turn off all the lights in the house before sprinting back to my room. It was as if I was a child again, running down to the basement to fetch something, then turning off the lights and bolting up the stairs before the demons could catch me.

Yesterday, in the woods, I heard some things that gave me chills. Not long after, I saw... or thought I saw... The Beast.

No wonder Luke was found mauled to death shortly before. The Beast must have done it. But how could I explain to the police without them sending me to a mental institution? I had to play it safe. Only answer their questions. Avoid sharing any far-fetched ideas.

After a restful night's sleep, I dragged myself out of bed and dressed in my most comfortable clothes. The drive up the mountain to the police station felt shorter than usual, but I wanted it to last as long as possible.

When I arrived, I sat in my car for a few minutes to collect myself before heading inside. As I watched a plump older man step outside for a smoke, I noted his movements with a calculating eye.

By 11:05, he was back inside, and I took that as my cue to enter the building.

The receptionist greeted me, "Good morning! Do you have a meeting scheduled?"

I gave a small smile, the only one I could muster, "I'm here to see Detective Ambrose."

The same man from earlier emerged from his office. "Miss Lincoln?"

"Yes, please, call me Cora."

"Why don't we chat in one of the other rooms?" His soft southern accent was thicker in person than it was over the phone.

I followed behind, and we entered an interrogation room. The anxiety bubbled in my stomach, much more intense than I had anticipated. I thought I was just here to answer a few questions about Luke's potential stay, not answer the hard questions.

The anxiety was plastered on my face when we sat, evident by his comment.

"Cora, you can relax. I promise this room is much scarier than the conversation we're about to have." There's something about a southern accent that makes it feel like the truth.

"Would you mind telling me about your interactions with Mr. Anderson?"

Good! An easy question.

"He booked a stay at my cabin up here in Byglass. According to the reservation, he and two friends would be staying there. My first interaction with him was last weekend when I sent him a message thanking him for booking with me. He messaged back. Then, an hour before they were supposed to arrive, I sent the code for the lockbox. Then, it was radio silence. When they didn't show up, I messaged him through the app several times before he responded. He said something had come up, and they weren't going to make it, but I could keep the money, and he would leave me a good rating."

His ice-blue eyes pierced my soul. "And was that the last communication with him?"

"Yes, aside from thanking him."

He nodded. His eyes squinted at me.

I took this as my cue to continue, "There is one more thing."

"What is it?" he asked, genuinely interested.

"His wife, Cathleen, was here the Sunday, the day after he was supposed to check in. She thought he was having an affair. I don't know if that's relevant or not."

"Mrs. Anderson is here, we've spoken with her, and she told us she went there."

"How is Cathleen doing?"

"Not well, but she has a community surrounding her that will provide love and support."

I nodded, not having anything else to say. We sat silently for a minute while Detective Ambrose stared at his notepad, twiddling the pen in his fingers.

"Have you heard many details of this case?"

This seemed like a probing question, and I felt my blood run cold.

"No, sir. I haven't." I lied. I had done my research.

"Luke was found about a quarter mile from the cabin, completely mauled. I'll leave out the gruesome details, but some hikers found him Friday morning. They all need therapy after the scene they stumbled upon. They called us immediately, but obviously, he was long gone. We had to identify him with his dental records."

My eyes went wide, not knowing they couldn't identify him. "I hadn't heard all those details."

"This is a sad case for sure. Hopefully, we can get to the bottom of it, bring his family and friends some closure. So, do you have anything else you wanted to talk about, Cora?" his eyes were inquisitive.

My knee bounced nervously. I wanted to spill the beans, but picked at the corner of my nail, peeling up the black gel nail polish.

"No, sir. I think that's it."

He had more he wanted to talk about. I was sure of it. "Have you heard anything about that girl, Linsey, that just went missing?"

I visibly tensed. I remembered her name from last night's research. Linsey is a twenty-three-year-old woman who went missing a few weeks ago, a little higher up on the mountain. A natural-born hiker, she went out with three of her friends, and only her friends returned home.

Their story stated they were overlooking one valley, and Linsey said she would backtrack a bit and see if she could find a different trail for them to take back for a change of scenery. They searched for her for hours, but there was no luck. They only heard a lot of rustling around in the trees and didn't see or hear anything else.

"Yes, sir, I have. It's such a sad case. Do you all have any leads?" The Internet was abuzz with how this could be The Beast.

While some people believed that the woman might have simply fallen and been unable to call for help, the residents of Byglass County were convinced The Beast was responsible for her disappearance. I've got to give it to them, they were dedicated to catching that creature…whatever it was.

"There are some, but not many."

I was lost in my thoughts and missed my cue to nod, feeling uncomfortable and unsure of what to say. I wanted to tell him everything I had seen, heard, and felt.

"Cora, you seem like you're not telling us the whole truth. I hope you know we don't suspect you, so please, fill us in on your thoughts because we're hitting dead ends in this case left and right." Detective Ambrose twirled his white handlebar mustache.

I inhaled sharply, knowing I was doing all of Byglass County, North Carolina, a disservice by keeping everything in. "Detective Ambrose, you're probably not going to believe me, but have you ever heard of the Appalachian folklore of The Beast?"

CHAPTER 11

"WHAT DID YOU SAY?" DETECTIVE AMBROSE'S EYEBROW was raised, beckoning me to continue my thought.

How do I get him to believe me?

No matter what I said, it would be met with a barrage of questions, so I braced myself and inhaled sharply. "I asked if you had ever heard of the folklore of The Beast?"

His eyes narrowed, and he was skeptical. "I have, but what are you getting at, Cora?"

I shrugged, unsure if I should even continue. I could already tell he thought I was crazy.

Detective Ambrose's face softened, "Go ahead. I'm not judging. This is my concentration face." He laughed and his eyes crinkled. His white beard made him look like Santa Claus. It was fitting because he always dressed up as Santa for the Byglass Christmas Festival.

"I know you'll brush this off, but I think all those stories are true. I think there might be something out there in the woods. Something that's not an animal that's killing people." I paused, giving him time to refute before continuing. "Think of how many people have gone missing over the last few years. Not just people we know that lived here but the out-of-town visitors. Some are never found. Others are just piles of bones when y'all find them."

I watched as Detective Ambrose chewed on his bottom lip, waiting for him to break his silence. My knee bounced under the table, this whole situation was uncomfortable. I was making myself look like a fool, I should've just stuck to my script.

What felt like a lifetime had passed before he started nodding, understanding what I was saying.

I had to break the silence before I drove myself into insanity. "I know you think I'm crazy, I know. I think I'm crazy too, saying it out loud, but I had my own encounter with…something." My heart rate sped up.

"What did you see?" He looked half-intrigued, half-suspicious. I was hoping the intrigue would win.

"A creature? I'm not sure what to call it. All I know is it was tall, had black skin that was covered in fur, and glowing white eyes."

Detective Ambrose stopped writing and stared at me. "And, you're sure it wasn't a bear or something?"

"I mean, I think it was a bear, or something, but it didn't look like any of the bears I've seen around Byglass, that's for sure. It was just staring at me."

"When was this?"

"Yesterday. I went up to the cabin to see if I could find anything that would be helpful to share today. On my way back down the mountain, there was a tree limb in the road, so I had to get out to move it. That's when I saw it just past the tree line." I crossed my legs, a nervous habit of mine, and my foot shook.

I was met with narrowed eyes again. "Why didn't you call us?"

"For starters, I knew I was coming here today. But also because I knew this is how the conversation would go. I would share all this random information and it would just be passed off as 'Cora has lost her mind.'" That garnered a slow nod and more notes written on the small notepad he's been writing in since I sat down.

"You're not saying anything, Detective Ambrose, you're just writing stuff down and nodding at me. Do you think I'm crazy or no? If so, I would like to leave."

He took a deep breath. "I don't think you're crazy. Don't you think that was my first thought as well?" His eyes fell. "Every time we have a missing person's case called in, that's all I can think about. These trails aren't difficult to navigate, so how do all these people keep going missing?"

"It just feels awfully coincidental that Linsey went missing and all her friends heard were the trees rustling. Luke was missing, then showed up dead, and mauled to death. Bad things happen in threes. We're just waiting for it to happen at this point."

"This is all pure speculation though, Cora. I don't want to discredit what you saw, but we have to treat this like a legitimate murder investigation and not like it's part of a folklore. How do you think the Lieutenant or Captain would react if I told them we were going after The Beast and not some sick human being who did this?"

My eyes fell at what he was saying.

"Trust me, I don't want to discredit you. I need you to know that while I believe you saw something, I can't bring that up to anyone. There's a person out there that did this and needs to be caught."

"Yes, sir." I was defeated and had completely lost my mind. What if he was right? What if there really wasn't anything there? Cue the doubt setting in.

"I want you to rest assured that we will do everything in our power to catch this monster so you feel safe going up to your cabin again."

I nodded, not wanting to make myself seem any less credible.

I had already embarrassed myself enough for the day. "I should be on my way if we're done here."

"Of course. I'll give you a call if we need any further information from you."

I wiped my hands on my jeans before shaking Detective Ambrose's hand. "Have a great day, sir."

"You too, Cora! If you need anything, just give me a call."

I left the police station and headed back down the mountain to calm my racing mind. Was I really *that* off point? Had I let my mind get the best of me?

As I drove, my eyes were plastered on the road. I didn't let them wander passed the tree line. I didn't trust my eyes anymore. I dialed the one person I knew would believe me, my childhood best friend, Kendra.

It rang three times before she picked up, out of breath. "Hello?"

"Do you have a few minutes?" I asked, hoping she did.

"Cora? Are you there? You're breaking up."

I looked at my phone and had no cell service. I hung up, waited until I was closer to the bottom of the mountain and had service again.

"Can you hear me now?" I asked as soon as Kendra answered.

"Are we in that old Verizon commercial?" she laughed. "But yes, I can hear you loud and clear. What's up?"

"So, do you remember how you ruined my life all those years ago?" I asked, hoping she knew exactly what I was talking about.

"Do you mean the failed hair dye incident?"

"Not quite..."

"When we went to that carnival and I forced you on that rickety roller coaster?"

"No, but thank you for reminding me of that nauseating experience. I was more referring to the story of The Beast."

"Wow, that's a story I've not thought about in years. Since moving, really. Why do you bring that up?"

Kendra moved away as soon as we graduated high school because she had dreams that were bigger than Byglass County. As much as it killed me when she packed up and moved to Pittsburgh, it was the right thing for her, so I was always there as support.

"You know how I told you that guest never showed up?"

"Yeah. Did he ever give an explanation?"

"Umm, not quite?"

"That was a question and not a statement. What happened?" Kendra was ready for some good gossip and boy do I have some.

"I got a message saying that he and his friends wouldn't be able to make it, but they were still going to pay and leave a good review. Then, I go to New York for work and I get a call from Miranda that the guy was found dead near the property."

"Oh my..." Kendra trailed off, expecting me to continue.

"Oh, just wait. He was found mauled to death."

"You don't think...?" she asked cautiously.

"Oh, I do think. I very much think so. I was at the cabin yesterday, and I felt so awful and unsettled. I kept thinking that I saw something and nothing was there. Then, I was leaving, and as I was driving back down the mountain, there was a branch in the road, so I had to get out." I paused, a massive sigh escaping my lips, "I got out to move it and something was staring at me in the woods. It was a tall figure, glowing eyes, black furry skin. I freaked the hell out and jumped back in the car." I was met with silence. "Kendra, you there?"

"Yeah, just trying to understand. Are you sure you saw something?" Kendra was at a loss for words, which rarely happened.

"Yes! I was sure until everyone started questioning me about it."

"Who else have you talked to?" I could tell she was hoping I hadn't told many people.

"Just Miranda and the detective in charge of the case."

"What did Miranda think?"

"Honestly, I'm not sure she knew what to think. She was speechless."

"Interesting. And what did the detective say? How did that even come up?

"I was dumb and brought it up. I'm pretty sure he thinks I've completely lost my mind. Even though this all happened on my property, I brought up a damn folklore as a suggestion as to why this guy was found dead."

"For what it's worth, I believe you." Kendra comforted.

"I appreciate that more than you know. When I was at the cabin yesterday, I kept feeling like something was watching me. I also heard someone knocking on the door, but no one was there. I just…I don't know. I'm confused and exhausted."

"You certainly sound like it. Why don't you take some time off and come visit me? We'll get you out of your routine and do some fun stuff."

I pulled up to the stop light, entering the downtown area and I could finally breathe, again. I thought about Kendra's proposition, it wasn't a bad idea.

"That actually sounds really nice. I can look into it this afternoon. Can you text me any dates that won't work for you?"

"I have open availability in December, so why don't you plan on taking some time off before the holidays."

"I love this plan!" My mood immediately improved. "I'll check my work calendar as well and we can make this happen." Even though it's Sunday, I needed to work this afternoon if I wanted to be able to make Thanksgiving dinner this Thursday and not sit on my parent's couch, answering emails between dinner and dessert.

"I can't wait! I'm going to smush the shit out of you when I see you."

Kendra and I hadn't seen each other in over a year. We tried our best to take a trip once per year, but last year, we couldn't find dates that worked.

"We can talk later about everything. I'm about to go see if Miranda can give me a drip IV of coffee."

"Did you sleep at all, last night?" she asked, already knowing my answer.

"Last night? Not at all. I slept once the sun came up, though."

"Good grief. Go get your damn coffee, take a nap, and then, plan a trip to see me!"

We hung up and I pulled into my driveway with my sights set on coffee. I walked up the hill towards The Higher Ground and hoped Miranda hadn't left for the day. Walking in, the aroma of coffee hit my nose, as always, it was intoxicating. The warm air hit my face while some tension left my body. I ordered my coffee and found a seat towards the back of the shop.

I popped my headphones in, hoping no one would strike up a conversation. Normally, I'm a chatty person, but after this morning's conversation with Detective Ambrose, I didn't have it in me to make small-talk with people. With my back facing the coffee bar, I felt a tap on the shoulder, pulling me back to reality.

"A large hot coffee for Cora, the princess of Byglass." Miranda joked, handing my coffee over.

"Thanks!" I tried to smile, but it came out as some half-assed smirk.

"Well, that's a face, if I've ever seen one. Let me go clock out and I'll join you. I want to hear all about how it went this morning."

Miranda's blonde hair was curled and bounced when she walked. She had that 'no makeup' makeup look down and I had always been jealous. When that first sip of coffee hit my lips, I was reinvigorated and ready to talk.

Miranda plopped in the leather chair next to me. By the way she had her hand perched on her cheek, she was ready to hear the details of what happened earlier.

"Spill." *Right to the point.*

"I talked with Detective Ambrose and it was weird. I don't

know how else to put it. I answered his questions and then it almost felt like he thought I was hiding something, so I brought up The Beast."

Her eyebrows shot up. "You did what?!"

"I told him that I had seen what I thought was The Beast and that they should look into it."

"And how did he respond?"

"About as well as you'd expect. He did seem to believe me and didn't brush it off right away, but who knows. Now I'm questioning everything I saw…or, thought I saw." I took a long sip of my coffee to hide my shame.

"I've been thinking about it, maybe it was just a large animal of some sort. It could've been a deformed deer or something. You know anything is possible."

I nodded. "It could've been for sure. I'm going to give myself some time away from the cabin for the next few days. Maybe I'll head up there next week."

"I think that's a good idea. You've been going non-stop the last two years. Between work and renovating the cabin, you've been wearing yourself so thin."

"Work should calm down once we get through the holidays. If I can get the time off mid-December, I'm going to visit Kendra."

"That'll be really good for you. Take some time off, head up to Pittsburgh to freeze, and spend time with a good friend. It has all the makings to be a great trip."

"I agree. I'm not sure how I'm going to take the time off with such short notice, but I'll try."

"You've taken like three days off this entire year and I'm sure you checked your emails the entire time."

My eyes darted down and I shrugged. I knew she was right, I needed to start taking better care of myself. I was overworked, which, to be fair, is my own doing. I tend to put too much pressure on myself and take on whatever is asked of me. Hell, I volunteer to take things on because I know if I don't, no one else will.

Miranda glanced at her watch. "I have to run. I'm due at my parent's house in fifteen minutes for dinner. We'll talk later, okay?"

"Tell them I said hello!" I waved as she walked away.

I stared at my coffee cup, getting lost in my thoughts. When I started at Alliteration, I was the new hire who, even though I had a full-time job, I was still the one who was sent out on errands or to go pick up coffee.

Think of Anne Hathaway's character in *The Devil Wears Prada*, well, before she got her makeover.

As I started to prove myself within the marketing department, I started to gain the respect of the higher-ups and my coffee trips slowed substantially. My director started asking my opinions on certain campaigns and brought me into meetings no one else on my level was in.

Did I make enemies? Of course, that's human nature. Toss in a corporate setting and it was exacerbated.

Within two years, I was a manager in my department. Two years after that, I was a senior manager. Fast forward to earlier this year, I was once again promoted to director. I worked my hardest to change the culture within Marketing. I didn't want anyone else to feel like just because they were just starting out in their careers, their opinions weren't valuable. I am a firm believer all opinions matter in the workplace.

Taking on this leadership role also meant that I had bigger decisions to make. Instead of deciding on a campaign now, I was deciding what platforms and programs we would be using—which I love. Being the head of the team also meant that I covered for anyone if they needed it. In addition to our personal inboxes, we also have a shared inbox that we use for general requests and inquiries. Over the weekends and on holidays, people from overseas are still working, so I manage the inbox. I don't want my team members to have to change their plans to accommodate the mailbox, so I take care of it. I don't mind, really, it's usually pretty quiet.

I pulled myself out of my work thoughts and finished off my coffee before heading back home. The chill in the air went right through my jacket and hit my bones. When the lock clicked and the warm air hit my face, I was relieved to be home. I made my way to the couch and grabbed my work laptop, determined to get a few hours done in a desperate attempt to not check my email while at Thanksgiving dinner.

Since we're in the publishing industry, we have a bare-bones crew on standby just in case something happens. Each holiday every year, I volunteer to be on the crew. I'm not in a relationship, so it's easy for me to adjust my plans. For Christmas, the only plans I have to work around are the Christmas Eve dinner, movie and, Christmas Day until six at night.

I had finished clearing out my inbox when my stomach alerted me it was time to eat dinner. While I ate and watched television, I sent money to each of the managers that report to me. I did this every Sunday night. They were responsible for taking each of their employees out separately for the week and get coffee. They didn't have to talk about work, they could use that time however they wanted, but they had to be out of the building.

For the remote employees, they did virtual coffee chats. I wanted a culture where everyone enjoyed being around each other and collaborating. I set my phone aside and focused in on the new episode of *The Great British Bake Off* while looking at flights up to Pittsburgh.

CHAPTER 12

I WAS UP BEFORE THE SUN THIS MORNING. I HAD A CALL with my colleagues in London, so their ten o'clock meeting meant a four-thirty wakeup call for me. As much as it sucked being up that early, I could take a chilly walk to get coffee and watch the sunrise after I had successfully conquered that call. Let's not mince words, I was by no stretch of the imagination an early bird, but I could get up early when I needed to.

If my alarm hadn't started beeping, I would have been subjected to the continuation of the same nightmare I always had—being framed for a murder I didn't commit. This time, I was saved by my alarm before the dead body came into view.

While these nightmares used to be far and few between, it's becoming more of a recurring thing now. Every two to three nights I'm having the same dream.

I've searched for everything.

What is the meaning if you see a dead body in your dreams?

What does it mean if you are framed for a murder in a dream?

Lucid dreaming.

Recurring nightmare.

If you see a forest in your dream.

None of these searches were helpful because how was Google to know what was wrong with me? I gave up on researching a few months ago. When I told Miranda, what was going on, she immediately offered some suggestions: take a warm bath before bed, meditate, do yoga, have a cup of tea, see a psychiatrist. When she had offered up her psychiatrist's contact information, my blood ran cold.

I went to a psychiatrist a while back to work through some anxiety and depression issues I had been dealing with for years. The psychiatrist came highly recommended from multiple people in Byglass County, so I went to her.

The first visit went fine. Back, a week later to continue the conversation and that was the first time she asked me, "and, how does that make you feel?" I always saw that in movies, but I didn't think they *actually* asked that.

It makes me feel like shit; does that answer the question?

The following week, I returned and finally found the courage to confide in her about a disturbing incident. A man had pursued me to my car after I left a store and attempted to assault me. Despite my desperate cries for help, I only managed to escape unharmed thanks to the intervention of another man who was putting away his groceries nearby.

Until then, I had not shared this experience with anyone, not even my loved ones, due to a deep sense of shame that wasn't my own.

The morning after, I confided in the psychiatrist. I woke up feeling happy, as if the burden I had been carrying had been lifted.

However, my newfound sense of relief was short-lived.

An hour later, my aunt called me, having heard my story from the psychiatrist. She had violated doctor-patient confidentiality and spread my personal information throughout the town. Unfortunately, reporting her to the board yielded no consequences.

It was a valuable lesson for me: never see a psychiatrist who has personal connections to your family.

As I sat in my desk chair, gazing out the window, Mrs. Bethel walked by again, right on schedule. I jotted a note to remind myself to have tea with her sometime that week. Just as I finished, my laptop beeped, signaling it was time for me to join another meeting.

I glanced at the clock and saw it was just past seven. The workday was finally over. I was ready to make dinner and unwind on the couch with my laptop.

It had been a long day, with over three hundred emails to sort through and back-to-back meetings. I loved my job and had worked hard to get to where I was, but the workload was starting to take its toll.

As a Vice President, I couldn't imagine managing even more people. I used to make it a point to leave work by six, but my responsibilities had increased, and so had my hours.

Today, I started at 4:45 AM and just finished at 7:45 PM. I barely took any breaks, only stepping out for coffee in the morning and two quick bathroom breaks. This was all self-induced and I decided to make a New Year's Resolution to set stricter boundaries with work creating some work-life balance.

I checked my schedule and the week prior to Christmas appeared to be relatively calm, so I figured I could take a day or two off to visit Kendra. I blocked off my calendar for three days, closed my work laptop, and returned it to my office.

Next, I picked up my iPad and began searching for flights, which turned out to be less expensive than I had anticipated. Either people weren't interested in traveling to Pittsburgh during winter or I was simply fortunate. I don't consider myself a lucky person, so it was probably the former.

I called Kendra to confirm the dates. "Are you free in December?"

"Are you coming up? If the answer is yes, then I am more than free," I could tell by her tone she already knew, "But if the answer is no, then I'm not."

"Flights are cheap! I was hoping to book them tonight."

"Do it!" Kendra let out a squeal. "I'm so excited!"

"And, I can stay with you, right?" I wanted to confirm, just in case.

"Don't be stupid, of course! I wasn't going to make you stay at a hotel like a peasant."

A wide smile spread across my face. "I appreciate that."

"I'll have to start planning what we're going to do! I have many days to fill." I could almost hear the wheels turning in Kendra's head.

"Just remember that I am *more* than fine with just hanging out at home."

"Sounds good! I'll think of something for us to do. Just send me the flight info."

"As soon as I book it, I'll forward it over."

We chatted for a bit longer about Kendra's terrible new neighbor and how she's convinced he's a murder before hanging up. Having conversations like that made me happy, all my neighbors are very sweet and none of them could hurt a fly.

I booked my flight and called it a night because midnight was fast-approaching; I needed to be up at six to practice yoga, shower, and get ready for my seven-thirty video call with my boss's boss, Eve.

Early calls with co-workers living in the United States aren't common, but sometimes, they were inevitable.

Like this one. Eve apologized profusely, but we needed to meet to discuss a new system we were implementing.

By seven-twenty-five, I was in my desk chair, ready to turn the camera on and flash her my hundred-watt smile, pretending like I hadn't only slept for three hours because a certain nightmare woke me up.

When the nightmares started, I was able to shake them off quickly. Now that they're happening more frequently, they're getting harder to push out of my mind.

The dead man's face stays imprinted in my brain for an hour after I wake up. His lifeless amber eyes are open, piercing my soul. I scan to his neck, it's covered in fresh, bright red blood. His abdomen is sliced open. I snap back to reality and joined the call.

"Good morning, Cora!" Eve had her signature navy blue blazer on. She was a creature of habit and alternated between the same five or six blazers each week.

I threw on my biggest fake smile before I turned my camera on. "Good morning, Eve! How was your weekend?"

Eve tended to fill our meetings with stories about her kids, the latest family trip, or weekend activities. It could be nice if I was feeling exhausted on a Monday morning and not quite up to tackling important decisions.

I listened as she described the picturesque bed and breakfast they visited in Vermont, before steering the conversation back to the matter at hand.

"Enough about me! How was your weekend? How are you doing with everything going on?" I forgot I had mentioned it to both Eve and my direct manager, Jill.

"I guess, I'm better than I thought I would be?" It came out as more of a question than a statement. "I spoke with the detective yesterday, so I think my part is done. I need some time away from the cabin, so I'm going to try to spend the next few weeks home and clearing my mind. I took a few days off before Christmas to go visit my best friend, so that'll help."

"Good. Take whatever time you need. We know how much you work." Eve flashed a quick closed-lip smile, sympathetic to my current situation. "It looks like we have about twenty minutes left, so why don't we go ahead and talk about this new program."

We chatted about how we were going to implement the new

marketing program as I furiously jotted down every thought that came out of Eve's mouth. I needed to schedule meetings with my contact at the company we were partnering with, talk with our IT department to figure how to work out all the bugs in the system to make the program actually work, and have this done within the next three weeks.

This was going to be nearly impossible. System integrations took months, not weeks. My stress skyrocket off the chart, even though Eve was putting these incredibly outlandish timetables on. I respected Eve. She trusted her employees to make decisions that bettered the company. She never [really] questioned anyone and it was fantastic.

I've heard horror stories from Kendra of managers she had that were the devil reincarnated. I realized the fake smile was still dancing on my lips. I let it fall and started on some work.

I came up for air around two. One of the meetings I was on was cancelled, so I had an hour back in my day. Normally, I would take this time to get some work done, but today, I needed fresh air, some food, and a large coffee.

I stood up and stretched my long limbs, something I was trying to be better about—taking breaks within the day. If it was up to me, I would spend my entire life working.

Is that healthy? Not at all, but it was personal preference.

During my college years, I put in a lot of effort and dedication to my studies, and continued to do the same during my internships. Because of my hard work, I achieved a successful career path. Although my friends prioritize work-life balance, I prioritized my work over other activities.

My mom expressed concern I work too much, but in reality, she doesn't know the extent of it as she only sees me at family gatherings. Miranda urged me to take breaks during the day and prioritize my well-being.

I was resistant to her advice and frustrated when people try to tell me what's best for me. I believe my life is fulfilling, despite not following the conventional path of marriage and kids.

I own two beautiful homes, have a wonderful group of friends, and a successful career. Although my version of a fulfilling life may be different from others, it is meaningful to me.

As I looked out the window, it had started snowing, which was unusual for this time of the year. I was elated because I love the snow, even though some people dislike it. I put on my warm coat, a hat with a pom-pom, and the mittens I had sewed earlier in the year, and locked the door. The cold was so piercing penetrating through all the layers of clothing. Looking up, I saw the trees were bare and had icicles hanging from the branches.

Beautiful.

There was a light dusting of snow on the grass that glistened as I walked by on my way to The Higher Ground.

My eyes were down in a desperate attempt to not trip on the sidewalk. When I was younger, my parents joked I could trip going up the stairs… and it happened one day. The new joke was I could trip over air. While that's not happened [yet], I am the clumsiest of everyone in our family and out of my small group of friends. A badge I don't wear with honor.

Mid-step, I heard my name being called in front of me. I adjusted my gaze, taking a snowflake to the eye.

"Cora! Isn't this snow just beautiful?" Mrs. Bethel was walking towards me, a bright smile plastered across her face.

I smiled involuntarily. "Yes, it is. How are you doing today?"

We met in the middle. "I'm good." Her southern drawl was evident. "Just had to walk up to pick up a new book from Sharon." Sharon was the local librarian. It was a short walk to the library, so Mrs. Bethel frequented it multiple times per week.

"What'd you pick up?" I shoved my hands in my pockets. The chill had started to permeate my many layers.

"Just a new release from one of my favorite romance authors."

She looked longingly at the cover. Her husband had passed away a few years ago and she was lonely, she didn't make much of an effort to hide it. Her grandson, Griffin, visited somewhat often, but that was it.

I nodded towards the book. "It looks like a good one!"

"It's supposed to be!" A sharp wind gust almost knocked Mrs. Bethel's small frame over. "Oh goodness! I should get back home."

"Do you want me to walk with you?" I was actually concerned she would be blown over.

"You're so sweet, Cora. I'm good, though. Just another block to go!"

"Alright, you have my number if you need anything, right?"

"I do. Why don't you come by later and have some tea. Griffin is coming to town tomorrow, so I need to talk him up before you meet him."

A laugh escaped. "That sounds good. I'll be over around eight?"

"I'll have tea and cookies waiting." A soft smile spread across her face, she was so happy to have company coming over.

We parted ways and I continued on to the coffee shop. As I waited for my cue to cross the street, I glanced over my shoulder to make sure Mrs. Bethel made it into her house.

I entered The Higher Ground and the aroma of coffee wafted into my nose. I was convinced the only smell better than a fresh cut Frasier Fir tree is freshly roasted and brewed coffee. I made my way to the counter and ordered a coffee. I waited at the end of the bar for it to be ready and observed my fellow patrons.

Since it was the week of Thanksgiving, the coffee shop was more busy than usual. There were families and friends enjoying time together, catching up on their lives. I looked at the couple in the corner, snuggled up, laughing and drinking their coffee. A pang of wanting hit me in the chest.

The barista called my name just in time to pull me out of

my thoughts about why I needed to be in a relationship. I took my coffee and went next door to the sandwich shop to get some lunch. Deciding to order a large sandwich, I planned to save the leftovers for dinner.

With coffee and sandwich in hand, I walked back home. Upon arriving, I was greeted by a cozy warmth and the delightful fragrance of a pot of cranberries, cinnamon, oranges, and cloves simmering on the stove.

I sat at the island in my kitchen to keep myself away from my laptop. If I ate in my office, even though, I planned on scrolling on my phone, I would get sucked into my black hole of an email inbox. Five minutes before my next block of meetings, I made my way back into my office to finish out my day.

My office was getting darker as the sun fell below the horizon. For many people, they had already logged off for the day, but for me, I still had two more hours of work to get done to account for the lunch break I took earlier. I glanced at the clock and it was just after seven. The street lights were on and the snow had stopped, leaving behind a dusting of white all over the long-dead grass. I admired the way the icicles on the trees sparkled under the lights.

Log-off, Cora. It's not that important. These emails will be there tomorrow.

I had to force myself to log off most evenings.

The words of Taylor Swift echoed in my brain, "You're on your own, kid. You have always been."

Finishing my sandwich, I walked to Mrs. Bethel's house as she lived a few doors down. I arrived right on time. Before the door opened I was met with Mrs. Bethel standing there in a matching sweatsuit and curlers in her hand.

"Come in, dear! It's gotten chillier out there." She moved aside to welcome me in.

Stepping into her house was like visiting my grandparents—the house was cozy, had some eclectic décor she had accumulated over her years. It had a faint smell of mothballs.

I hung my coat in the hall closet and followed her into the living room where she had two teacups waiting for tea and a large plate of chocolate chip cookies.

"Did you make these because I was coming over?"

"I love you dearly, but don't flatter yourself. I made them for both you and Griffin."

Don't feel so self-important.

I sat on the floral print couch, reaching for a warm cookie. "Are you looking forward to his visit?"

I already knew the answer, but it was nice to ask.

"Very much so. It's been almost a year since I last saw him, so it'll be nice to catch up and have some company around the house." Mrs. Bethel disappeared into the kitchen and brought back the tea kettle, pouring us both a cup before sitting down.

"So, what's new with you, Cora Grace? How's work?"

I wished I could jump in there and hide from this question. "It's been fine, busy as usual."

"You work way too much. Between you and Griffin, I'm not sure which one of you is worse."

"What does Griffin do?" She had been trying to set us up for a while, maybe this is the time I actually follow-through and meet him.

"He's an architect down in Charlotte."

My eyebrow raised involuntarily. "Wow, that's impressive! You must be proud."

"I'd be prouder if he was married and giving me great grand-babies." She laughed, but I could tell she partially meant it.

"You're not going to find me judging him. I'm in the same boat."

"I need the two of you to meet. Are you around Wednesday night? Maybe the three of us could get dinner out."

"That would be great, I'd like that. Let's aim for seven?" *Not a lie.*

She nodded. We sat in silence for a moment, enjoying our tea and each other's company.

"Has work been busy?" She broke the silence first.

"Yeah, it has. Not more than usual though."

"Then, why do you seem like something is bothering you?" *Because it is.*

"Just running on fumes, is all."

She nodded before pressing on. "Are you sure? You don't seem like your bright, happy self. Is it because of the holidays?"

I shrugged and shook my head. "I'm not sure what's going on with me. Maybe I'm just getting older and starting to realize that there's more to life than working. I feel like I did life backwards. I should've dated more seriously while I was still in school. Maybe I'd be sitting at home with my husband right now, no offense."

"Absolutely none taken." Mrs. Bethel took a bite of a cookie. "When Griffin Sr. and I met all those years ago, I knew it was love at first sight. We got engaged quickly and then married shortly after. Want to know a secret?"

I nodded, encouraging her to finish her thought.

"Even though he was the love of my life and I wouldn't trade a moment of our lives together, sometimes, I wish I had met him later in life so I would have had a career. I got married at nineteen, I had practically just graduated high school, and there I was walking down the aisle. Griffin went to work and I stayed home with the kids."

It was oddly refreshing to hear. Maybe I hadn't screwed up my life.

"What did you want to do?"

"I wanted to be a teacher. Which, I eventually was able to do when we homeschooled our two kids."

She had the best of both worlds.

We chatted about work and her life for a while before she turned the conversation back onto me.

"Is anything new with you?"

Do I tell her about Luke and everything that happened?

"Well…"

"I sense a story!" She snuggled further into the chair.

"A crazy one."

"Even better."

"That would explain it then." For both of our sakes, we took this as our answer. I didn't need to let my creative mind wander anymore.

We chatted for a while longer about Luke. "You've lived in the mountains for a while, right?"

She nodded. "My entire life."

"So you've heard all the crazy folklores?"

"Oh have I! My favorite was this one I heard maybe thirty or so years ago. I had heard about it when I was a child, but it died off. Until one day a girl went missing on her way to school and was found in the woods…"

I cut her off. "Mauled to death."

"Yes! That one. It creeped me out, even at almost fifty years old. What relevance does this have to your story? Or, were you going to tell me that story of the folklore?"

"My story involves the folklore about the Beast."

Her eyes went wide. Unless she spoke with some of our neighbors that had seen it on the news, I knew Mrs. Bethel wouldn't have known about what's been going on in my life the last week and some change.

"You know the cabin I renovated?" I didn't wait for an answer because she knew what I was talking about. "I had a guy that booked it for a weekend with his friends, which might have been a cover-up for an affair, but he never showed up. He sent me a message saying that they weren't able to make it, but he was still going to pay me. His body was found mauled not too far from the cabin."

Her eyes went wide and she wiped her hands on her pants, her knee bounced. "Surely it was just a coincidence."

"It could have been. But I think I saw something while I was up there. It looked an awful lot like the drawings people have done and it matched the description perfectly."

"And, you were of sound mind when all this happened?"

I nodded. "I think so."

"I see."

"You think I'm crazy."

"No, I don't, actually. I had an ...experience when I was a young girl."

My mouth fell open. *Was she trying to make me feel better?*

"I think I was ten years old. I was outside playing hide and seek with my friends, something you should never do in a forest. I ran off in a different direction from the group and didn't realize until it was too late. I had wandered off to a sharp cliff. I heard some yelling, so I ran back towards where I came from, or so I thought. I ended up in a heavily wooded area and couldn't see or hear anything, until I did." She crossed her legs and her foot bounced. "I kept walking until I heard a voice. It sounded like a woman, so I walked towards it."

She took a sip of her tea. "I heard a lot of rustling in front of me and then was face-to-face with a creature." She shuddered. "So, no, I don't think you're crazy."

"How did you get away?" I broke my silence.

"I started screaming. Once I did, it ran away on two feet."

It was my turn to shudder. "Did you tell anyone about it?"

She nodded. "I did. And everyone thought I was crazy. Do you blame them? Would you believe it if someone told you that?"

I shook my head.

"Did you tell the police?" she finally asked.

"I did. I'm not sure if they believed me or thought I was crazy."

"I mean, probably a little bit of both, if I'm honest. So what are you going to do now? Are you going to sell the cabin?"

"I'm not sure yet. I can't even be sure of what I saw. I've been so busy with work and I've been having some nightmares, I can't even picture it anymore."

Mrs. Bethel relaxed her forehead. "You probably saw a deformed bear or something. I read an article not too long ago about animal mutations because they were drinking some chemical-filled water. I don't remember the whole story, but it basically said some animals were mutating."

We were talking about Luke and the unfortunate situation when I saw a small yawn escape her mouth.

I looked at my watch. "It's getting late, I should get home." I headed for the door, grabbing my jacket. "Thank you for the tea and cookies. And the talk. I appreciate them more than you know."

"You know you're always welcome here."

Her small frame made its way over to me and enveloped me in a hug. A much-needed hug for both of us, if I'm honest. My grandma had passed away a few years ago and I loved anytime I could spend some time, with people, around her age. While no one could replace my grandma, Mrs. Bethel helped to fill the void, well.

When I walked in the door to my home, I breathed a sigh of relief. Mrs. Bethel was probably right, I probably had seen some kind of mutated bear. I still didn't have answers on why Luke bailed on the reservation. They were still up there, but that was a problem for Detective Ambrose and not me. As far as I was concerned, I had nothing to do with the case at all.

I was an innocent bystander in all this.

CHAPTER 13

I DIDN'T HAVE ANY WORK CALLS UNTIL EIGHT-THIRTY AND no camera needed on this morning, so I was able to roll out of bed with my alarm in my pajamas.

Perks of it being the week of Thanksgiving: not many people are in, which means not many meetings. I had gotten through the hard day of the week, so the next two days will be status quo and I'll be smooth sailing to a much-needed day off.

This morning went off without a hitch, some of my meetings were even cancelled. The afternoon flew by and before I knew it, I was done with calls and I had gotten caught up on some of my inbox. I logged off at six, which was extraordinarily early for me and remembered I had nothing to wear for Thanksgiving. I was on the hunt for a new dress, so a trip to the mall was a must... two days before Thanksgiving.

Brilliant.

I've always hated going shopping alone because I tend to second-guess myself and leave with nothing. I needed to recruit Miranda, so I sent her a text asking her what she was doing.

My phone rang immediately. "I'm free. What are we doing?"

I loved how there were never any hesitations with her. She was always ready for anything.

"I need a dress for Thursday. Help me?"

"I'll be at your place in five. Let me put on real pants."

A few years ago when I bought my house, it was love at first sight. It was a beautiful Fall day and I had just picked up a book from the library and had decided to walk around and enjoy the fresh air. I lived in an apartment, but I wanted my own space, so I had started looking at houses.

I had no intention of buying anything that quickly, but the black fence lured me in and the white brick two-story home with blue shutters sold me. The front yard was fenced in and bushes lined the front of the fence giving me privacy. There were even big, beautiful old trees surrounding the house.

There happened to be an open house that day, so I was able to go inside and fell in love with the modern, clean style. I put an offer in on it immediately and a week later, after much negotiation, the sellers accepted my offer.

The day I found out it was going to be mine, Miranda and I drove over so I could show her the house. We drove around the neighborhood when a red brick house just down the street caught her eye. Three months later, we were both new homeowners and lived walking distance from each other.

For the holidays, I put holly and Christmas tree scraps in the window boxes and line the windows and door with string lights. I put fresh garland on the railing up the front stairs. As stressful as it can be, the holidays are my favorite time of the year. I decorate the inside of my house, too, and as I watch television on the couch with the fire roaring, sipping on tea, while the aroma of pine mixed with the burning embers.

Four minutes later, Miranda was there, knocking on the front door.

"Let's go!" she ushered us to the car while I locked up.

"What type of dress are we looking for?" Miranda asked, getting in the car.

The engine roared to life. "Something casual. It's just the immediate family this year."

"After last year, that is a good thing." Last Thanksgiving, my aunts and uncles came over and there was a screaming match amongst them.

Someone owed someone else money and it just spiraled from there. It got ugly quick.

We pulled up to the mall and found a front space. We took off our coats because our mall kept the temperature at 80 degrees in the winter. It was cold out, but 80 with a jacket on would kill you. Our first stop was a bust and we chatted about my upcoming trip to Pittsburgh.

"What else is new with you?" Miranda asked, holding out a cute plaid jumper and black long-sleeve top. I reached for it, adding it to the pile of potential purchases I was carrying around.

"I went over to Mrs. Bethel's last night."

"And, how did that go?" She's always been skeptical of her for some reason.

"It was good. We chatted about her grandson a little bit. I'm meeting him tomorrow night."

A look of shock spread across her face. "Are you going on a date?"

"Not unless you count Mrs. Bethel also being there as a date."

"Oof. Never mind then."

"The three of us are going out for dinner. I'm not expecting anything to come from it. If nothing else, it'll be good practice. I think it's time I start dating."

"Does this mean you'll actually stop working so much?" Miranda raised an eyebrow, skeptical.

"I think so. Today was a nice change of pace. Meetings were

cancelled, I was able to get stuff done, and I logged off way earlier than usual."

"I've heard this before. I'll believe it after it happens."

I made my way to the changing rooms to try on the dresses we had pulled from the racks. With each outfit, I either got a thumbs up or thumbs down from Miranda. Almost everything was returned to the rack, but the jumper she had picked was extremely flattering, so that was coming home with me.

"Do you want to grab some dinner?" I asked, swiping my card.

"To whom do I owe this honor? First, shopping. Now dinner!"

"You're an ass sometimes." I shot back.

Thanksgiving outfit in-hand, we walked around for a bit more because Miranda was convinced that I needed a new top to meet Griffin in.

She pulled sparkly tops off the racks and I vetoed each one. "When do you ever know me to wear sparkles?"

"Never. But maybe you should start."

"Won't happen. Let's tone it down a notch."

I pulled an oatmeal-colored long cardigan off the rack and waved Miranda over to get her opinion. She tapped her chin and walked away, returning a minute later with a shimmery nude-colored cami.

"Put this under that and that's perfect."

I wouldn't admit it, but it was a pretty combination. I admired my reflection in the fitting room mirror before coming out to show Miranda. *I felt pretty.* The shimmer in the cami complimented the color in the cardigan perfectly. I stepped out of the room to get Miranda's opinion.

"You're buying that. It looks amazing on you. If you wear that with those dark wash skinny jeans you have and maybe a pair of brown heeled boots, you'll be a smoke show."

"I feel really good in it. It's coming home with me!"

I paid and we left to go get dinner, making small talk on the way to the restaurant. We were seated immediately and a waiter came over to take our drink order.

"What's new in Miranda Land?" I asked, sipping on my Dr. Pepper.

"Not a whole bunch. Same shit, different day. What about you? Anything else aside from dinner tomorrow? Any family gossip for me?"

"No family gossip, at least yet. I'll get the low-down from my mom on Thursday." I took a long sip of my drink, unsure if I should tell Miranda about the story Mrs. Bethel told me. She was already skeptical of this woman, I don't know if she'd believe it.

"I look forward to hearing it all on Friday! I'm working, so come in and give me the scoop." Since we've been friends since high school, Miranda knew all my family members, so when I brought family drama to dinner, she was here for it.

"Mrs. Bethel told me an interesting story today."

"What was it about?"

"The Beast…" My pulse pounded in my ears.

Miranda choked on her drink. "What?"

"She told me about her encounter with something similar when she was young. It sounded exactly like what I saw and she seemed to believe me, but then she told me it was probably a mutated animal. So, I'm not sure what to think."

"Hm. Interesting." Her eyes wandered around the restaurant. "It's not that I don't believe you, because I do. You've had such bad nightmares and haven't been sleeping well. Don't you think maybe you were seeing things?"

"So you don't believe me."

"I believe you saw something, but maybe it was a regular animal. It was raining and foggy, it could have distorted what you were actually seeing."

She doesn't believe me. I couldn't make eye contact, I felt crazy.

What if she's right, what if I hadn't actually seen anything—it very well could've been an animal, it was far enough away.

My mind immediately went to Detective Ambrose and how as soon as I left, I was probably the laughingstock of the police department.

"You're probably right." I thought about it for a moment. "Why did you seem to believe me the other day, then?"

"Because I figured you were having some kind of trauma response. A man was found dead on your property—that's pretty dramatic."

I nodded because she was right. Maybe I saw what I wanted to see. We enjoyed our food and we stuck to lighter topics—when Miranda was going to host her holiday party with me going out of town the week before Christmas, this dinner with Griffin, and what was going on with her family.

We finished dinner and I dropped her back off at her house so she didn't have to walk back home in the dark and cold. The sidewalks had iced over slightly from the melting snow. I brought my purchases inside and hung them up before stepping into a scalding shower. I needed to steam my mind clear of all the negativity.

The bathroom fogged up and I stripped out of my clothes and into the hot shower, letting the water hit my neck. I rested my head on the back wall of the shower stall. I could feel the muscles in my neck starting to loosen and felt the stress of the last few weeks, hell, months, float away.

I turned the handle towards the hot side a little bit more. The shower steamed up even more and I washed my body and hair. I reached for the shower handle when the world went black.

CHAPTER 14

WOKE UP WITH A THROBBING HEAD THIS MORNING.
I don't know what happened last night, one minute I was reaching for the shower handle to turn it off and the next I was lying on the bathroom floor, my feet still in the shower. I reached for my phone on the counter and I had only been out for a few minutes. I must have made the water too hot and over-heated. I had some water and went to bed.

I wish I could say I had a restful night of sleep. *Ha.*

I don't even know what that is anymore. These nightmares are ruining my life. As soon as I fell asleep, the nightmare started. I was able to wake myself up towards the end, but as soon as I fell back to sleep, it happened, again. This cycle repeated five times over the course of seven hours.

I'm exhausted, but it should be another slow day at work.

I reached for my work phone to see what my calendar looked like for the day. I originally had eight meetings today and now I only have three. *I love holidays.* I worked from my phone in my bed, just answering emails until my call at ten. I showered and got ready for the day around nine-thirty and started to feel better.

Around eleven, I really wanted to go back to bed, so I took my laptop and worked from my bed with a movie on. I finished my meetings at three, so I took the open window in my calendar to call Kendra.

She picked up on the first ring. "Are you okay?"

"Yes! Just because I call in the middle of the day, it doesn't mean I'm dying, Kendra."

"Whatever you say. What's up?"

"I have a dinner tonight." *I'm excited.*

"With who?"

"Mrs. Bethel and her grandson."

"The one she's been trying to set you up with for years?" I could hear the smile through the phone. Kendra had been dying for me to meet this guy ever since the first time Mrs. Bethel brought it up right after I moved in.

"Yep, that one."

"Are you nervous?" I could hear her practically tossing her laptop aside, sitting crossed legged on her bed.

"A little bit. It's not a date because his freakin' grandma will be there, but I feel like I don't know how to even act anymore. I'm not an interesting person." It felt good to finally admit that.

"It's going to be just fine. You know she'll be there to fill the conversation. I'd be surprised if you two actually even talk by yourselves. Try to stay calm."

I couldn't hold in a yawn. "Sorry, I'm exhausted."

"Nightmare again?"

"Nightmares, yeah." I hoped she didn't pick up on the multiple.

"Nightmares?" Kendra emphasized the 's.'

"Yeah. It happened a few times last night."

"Has that happened before?"

"Not really." *A lie.*

"Did anything happen last night that could've caused it?"

"Other than me passing out, no."

"Excuse me?"

"I made the shower too hot last night and overheated. I was only out for three minutes, I'm fine."

"Cora, you should have gone to the hospital to get checked out! You could have a concussion."

"My head hit my pile of clothes, I'm fine. I promise."

"You just need to start taking care of yourself more. I sure hope that you and Griffin hit it off. You need a distraction from this damn job."

"I know. He's an architect, so that's pretty cool. I just, I don't know. I feel so weird."

"You're exhausted. Just be yourself and it'll be great. What do you have to lose? This guy doesn't even live close, does he?"

"That's a great question. I don't think so."

"I rest my case." I could practically hear Kendra's smirk through the phone.

"You're right. I'm putting too much pressure on this situation unnecessarily. If I don't make a complete fool of myself, maybe when I'm up there we can create some dating app profiles for me."

A squeal escaped Kendra's mouth and I had to pull the phone away from my ear.

"And, now I'm deaf."

"You're dramatic. But are you serious? I can create profiles for you?"

"Yep. *Only* if tonight goes well." My stomach turned.

"I can work with this! I'm excited that this is finally happening."

Kendra and Miranda had both been trying to get me on dating apps for years much to my dismay. I was a firm believer that you couldn't meet someone via a phone, you needed to meet in person; but I wasn't cool and with the times, so I had to rely on them for help now. I didn't like admitting defeat, but knew they were right. With my work schedule, I needed to try the apps first so I could talk with guys on my time from the safety of my own home.

"Don't get too excited. I didn't say I would use them; I just said you could create the profiles." I had every intention of actually using them, I just wanted to mess with Kendra.

"Whatever, I'll take what I can get." I heard her laptop make a noise. "Ugh, I have a meeting I need to get to. Text me later and let me know how dinner goes?"

I agreed and let her go to her meeting. This was weird, this is the first time I've had to let someone go and it wasn't me that was running off to another meeting. I finished out my day at five, the earliest time in months, if not all year. It was weird not having anything to do.

I took the time I had to sit down and watch some television. Not that I didn't do that, but now I was able to sit down and watch the show, not just listen while I was coming up with strategies or answering emails.

I could get used to this.

An hour before I was supposed to leave, I started getting ready. I took Miranda's fashion advice and wore the exact outfit she said I should. I swiped makeup across my pale skin and curled my hair. While I always did hair and makeup and went the full nine yards when I was on a work trip, I didn't while I was at home. It had been ages since I had taken my time at home and gotten ready. I looked at my reflection in the mirror and didn't hate it.

Concealer works wonders.

Normally, I look at myself with disgust because all I see are the tired eyes, ratty sweatpants, and dark circles, but tonight I looked like I was full of life. Despite not getting much sleep last night. Right on time, I was heading out the door to walk down to Mrs. Bethel's house.

As I approached the stairs, I caught a glimpse of Mrs. Bethel in the window, presumably waiting for me. I took a deep breath. *You've got this, Cora.*

Barely on the second step, the heavy front door swung open. "Cora!"

"Hi, Mrs. Bethel." I leaned down for a hug.

"Come in, dear. Griffin is just inside."

My stomach lurched, nervously picking at my nail polish as I followed her into the living room to meet Griffin. My eyes trailed up to his inviting face. His sharp blue eyes met mine and pierced into my soul. *He was trouble.*

He stood up and extended his hand. "I'm Griffin, it's nice to finally meet you, Cora."

An involuntary smile spread across my lips. "It's nice to meet you as well. Your grandma has spoken *very* highly of you."

"She tends to oversell." He laughed and I took note of the smile lines around his eyes. The bottom half of his face was angular and covered by brown stubble, the same color as his perfectly quaffed hair. *I hit the jackpot.*

"We'll see about that." I smirked. Who did I think I was just flirting like that? That came way more naturally than I had anticipated.

"Shall we head out, kids?" Mrs. Bethel stood by the door, smiling from ear-to-ear.

"After you." Griffin motioned for me to go in front of him.

I smiled in his direction, a silent thank you.

Mrs. Bethel bolted for her car, leaving Griffin to lock up. Unsure of where to go—is it awkward to stay with him? Is it more awkward to go? Just as I felt the blush creep up in my cheeks, Mrs. Bethel called out from her car.

"I'm driving!"

"No, grandma, you're not. You have a very capable grandson and a more than capable neighbor—both of which will not let you drive right now."

"You always have to ruin my fun. Let's go ride in your fancy car."

He rolled his eyes playfully at her. They had a sweet bond. We got in the car and Mrs. Bethel rattled off directions to Griffin, causing him to make three wrong turns. I wasn't about to get in the middle of their argument, I sat in the back seat for a reason. I hope I'm that sassy when I'm eighty. We arrived at the diner and were seated and ordered, all within being in the building for eight minutes.

Yes, I looked.

We settled into a comfortable conversation, Mrs. Bethel bridging the gap between the two of us. He talked about work and the building he's designing in Charlotte. He only lives two hours away, that's not bad. After we finished eating, Griffin drove us back to the house.

I got out, not wanting to intrude on any more of their evening. "It was really nice to meet you, Griffin."

"Where are you going?" Mrs. Bethel asked, standing on the stairs, Griffin holding her back.

"Home. I know y'all don't have much time together. I don't want to intrude!" *I don't want to.* I was enjoying the conversation.

I swore I could see the corner of Griffin's mouth droop.

"You know, I could use some time alone. This guy has been here all day and he's been up my butt. Why don't you kids head back over to Cora's to get to know each other better."

He looked in my direction. "I'm not sure if I should be offended or thankful."

"I think a little bit of both!" I glanced down the block, trying to remember if I had any embarrassing things lying out at home. "You're more than welcome to come over to my place. I have wine."

"Are you sure?" Griffin asked, not wanting to impose on my evening.

"Griffin Brooks, she said she has wine. Go on over." Mrs. Bethel called from the front door.

I lowered my voice so only he could hear. "She used your middle name, you should probably come back to my place."

He laughed. "Alright, let's go. Did you want me to drive?"

"It's only down the street, I think we can walk."

We walked back to my house and I said a silent prayer that it didn't still smell like the Chinese takeout leftovers that I had forgotten about in my fridge. I wasn't expecting company, so there were dishes in the sink, blankets and pillows all over the couch, and mail on the counters.

If the mess didn't scare him away, then he was truly a saint. I know I'm not a messy person, but some guys are repulsed by women who didn't keep their house in pristine condition. My house was lived in and that's how it was going to stay.

"Come on in. Make yourself at home." I reached for the jacket he was taking off, so I could hang it up for him.

"Thank you." He looked around the foyer and into the living room. I cringed, hoping he didn't make a snide comment about the shit everywhere.

"This is a beautiful home. Do you know when it was built?" He ran his long, slender fingers over the molding on the doorframe.

"Thank you. I think it was around 1930 or so." I walked into the kitchen, hoping he would follow. That's exactly what he did.

"Would you like some wine? I have red and white."

"Whatever you prefer is fine with me." Griffin leaned against the island in the kitchen, watching me as I reached for a bottle of red.

I poured two small glasses and we made our way to the couch.

"So, Cora Grace, tell me more about you now that my nosey grandmother isn't here." His blue eyes stared into mine, searching for more information.

"It's just Cora, you can drop the Grace." I laughed, I knew exactly where he got it from.

"Sorry, you know where I got it from."

"It's totally fine, I promise. She's the only one who calls me that." I smiled warmly, easing the tension. "I'm pretty boring, honestly. I spend most of my time working, which I'm trying to be better about. I was renovating a house in the mountains, but since that's done now, I spend whatever free time I have reading."

"A mountain house, I didn't know that." Griffin's eyes lit up.

My stomach turned. I didn't want to talk about The Widow's Peak more than I had to. "Yep, I finished up last month and now I'm just waiting for a booking."

And, for someone to not show up dead.

"That's so cool! Is it nearby? I'd love to check it out."

"It's about a half hour away. I can take you there if you'd like."

"Can we? That would be awesome. Obviously, as an architect, I love to look at homes and their details."

I placed my glass of wine that was only missing one sip on the coffee table and looked at the time on my phone, it was only eight, so we could be there for a bit. "Sure. We can go now if you'd like."

Like a kid on Christmas morning, Griffin sprung up from the couch and bounded for the closet to grab our coats. He brought life into my quiet house and I liked that.

We made our way to my car and I tried my best to hide my thumping chest—thank goodness for this puffy coat. My hands were sweating and I felt like I was going to be sick. Griffin took notice.

"Are you okay? You look like you don't feel well."

"Sometimes the winding road makes me a little carsick, I'll be fine once we get there." That lie came out easily.

"If you want me to drive, I'd be happy to."

"We're only five minutes away, I'll be fine. But thank you." I kept my eyes on the road and refused to look off to the side into the trees.

What if everyone was wrong and I did actually see something out here?

CHAPTER 15

E PULLED UP THE LONG DRIVEWAY AND THE HOUSE CAME into view. Everything looked as it had when I left, nothing was out of place. I held my breath as I unlocked the front door—I needed to conquer this fear.

This is *my* house.

Griffin insisted on going in first, the polite thing to do. I trailed right behind, compulsively picking my nails.

He looked around, taking in all the work I had done. "Cora, this is incredible. Did you do all this by yourself?"

"No, I had a bunch of help. I could maybe take credit for 50% of it." I forced a smile.

"You should be proud of yourself, this is a huge feat." His eyes danced around the house. "Do you mind if I take a look around?"

"Of course not, go right ahead."

I took off my jacket and hung it up by the door, making my way to the kitchen to turn on a light. I wanted to spend time with Griffin, but I wanted to get the hell out of this house. Just being here, even with another human, was unnerving. I leaned my elbows on the counter and put my head in my hands, staring out the back window.

"Cora, you're bleeding."

I snapped out of my thoughts, I had zoned out. "What?"

He motioned towards my thumb, there was blood dropping onto the counter. I had picked at my cuticles enough to make it bleed, a new one—even for me.

"Oh. I do that sometimes. Nervous tick."

"My mom used to do that. I get it." Griffin's words were comforting. I've never had people understand my nervous habits before. People usually try to fix it, not try to understand.

"It hurts like a bitch. I wish I picked up the normal anxious habit of bouncing my knee or something."

"It's less conspicuous than bouncing your knee. My guess is you pick at your fingers during work calls?"

I nodded.

"What are you anxious about?" Griffin sat across from me at the kitchen island.

Do I tell him everything and inevitably scare him off? Or, do I just blame it on work?

"Work has been busier than usual. I think I've just internalized it."

Griffin narrowed his eyes and I wondered if Mrs. Bethel had told him everything that had gone on over the last week and a half.

"Did you want to stay for a while?"

"Yeah, I'd like that. This is a cool place you've got here."

"Thank you. I'll go get a fire started." I started for the fireplace.

"I can take care of that." Griffin tinkered around the fireplace while I sat on the couch and turned on a coffee shop acoustic playlist. Within a few minutes, there was a roaring fire in the fireplace.

"You were able to do that so quickly! It would've taken me at least a half hour to get the logs lit."

"Just call me an expert fire builder." Griffin winked, still crouched by the fire.

He made his way over to the other side of the couch and sat down, admiring his fire before turning and facing me. "Tell me something about yourself that not many people know."

Here we go.

"I have nightmares." Why am I telling a stranger my secret?

"What kind of nightmares?" Griffin's eyebrow raised involuntarily.

"It's the same one over and over. It never varies."

"So, is it like you're watching the same horror movie over and over?"

"Pretty much."

"What's it about? Maybe talking about it will help you work through it."

"It doesn't happen every night. Some nights are worse than others. If I told you, you'd think I was crazy."

"I could never." He paused before continuing, "Unless you put pineapple on your pizza, and then I would."

I motioned like I was writing something in a notebook, "Do not put pineapple on pizza."

"Do you actually do that?" Griffin's eyes went wide.

"No. Although I wouldn't think someone was crazy if they did."

"Did I just hit a sore spot?"

"Not at all." I smiled. "Just standing up for those who like pizza with something sweet and tangy."

"Then that's fine. I won't pressure you into telling me. I can tell that it's a tough subject for you to talk about, so I'm here if you want to talk."

He was being really kind and I could tell him, "The dream starts off the same each time. I'm walking through a forest, look-ing for something. I can never remember what. I walk for a while and find a shoe in the same place each time. I look to the left and there's a man's body lying there, covered in blood. Clearly, he's dead. I scream and then sprint down the mountain to the police station. I tell them everything that's happened and when I look down at my body, there's blood everywhere." I took a deep breath and continued. "It doesn't feel like any time has passed and I have handcuffs around my wrists and I just can't talk."

"Wow, that's some heavy stuff. I'm sorry you're having to deal with that." Griffin caught my gaze. "Probably a stupid question, but do you know the dead guy?"

I shake my head. "I don't. I used to see his face so clearly, but lately, it's getting a little bit fuzzy."

"Next silly question. Did you look any of that up in a dream dictionary?"

"I have. The only helpful thing I was able to find was that if you dream that you're lost in a forest, it signifies that you are searching through your subconscious for a better understanding of yourself." I took a sip of my water. "I don't know if that's true or not."

"Are you struggling with figuring out who you are?"

"Are you a psychiatrist instead of an architect all of a sudden?" It was a joke, but I really did appreciate the interest Griffin had taken in my brain.

"I'm a man of many talents." At that, we both laughed and the conversation became much more light-hearted.

We lost track of time because when Griffin checked his phone, it was nearing midnight and the fire had died out an hour earlier. "We should probably head home. I know you have dinner with your family tomorrow…er, today."

A yawn snuck out of my mouth. "Yeah, we should get back. Your grandma is probably stressed with your whereabouts."

"Are you kidding me? She was thrilled that I was going back

to your house. This has been her plan all along. She's like that Taylor Swift song—Mastermind."

My jaw dropped. "You're a Swiftie?"

"I did *not* say that. I think some of her songs are catchy and nothing more."

"Whatever you say. All I heard was that you knew one of her songs." I smirked, locking up behind us.

We walked to the car and I started to get in when I looked up at the balcony. A large creature was standing there, watching us. I was frozen.

I looked over at him and swallowed hard, my heart pounding in my ears. "Griffin, do you see that?"

"See what?" He slammed the car door closed.

"That." I pointed in the direction of whatever it was I saw.

I followed his gaze…nothing was there.

"What was it?" he asked, curious.

"It looked like an animal. It must have walked away."

I picked at the cuticles on my left hand the entire way home. I couldn't let Griffin see.

CHAPTER 16

THE SOUND OF RAIN PUMMELED MY WINDOW BEFORE I EVEN opened my eyes. Not only did I have to sit through a family gathering, but it was also disgusting out. The things I would do to be able to stay home today.

If I'm honest with myself, I was only going so I could visit with my brother, James, and his wife, Charlotte. They moved to Florida last year, so we only saw each other for holidays. I hadn't seen them since last Christmas, so that was the one factor that was pushing me to get out of bed.

I got ready and was pulling into my parent's driveway by ten. My mom loved to have everyone there early to socialize and have thirty-five different appetizers. The woman didn't know the definition of excess.

I entered the beehive of activity—my mom was bustling around the kitchen, yelling at my dad. My extended family was gathered around the dining room table, snacking on the appetizers. My brother and sister-in-law were nowhere in sight, which meant they were already hiding from family.

Gathering the rest of my courage, I entered the kitchen to say hello to my parents and relatives.

They're all great people, but extended family…ya know?

"Cora!" a cacophony of voices called out as I made my presence known.

Ugh.

I made my way to everyone, partaking in small talk about my new role with Alliteration, the cabin renovations, and miscellaneous other trivial things. I was thanking my lucky stars that no one brought up Luke Anderson because I hadn't rehearsed any answers.

I made my way back to my parents. "Where are James and Lottie?"

"Upstairs hiding. Go on ahead, we'll call y'all when dinner is ready."

I bounded up the stairs; I could hear their voices coming from what was James' room. I walked over to the ajar door quietly, they were looking at old pictures.

"Knock, knock." I tapped on the door.

"Cora!" Charlotte, or as I called her, Lottie, jumped up from her spot on the bed and embraced me. I squeezed her back tightly. All my life, I wanted a sister and two years ago, my brother got married and gave me the best one I could've asked for. We're creepily similar, so now he has two of us to gang-up on him.

"Hey, little sister." James came over to hug me as well.

The three of us sat on James' old bed, catching up on life over the last year. I wanted to hear all about Lottie's new job, so I did my best to always direct the conversation away from me.

"Cora, why don't we go to the cabin between dinner and dessert? We're dying to see it!"

Poor choice of wording.

It was evident I didn't want to talk about it. "Maybe next time."

"We leave tomorrow morning. We won't be back for a while." James' brow furrowed. "Let's just go today."

"It's a mess, we really should go another time."

"Cora, what's wrong?" My brother was one of the few people who could pick up when something was wrong. I was thankful, my parents were just oblivious enough to never pry.

"I just don't want to go, okay? I was there last night." I was short.

"You're just acting weird. Why don't you tell us what's going on."

I finally snapped. "Can you *please* just leave it alone?"

Both James and Lottie stared at me with wide eyes.

"James, she doesn't want to go. Don't push the issue." Lottie interjected.

"Something is wrong and she won't tell us." James snapped back.

"Fine! You want to know what's wrong, James? I'll tell you. Remember that story of The Beast Kendra told me all those years ago?" I didn't wait for a response. "I think I saw it…twice now. And I think it's responsible for killing Luke Anderson, my first freaking guest at The Widow's Peak."

Both of them sat there, mouths open.

"And, to add a nice cherry on top, I've been having graphic nightmares for the last few months about a dead guy. So, no. I don't want to go there."

They blinked and looked at each other and back at me.

"That's…" Lottie started.

"A lot." James finished.

"I feel like I'm losing my mind. I love the cabin, I just can't go there without feeling weird. I was there last night with my neighbor's grandson and it was fine until we went to leave and I saw something on the balcony."

"How many times have you seen whatever it is?" James asked.

"Twice. The first time was when I was at the cabin after Luke was found. I saw it in the trees."

"Are you sure it wasn't just a wild animal of some sort?" Lottie asked.

"No. I'm not. I feel like I'm going crazy."

"I'm sure it was just a bear or something. Try to relax." Lottie patted my shoulder, in an attempt to comfort me.

"Have there been any leads in the murder investigation?" James pried.

"No. At least last I heard."

The three of us sat in silence for a minute before James piped up, again. "Why don't the three of us go up there? It'll be daytime and we'll be with you. I can go out and check everything—make sure it's all okay."

That wasn't one of his worst ideas. "Fine. Only if mom signs off on it. You know how she is about holidays."

"I'll go ask." Suddenly, it was like we were ten again and not in our early thirties, running down the stairs to go ask our mom something in the kitchen.

She didn't even turn from the sink. "What do you two need?"

James and I looked at each other. "You might be three times the size in which you used to do this, but nothing has changed. I can hear you two small elephants running down the stairs like the house was on fire."

We rolled our eyes. "Can the three of us go to the cabin between dinner and dessert?"

There was a long sigh and then she spoke. "Sure. Only if you promise to be back by the time we sit down for dessert."

I took this as my cue to speak. "Can you or dad text us a half hour before dessert?"

"Yes. Now go sit down, we're about to eat dinner."

For a Thanksgiving meal, there was minimal drama. Aside from an aunt that picked apart the entire meal and told my mom all the things she could have improved upon, everyone was well behaved. Once the critiquing started, Lottie, James, and I took that as our cue to leave.

We hopped in James's pickup truck and he drove us to the cabin while I gave directions from the passenger seat. As we got closer and the house came into view, my stomach flipped.

"Cora, it's beautiful!" Lottie was staring out the window, in awe of the cabin.

"Wow, my sister does some good work." James chimed in.

We got out of the truck and they were so eager to go in and see the inside, they practically ran to the front door. I unlocked it and let them inside, each of them going in opposite directions. James made a beeline for the balcony while Lottie admired the kitchen and living room.

Lottie and I chatted about the furnishings while James did as he promised and checked around the house.

"It's all clear. I didn't see anything suspicious." He dropped a knife down on the counter. "You really need to be more careful with where you leave things, though."

My face scrunched. "Where did you find that?"

"Upstairs. It was under one of the beds."

I picked it up, examining it. "This isn't mine."

My blood ran cold.

"What?" James was perplexed.

"This knife isn't mine. I've not seen it before."

"I'm sure it is. You probably just don't remember it." James held it up to the knife block in the kitchen. "Alright, that's not a match. It's probably one you borrowed and just forgot about."

I pleaded with myself to believe that it was someone else's and I had just forgotten to return it. I knew better. I had never seen that knife before.

"I think I need to call the police."

"For what?" Lottie asked.

"This isn't my knife. What if this was the murder weapon? They need to know."

I reached for my phone and dialed Detective Ambrose. It rang a few times and then his southern drawl echoed through the phone.

"Detective Ambrose speaking."

"Hi, Detective. This is Cora Lincoln."

"Cora! Happy Thanksgiving! I was going to give you a call tomorrow. We have some breaking news in the Luke Anderson case."

"Oh?"

"It's really great news. A guy was brought in for questioning over in Tennessee yesterday. There's a chance that he killed multiple people in a similar manner—one of which was Luke."

I wasn't sure how to feel. I was relieved that they had found someone, but that didn't explain the random knife James had just found.

"And, you're sure he's the right person?"

"We have enough to go on. Luke's body was found in the same state as someone else in Tennessee. We think the guy they're questioning might be a serial killer."

"That's horrible!"

"Unfortunately, we see things like this every day. I'm so sorry, what were you calling about?"

"I was just calling because I…" Last-minute decision to make. "I was just curious to see if you had any updates on the case."

"Just that. Nothing else, yet. I will call and keep you updated. Don't you worry."

"I appreciate that. Happy Thanksgiving." I ended the call.

"How come you didn't tell him?" James asked, eyes darting between me and the knife.

"They think they found someone. Apparently the guy could be a serial killer." My throat was dry.

"Oh my gosh!" Lottie pulled her hands to her mouth.

"He's in Tennessee, so we should be good." I looked down at the knife on the counter. "You're probably right. I probably used that knife to cut open a box and it slid under the bed or something."

That's the likely explanation.

I placed the knife in the drawer just as each of our phones beeped. It was a text message from my dad telling us dessert would be within the next hour and for us to start heading back.

The car ride back to my parents' house was quiet. I sat there, wondering where that knife came from. I knew in my heart that I would never leave a knife on the floor, no matter how forgetful I was.

We pulled back into the driveway forty minutes later and I went about dessert like nothing had happened. Lottie and James didn't seem to think it was a big deal, but it just didn't sit right with me.

CHAPTER 17

WHEN MY ALARM BLARED THIS MORNING, MY EYES WERE already wide open. Another night of no sleep thanks to the nightmares. Only this time, it continued. It typically ended right when they were handcuffing me. However, last night, after I was handcuffed, I had to go through a questioning. I was the prime suspect in the case.

No matter how many times I tried to tell the detectives that I had nothing to do with it, the more they pressed on. I was exhausted from all the work sleeping Cora had to do.

I was thankful though, today should be a quiet workday, so I planned on spending my morning reading and the afternoon checking out some sales with Miranda.

I reached for my work phone to check my emails. Imagine my surprise when I found my inbox filled with frantic emails. I scrolled to the bottom of my inbox to one thread that was marked as high importance.

It was an email from Eve.

Directors,

As much as it pains me to do this, especially around the holidays, Alliteration is laying off fifteen percent of its workforce due to a restructuring. I have the unfortunate job of delegating this to you all. By end of day Monday, I will need each of you to come up with a list of names of people that can be cut from your team. Please pick employees that have lower impact roles first, then work your way up accordingly. The salaries of those employees must equal around $500,000.

I'm so sorry to spring this on all of you, but it unfortunately has to be done. I'm available all day today, if you have any questions, please just send me a message and we can talk.

A lay-off right after Thanksgiving and right before the holidays? That was just cruel. I know that this wasn't Eve's doing—it was company-wide.

How was I going to figure out who would stay and who would go? My once peaceful day was no more.

I texted Miranda and told her what was happening and she agreed to go out after work to search for deals. I turned my attention to my laptop and pulled up my organization's personnel chart. I looked at all the bright, smiling faces.

How could I let some of them go?

This is one of the things that I knew would eventually come with being in my role, but was not prepared for.

I agonized over the chart for two hours, not coming up with a single person to let go. I had formed relationships with each of them, this felt like the ultimate betrayal of trust. I reached for my phone, pressing Kendra's name.

Before she could even say anything, I started talking. "I'm physically fine, but mentally, I'm in shambles."

"What's going on?" I could hear the concern in Kendra's voice.

"Alliteration is doing layoffs and I have to come up with a bunch of people to cut by Monday."

"That's tough. Do you have any ideas?"

"Not one. Everyone is valuable."

"That sounds like a tough position to be in. My best advice is to take the emotion out of it. Treat everyone like they're just a piece of paper with their accomplishments on the team on it."

"Yeah, that's a good idea." I admitted.

"So, are we going to completely gloss over the fact that you never told me how the date went with Griffin?"

I had hoped she wouldn't bring it up. "It went well. Mrs. Bethel bridged the gaps in conversation, but it wasn't weird. We had a good time and ended up at the cabin."

"And how did that go?"

"About as well as you'd expect." I didn't want to mention what I thought I saw.

"What does that mean?"

"It means I think I saw something while I was up there. As we were leaving, it was around midnight and I looked up at the balcony and," I breathed in deeply before I continued, "something was standing there. Whatever I saw in the woods last week, it looked the same. I pointed it out to Griffin, but by the time he looked, it was gone."

"You're sure that it wasn't just an animal? You know I believe you, I just want to make sure you think of all the logical options first."

"I don't know anymore. The eyes were glowing, but that could be anything. Then, Lottie, James, and I went back up yesterday and everything was fine. James did a once-over throughout the house and he found a knife."

I heard an audible gasp through the phone. "What kind of knife?"

"It looks like a big kitchen knife. I don't think it's mine, but James insisted it was."

"He's probably right. Where did he find it?"

"It was under one of the beds."

"Oh, then, it probably was you or maybe even your mom. Did you use knives to open boxes that the decorations and bedding came in?"

I had to think back to a few months ago when my mom and I were setting up the bedrooms. "I think so. Maybe?"

"One of you probably kicked it under the bed when you were moving things, I'm sure that's it." Kendra tried her best at comforting me.

"Yeah, you're probably right. That would make more sense."

"Do I even want to know what you were thinking?" Kendra asked, not sure she wanted an answer.

"Someone could have broken into the house and planted the knife there."

"You know I love you, but now you're starting to sound crazy. I never side with Jimmy boy, but I think this time I have to."

"I know you're both right. It was just poor timing." I cleared my throat, "So, how was your Thanksgiving?" I needed to turn the conversation away from me.

We chatted for a while about Kendra's cousin who showed up for Thanksgiving dinner after not being home for six years and told no one she was coming. Once we were all caught up, I dove back into my organization chart to see who we could let go.

This was the worst thing they've ever asked me to do. I would work for a week straight if it meant I didn't have to do this.

I cut the interns first, that freed up $100,000.

Only $400,000 left to go. I cut some of the duplicative roles. We had two people doing marketing analytics, I cut the newer person. We had three people doing Pinterest marketing, so I cut two.

I had worked my way up to my $500,000 and emailed my list over to Eve.

My phone rang, Eve's face on my screen. "Hello?"

"Hey, Cora. Thanks for getting those over to me so quickly."

"Yeah, no problem. Not exactly what I had hoped to be doing today."

"I know, I'm so sorry. That's actually why I'm calling—to apologize. I hate that we have to do this."

"I guess we're just doing as we're asked." I just wanted to get off the phone.

"So, how was your holiday?" Eve asked, making small talk.

I just want to go shopping. "It was really nice. How was yours?"

"It was good. I had the whole family over. It was a great day."

"Can I ask you a personal question, Eve? Like, as a person and not my boss?"

"Of course. Ask me anything."

"How do you work as much as you do and still have a family? I guess I struggle to believe it can be done."

"It's hard. I miss some events at my daughter's school, but I make it up to her. My husband is always there, so then, we have a mommy-Lilly date on the weekend. I let her pick everything we do."

"That's really sweet. Thank you for sharing that."

"Absolutely. Are you married, Cora?"

"I'm not. I'm not dating anyone, either."

"You're not? I thought you were!"

"No; single as can be. I met someone I might like to date eventually, so I was curious as to how you handled everything."

"You do know that you can hand off some of your responsibilities, right? And, we can get you an assistant. You're the only director that doesn't have one."

"I know. I'm not saying it'll even go anywhere. If he asks me out again, it'll be a miracle."

"Don't cut yourself so short. Give yourself a chance. Married life is wonderful."

I appreciated her honesty more than she knew. "Thank you for this. It means a lot."

"Anytime. You know you can always call if you need anything."

After the call, I felt a sense of clarity in my personal life. I picked up my phone and sent a text to Griffin.

Happy Thanksgiving, Griff! Thanks again for the other night. Hope you and Mabel are having a great day!

Having completed my unpleasant task for the day, I called Miranda to inform her that I was ready to go shopping whenever she was. Miranda kindly offered to drive, which was a relief after the terrible night's sleep I had. At around three, I put on my shoes and coat and made my way to her house.

I walked up to her fence, Miranda was already in the car and it was running. She was ready for some good Black Friday deals.

As I opened the passenger side door, I was hit in the face with dry heat and the smell of amber sunsets according to the air freshener she had hanging from the rearview mirror.

"So, how terrible was it?" Miranda asked, looking in her mirror, pulling out of her driveway.

"It was up there in the top five of miserable things I've had to do. I would rate it a solid two. The only thing that was worse was when I had to tell Matt in high school that I wasn't interested in dating him."

I thought back to the warm summer day in tenth grade when the sweetest guy in our grade, Matt Stone, that I wasn't interested in dating anyone. His infatuation with me started our freshman year and had only progressed into a full-blown obsession. While it was only slightly creepy, he was a really nice guy and the look on his face when I told him that I didn't feel the same way about him was heartbreaking. His face immediately drooped and he was defeated.

"Yeah, that was sad to watch." Miranda cleared her throat. "On a less depressing topic, how did it go with Griffin the other night?"

I recounted the story for the second time today and she was content with where we had left it. We pulled into the mall's parking lot and circled for what felt like a half hour before finding a spot at the very back of the lot.

On our mile trek to the mall's main entrance, I spoke, "Something weird happened at the cabin."

Miranda stopped in her tracks. Her head swiveled to look at me faster than when the girl's head spun around in that possession movie. "What happened?"

"Lottie, James, and I went to the cabin since they hadn't seen it since it's been done. James was checking everything out, making sure no one else was in the house and found a knife under the bed."

Her jaw dropped. "There has to be a reasonable explanation." I could see her mind was racing, searching for one. "If you used a knife to cut something open, maybe you accidentally kicked it under the bed."

I cocked my head to look at her as we walked through the entrance. "That's what both Lottie and James think, too."

"It makes the most sense." She insisted.

I just nodded. It wasn't worth bringing up the fact that I had never seen the knife before. I don't know what to believe anymore. I knew it wouldn't be worth it to let everyone into my thoughts, no one would believe me. I had already raised enough eyebrows with Detective Ambrose and my friends by mentioning The Beast.

I knew this was the limit of my crazy that I should mention, so I shut up and we started our shopping bonanza.

Our afternoon was filled with a lot of "what do you think of this?", a handful of "should I get this in another color?", and a smattering of "are you sweating, too?". It was the perfect way to take my mind off of everything that was going on in my life at the moment.

When Miranda dropped me off and I had to pull all my bags out of the trunk, that's when I realized how much retail therapy I had done. I dropped all the bags in the hallway all dramatic-like, how they do in the movies. I stepped over them and took off my coat and shoes before heading back to sort through my purchases.

I checked my online banking app. Apparently being stressed about work and a potential serial killer had caused me to spend $324 on things I didn't need.

Barnes and Noble was practically calling my name: "Cora, we have books that are buy one, get one 50% off!". Personally, I've always loved to escape into a good book when the rest of my life is in chaos.

I hung up my new clothes and placed my new books in a comfort pile on my nightstand, vowing to start on one of them tonight.

I took a long shower to wash all of my spending sins of the day away and slipped on my new pajamas set. I sorted through the stack of books I bought today, and sure enough, nothing sounded good at the moment.

Mood reader. So, I made my way to my office to check out what books I had on my shelves.

I reached for a lighthearted holiday romance, making my way to the couch to snuggle in and read. I needed to de-stress and fast. I was about 30% done with the book when I should probably order some take-out because I was about to go from zero to hungry fast.

I turned my attention back to my book until I heard a knock at the door. The pizza restaurant I ordered from said it would take over an hour. It had only been fifteen minutes. I checked the peephole and didn't see anyone out there.

I remembered I had a wreath on the door—that must have been it. *Right?*

That was a logical explanation, but the feeling in the pit of my stomach as I sat back down said otherwise. I went back to the front door and opened it, tapping the wreath on the door—just like wind would have done. I couldn't replicate the sound, no matter what I did.

Maybe someone rang the bell and then ran away?

I made my way back to the couch and checked the video from the camera by my front door. I rewound the camera footage from ten minutes ago.

Nothing.

My stomach sank.

I'm sure there's another very reasonable explanation. I lied to myself. I believed the lie enough because my heart stopped racing… until an hour later when I actually heard the knocking this time.

I grabbed the pizza and went into the kitchen.

As I passed through the hallway, there was a shadow outside the window. My breath caught in my throat, but I kept moving until I hit the kitchen where I was surrounded by closed blinds.

I put my head down on the cold counter.

What the hell was happening?

CHAPTER 18

I CONTINUED EATING MY PIZZA AS I SLOWLY CALMED myself, but my heart was still racing. The thought of someone watching me was unnerving, but I couldn't muster the courage to check outside again. Besides, calling the police on a hunch would make me seem foolish, like the boy who cried wolf...or BEAST, in this case.

To drown out the deafening silence, I switched on the TV and attempted to eat my meal without gazing out into my backyard. I ate, doing my best to not look outside. I didn't care for the shadow by the hallway window, I wasn't taking any chances by looking outside.

I slept for a bit because when I woke up, both the television and the lights were all turned off. It took me a minute to gather myself. It wasn't normal, the television always stays on, long after the show stops playing. That was the final nail in the coffin I needed to fully have a panic attack.

I still hadn't moved from my position on the couch; I was paralyzed with fear. I quietly searched for my phone under the blanket in the pitch-black room, just in case someone was inside the house with me.

What if the shadowy figure had somehow gotten inside?

I moved my foot and found my phone, pulling it to my chest to check the time. It was only a little after ten and I saw that Griffin had finally texted me back. I started typing a response, but something else caught my attention.

It sounded like there was a sharp object running along the pane of the hallway window. It sent a shiver down my spine. I gulped loudly, unable to determine if the noise was coming from inside or outside the house. I laid there, still as can be, waiting to hear it again. Sure enough, a minute later, there it was again. It sounded like a claw running across the window.

My blood ran cold.

I reached for the baseball bat underneath my couch (something my dad had me keep there in case of an emergency) and flicked on the lamp. I sat up, surveying as much of the downstairs as I could from my spot on the couch. I couldn't see anything, so I got up to check upstairs. Everything was clear. *Maybe* it was an animal's claw.

I went back downstairs and garnered enough courage to walk over to the hallway window—nothing was outside. From the way I was holding the bat, it was evident that I never played sports as a kid. I stuck to art classes, reading, and choreographing cringey dances to my favorite songs as my extracurriculars.

For my own sanity, I needed to go check the backyard. If I didn't see anyone or anything back there, it was likely just an animal. I peered through the blinds, trying not to move them much, but I couldn't see anything. I had to open them fully and turn on the small light to see anything.

I scanned the yard, there was nothing there. I breathed a sigh of relief and felt secure that there, in fact, was a logical explanation for all of this. I settled back in on the couch and lifted my phone to finish typing my message to Griffin, asking if he wanted to get some lunch tomorrow before he left town.

My eyelids grew heavy and I knew it was time for bed. I turned off the lights, checked that every door and window was locked, and headed up the wooden staircase to my bedroom. I went over to close the blinds when I noticed something in the backyard.

My heart fell to the floor.

What the fuck?

Staring back at me in the farthest corner of the yard was… The Beast.

The hair all over my body stood on edge. My throat tightened. It looked like it was the same creature I had seen in the woods up by the cabin. I stood there, paralyzed with fear when I noticed it had slowly started to walk backwards into the shadows of the yard. I could no longer see the large body, just the glowing eyes.

A bead of sweat ran down my back. I now understand what people mean when they say they have a cold sweat. I'm freezing, yet I'm sweating profusely.

Do I call someone? Do I go outside?

I stood there, still making eye contact with whatever this thing was. I blinked and couldn't see the outline or the glowing eyes anymore. Heart still racing, I shut the blinds and leapt into my bed, seeking refuge.

I grabbed my phone off the nightstand, calling Miranda. It rang four times before I heard her sleepy voice on the other end of the phone.

"Cora?" her voice was thick with sleep.

"Hey, are you awake?"

"I am now." Miranda cleared her throat. "What's up?"

"I think I just saw something in the backyard. Weird shit has been happening all night."

"What happened?"

"There was some weird knocking at the front door, which, to be fair, could've been the wreath. Even though I tried to replicate it and couldn't. I saw a shadow in the window on my way from the front door to the kitchen. Then I heard what sounded like a claw being dragged along the same window. And then just now, I came upstairs to go to bed and there was…something in the backyard."

"What did you see?" She sounded skeptical of everything.

"I think it was the same thing I saw near the cabin. It looked like The Beast."

"Cora…are you still on this? Have you slept at all?"

"I really do think it was the same creature I saw. The eyes were glowing, then, it just slunk back into the shadows and it wasn't there anymore. And, yes, I have gotten some sleep."

"I think you're just really stressed and your mind is getting the best of you. You had to make some really difficult work decisions and that took a toll on you. I promise, if you got a solid night of rest, you'd feel like a new person."

I chewed my bottom lip, internalizing what she had just said. She was right.

"I know. All I want is to get a solid eight hours of sleep, but the freaking nightmares won't let me."

"Tomorrow morning, when I'm somewhat coherent, I will text you the information for my psychiatrist. Just go once, I think it will do you some good."

"Okay, I'll go."

She immediately woke up. "You will?"

"Yeah, I think it's time."

"That's really great, Cora. I'm proud of you." Miranda yawned.

"I'll let you go back to sleep. Sorry for calling so late."

"I'm always here for you. Did you want me to come over?"

"No, it's okay. Talking it out helped. Thanks for being you, M."

The line went dead. I subconsciously picked at my nail, thinking about everything that just happened. I know what I saw, I just needed people to believe me. I laid down and turned on the television, turning up the volume so I couldn't hear anything outside. I didn't know where that creature lurked off to, but I didn't want to know—at least right now.

CHAPTER 19

LYING IN BED, THE SUN POKED OVER THE HORIZON. THE blinds were still closed, but I was awake as the room went from pitch-black with only the light of the television to a bright, sunny morning. Another night of only a few hours of interrupted sleep.

My nightmare had morphed last night:

It was the dead of winter and not summer. Instead of just wandering around in the forest, this time, I was being chased. I never caught a glimpse of what was chasing me, I just knew it was running on two legs and was some ways back. I knew I couldn't run for much longer, so I peeled off behind a tree. Back pressed up against the tree, I slid down, my butt in the snow, and caught my breath. I didn't hear anymore footsteps, so I figured whoever it was had given up—at least for the time being.

I looked to my left and saw a long mound of snow. I crawled over and as I got closer, I noticed there was a pool of something dark near the mound. I brushed away the light dusting of snow and was met with shoes. I brushed further up and there were pants.

A body. The realization hit me that the blood was coming from this person's head.

Should I leave it and call the police?

My hands shook and I continued brushing. I carefully scooped the snow away from the person's face. I was met with one of the most horrific sights I had ever seen. The body lying in front of me belonged to a woman. She was thin. Her face was drawn in, bright red blood pooled from her mouth. Her skin had color in it, her eyes were closed, and I dialed 9-1-1. As I pressed the last 1, her eyes opened and her mouth pulled up in a devious smile. Her eyes met mine. She reached up, grabbed my throat and I couldn't breathe.

I fell backwards, jolting awake. I shot up in bed, drenched in sweat, and my body shook from head to toe. I needed to get up and rinse my face but was too afraid to move across my room in the dark, despite the television being on. I never went back to sleep.

How could I, *could you?*

As the sun rose, I took this as my cue to get up. I opened the blinds and the morning sun cascaded in, illuminating the once-dark room. I looked around, everything that looked like a shadowy figure at night, now just looked normal. I slid out of bed and made my way to the bathroom to steam the nightmare from my head.

My phone buzzed as I stepped out of the shower. It was Miranda, sending over her psychiatrist's contact information. I had already decided in the wee hours of the morning I wasn't going to tell anyone about this dream. This one felt more personal than the others. I clicked the website and stood there, in the steamy bathroom in my towel, making an appointment for the following week.

I didn't want to do this, but I knew I had to.

I turned on my favorite playlist as I got ready for the day; the background noise was much needed to help pull me out of the trance I had been in. Feeling like a new person, I examined my reflection in the mirror—I looked like I hadn't slept in days, which could be very much due to the fact that I hadn't slept more than three hours each night. I flicked off the light and made my way to the entryway to head out to get coffee.

Typically, when it's cold like this, I walk so quickly I almost jog to The Higher Ground, but today, I needed to clear my head, so I walked slowly. The shower hadn't helped at all, I could still see the woman's face clear as day and could almost feel the hand around my throat. I shook my head as I entered the shop and was met with friendly faces.

"Cora!" Some customers chimed in unison.

I waved and pulled out one of my best fake smiles. I stood in line, staring at the menu, but not registering any of it. I had zoned out, solely focused on why the woman in my dream looked familiar.

"Cora. Cora. Cora?" the cashier, Rachel, called from behind the register.

I snapped back to reality and threw on the pretend smile again. "Hey! Sorry, I was daydreaming."

"Hopefully dreaming of someplace warm."

I wish.

"Can I have a large, hot mocha, please?"

She nodded. "Of course!"

I waited for my coffee, still deciding if I was going to stay and get some fresh air, or if I was going to spend my Saturday at home, paranoid. My phone buzzed in my purse. Reaching for it, I saw Griffin's name on the screen. A genuine, involuntary smile spread across my face.

Griffin: You look like you had a rough morning.

I turned around and saw him ordering, smiling at me. My stomach had butterflies flying around, a new feeling—one that made me feel alive. Griffin walked over and looked different than he had the other night.

Dare I say more attractive? Which, I'm attributing solely to the fact that my call with Eve yesterday helped ease any anxieties I had about the potential for a relationship.

"Good morning, sunshine. How are you?" He smelled like woodsy cologne and was dressed in jeans, Converse, and a wool coat. Not usually what I would go for, but it suited him so well.

"Tired, but good. How are you?"

"Good! Not ready to leave tomorrow, that's for sure."

My stomach dropped, I forgot he leaves Byglass tomorrow.

"Not ready to go back to work?"

"Something like that." He smiled warmly as my order was ready. "You left me hanging."

I raised an eyebrow, not sure what he was talking about.

"I texted you back last night and asked if you wanted to hang out today. You never answered."

"Shit, I'm sorry. It was a rough night."

"Do you want to sit down and talk about it?"

"I'd love to sit, but don't want to talk about it. If that's okay?"

"Absolutely. Want to go grab that table by the window and I'll meet you over there?"

I nodded and made my way over to the table. I sat there, staring out the window, looking at all the happy families that were out doing their holiday shopping.

"I want one of those one day." I didn't hear Griffin approach the table or sit down. Lost in my damn thoughts again.

"One of what?" I asked, wanting clarification.

"A family." His eyes darted down. "My mom passed away in a tragic car accident when I was young and my dad did all he could, but it just never felt like a full family again, ya know?"

I stared back, unsure of what to say.

"Sorry, I didn't mean to make this morbid. I'm not really sure why I blurted that out. It always gets me around the holidays. I see others posting about cutting down Christmas trees or driving around and looking at lights and I want that."

"I get it." I was about to admit something out loud for the first time. "The truth is, I do, too. I want a family, I'm tired of being alone. I give everything I have to work and I just don't want to do that anymore. It's taking a toll. I want the fun movie nights where the mom plans snacks around the movie. It's silly, I know."

Griffin chewed his bottom lip, listening to every word I said. "I get it. I see people post their themed movie nights on social media and I think it's cool." He took a sip from his coffee. "If you asked me five years ago when I was in my twenties, I would've told you it was lame." He laughed, revealing his bright smile.

"Yep, same with me." I wanted to get our conversation back on track because this whole being vulnerable thing just made me uncomfortable. "So, my plans for today? I have none. What did you have in mind?"

"I really just enjoy spending time with you, so I'm cool with whatever you'd like to do."

I looked outside and saw the clouds forming. "I have a suggestion based on what we were just talking about."

"I'm all ears."

"How about we head up to the cabin, start a fire, and watch some movies?"

"I'd love that."

"I have to take my grandma to the grocery store this morning, but I'm free any time after noon."

"Why don't you do that, I'll head home and read a bit and then get some snacks pulled together for our movie date."

Date. Why did you say date?

A broad smile spread across his face. "I'd enjoy that. I can come over when I'm done."

"That works for me. Are there any special snacks you'd like?" The butterflies were dancing in my stomach.

"I'm good with anything except Sun Chips. Those are a desperate attempt at healthy Doritos." Griffin laughed, but he had a valid point.

"Noted: no Sun Chips." I smiled back at him. There was something about his personality that calmed my anxious mind.

We finished the last sips of our coffees and parted ways. I was happy we were going to spend time together this afternoon because when I was around him, the world quieted down.

CHAPTER 20

AROUND TWELVE THIRTY, THERE WAS A KNOCK AT THE door—of course I jumped. I had gotten lost in my book and forgot that Griffin would be arriving…now. I had spent the few hours between our impromptu coffee meetup and now reading and gathering the few snacks I had in the pantry.

I opened the heavy front door, Griffin's smiling face was beaming at me. "I picked up some snacks as well. I felt bad eating all your food." He lifted his right arm and I took notice of the grocery bag in his hand.

"I didn't mind. I don't snack very much, so I make no promises that these are even still good." *I should've checked the expiration dates.*

"I think we'll have enough, now. Did you want to head up? I'd be happy to drive…. if you don't mind someone else driving your car."

"I wouldn't mind one bit." I slipped on my coat. "I actually hate driving. That's why I love living here. I can walk to basically anywhere I need to go, except to get groceries. It's the anxious driver's dream location." I tossed the bag of snacks on my shoulder and locked up.

Griffin sat down in the driver's seat and something felt weird in my stomach. I felt like I was playing pretend—a guy driving me around, this was a first. We pulled out of the driveway and started on the twisty path up the mountain.

"How was grocery shopping with grams?" I asked. The way he talked about her was so cute, the two of them had a solid bond.

"It was fine. She insisted she could push the cart, so I just followed her around. Occasionally grabbing boxes off the top shelf for her, but mainly looking like a jack ass because I was having this old, decrepit woman pushes her own cart."

"The majority of people in Byglass know of Mabel Bethel, so I don't think anyone was judging."

"Is she really that well-known here?"

"The woman has the same routine almost every day, I would say so."

We chatted about Mrs. Bethel and her coffee routine every day and before we both knew it, we were pulling up to The Widow's Peak.

"It's more stunning today than it was last time. Today, I can really see the exterior structure and what the original architect was hoping to encapsulate."

I glanced in Griffin's direction, not sure what to say.

"Just ignore me. I geek out on cool houses."

"It's okay. I'm just happy someone appreciates this place."

We got out of the car and made our way to the front door before going inside and getting settled. I brought the groceries into the kitchen while Griffin checked out the views on the wraparound deck.

"Cora! Come out here." He called from the deck.

"Be right there." I shoved the frozen pizza in the refrigerator and made my way next to Griffin.

"It's beautiful up here. How do you not spend every waking moment staring out over this peak?"

I thought back to everything that has happened over the last two weeks and shuddered. "There's no delivery service up here. I wouldn't make it more than a week." Jokes were my escape out of potentially awkward conversations mechanism.

"Do you not cook?" He looked at me dead in the eye and raised an eyebrow.

"Not well." I leaned my elbows on the railing and put my head in my hands. "My mom was a Michelin star chef in New York, and I can barely boil water for pasta."

Griffin laughed. "Did your mom never teach you?"

"She attempted over the years, but I just never had the attention span for it. She lived in New York long before I was even a thought."

"That's pretty cool, though. Surely that's a flex though. It's not every day you meet someone who knows a Michelin star chef."

I pulled my hair back in a bun. "It's cold out here." I rubbed my hands together. "Why don't we go in?"

Griffin went to the kitchen to grab the snacks while I set up the television. He came back with an armful of different chips, popcorn, and candy.

"What are *these*?" His face was drawn up in disgust as he held up a small bag of Sun Chips I had bought on my way home from the coffee shop, just to bother him.

"You told me you didn't like them, so naturally, I had to try them for myself."

"The chips taste like trash. Simple as that. Save yourself!" Griffin snickered under his breath.

"Just sit down and stop being so dramatic about the chip choices I've made. We have serious matters that we need to discuss—like what movie we're going to watch."

"Something funny would be good. You seem stressed today."

Griffin was very observant. He notices nuances about me that others don't tend to.

"Something funny. Got it." I scrolled through the potential choices until we settled on a new Christmas RomCom.

We sat in silence for a while, watching the movie. The only sounds to be heard were the rustling of chip bags, an occasional laugh, and the movie itself.

I internally panicked, what if he was having a terrible time? I'm boring as hell, Griffin is probably having a terrible time. He's probably regretting all of his life decisions right now.

I glanced over in his direction. I picked the worst time because he was already looking at me, so we made eye contact.

"Cora, are you okay? You really seem off today. I'm not judging or anything, I just—need to shut up."

I pulled my hand up into my sleeve and went to town on my cuticles. I was already anxious being up here, I didn't want to think about what happened last night, and I certainly didn't want to spill everything to Griffin. I feel it should be the first lesson in the "potential girlfriend handbook" don't let them see your crazy.

"Yeah, I'm fine! I just didn't sleep well last night, so I'm a little tired."

"Do you want to take a nap? I've been told my shoulder makes for a great pillow."

I smiled at him. "I'm okay but thank you."

His face fell, I think that was his way of trying to make a move. The movie was almost over and I could feel Griffin's occasional staring. I checked my phone, it was only a little after two. "I'm going to get a glass of wine. Would you like one?"

"That would be great."

I headed to the kitchen and poured us each a small glass of wine. I knew we would have to drive home eventually, so a small glass would be just fine.

"Your wine, sir." I handed Griffin his glass of red wine.

"Thank you."

"Cheers!" I held up my glass as he clinked them together.

We finished the remainder of the first movie when Griffin turned towards me. "Tell me something about yourself that not many people know."

I pulled my lip between my teeth. "I graduated at the top of both my high school and college class."

"That's boring. Try again." He was looking for a fun fact, not a boring schooling fact.

It took a minute, but I thought of one. One that not even Kendra or Miranda knew. "I once went up in a hot air balloon on a family vacation. I pleaded with my parents to not make me go because I was terrified of heights. They made me go and I cried the entire time up. The minute I looked down, I threw up over the side."

Griffin paused for a moment, then burst into a fit of laughter, which made me giggle. "I'm sorry, I know I shouldn't be laughing." He paused to catch his breath. "I'm sure that was traumatizing for you, but all I can picture is vomit falling from above onto unsuspecting bystanders."

"Oh, it was terrible. My mom was mortified. When we finally touched back down, I couldn't get out fast enough. I laid there on the grass for a while, just saying, 'sweet, sweet land'. I'm pretty sure my brother has a video of this whole thing."

"I'm going to need to see that video one day."

"I'll text my brother and see if he can send it to me for your viewing pleasure." All of the stress melted away. I'm not sure if it was the wine or the conversation, but I felt relaxed.

"Hold on, how long ago was this incident?" Griffin held a hand over his mouth, trying to hide the fact that he was laughing.

"We won't be discussing that." He reached for my wine glass, offering to go refill them both. I took that time to text James and ask if he could send that video along. I knew it was going to expose the timeframe, but it was a funny video.

When he returned, both glasses were filled. "So, was the hot air balloon trip recent?"

I handed over my phone. "See for yourself."

Ten. That's how many times Griffin watched the video with tears streaming down his face. I have to admit, the video was funnier than I remembered. Or maybe it was the wine.

"I'm sorry, this is gold. Pure gold."

We laughed about the fact that this video was only from three years ago. I looked over at Griffin hoping he'd share his embarrassing story.

"I think it was maybe three or four years ago. I was presenting my plan for a new banking headquarters building in Charlotte and was so confident in the design." Griffin paused, shaking his head, "The night before, I had a little too much fun celebrating and 75% of the way through my presentation, my stomach flipped and I knew I had moments to make it out of there. I somehow made it out of the conference room to the nearest trash can, but little did I know, it was one of those conference rooms where you could see out, but no one could see in…."

I slapped my hand over my mouth. "And everyone saw it…" It was my turn to burst into laughter. The wine had been free flowing at this point and we brought the nearly empty bottle to the table. I looked at my phone, it was nearing four o'clock.

I looked down at our empty glasses and the empty bottle. "We should probably stop drinking now so we can drive home later tonight once we've sobered up."

Griffin scooted closer to me. "Or, we could just…stay here?"

Forget the butterflies in my stomach, I felt like I had fireworks exploding. I think he was actually enjoying himself, and I was, too.

"That works for me. I brought a frozen pizza, so we can have that for dinner if that's okay?"

"Sounds good to me." With our new plans decided, Griffin got up and opened another bottle of wine, bringing it to the couch.

The conversation was free-flowing now; no topics were off the table. The new bottle of wine was half-gone when Griffin piped up again, starting a new conversation topic.

"So, why do you work so much?"

Those words felt like a dagger in the stomach. "Honestly, I think it was my way of proving to everyone that I was worth a damn. Not my family or friends, but the people I went to high school and college with. Everyone thought my dreams were too big for this town, so I made it my mission to prove them wrong." I sighed. "It cost me all of my twenties."

"Do you regret it?" Griffin asked gently.

"Yes." I didn't have to think twice about it. "Don't get me wrong, I love my job, but I feel like it cost me a family. I know I'm still young enough, but I definitely feel like I'm late to the game. I never even really dated anyone seriously."

"I think it's brave."

I raised my eyebrow, cueing Griffin to continue.

"It's brave because you knew you could do it and you did."

"I guess you're right. It still sucks though."

"Yeah, it does." I tucked a stray strand of my hair behind my ear.

"I don't know how to back-off, though. I feel like a certain level of expectation has been set and if I don't continue to live up to it, they'll get rid of me."

"From what you've told me, they would be silly to get rid of you."

I nodded, unsure of what else to say. I looked up and could see the sunset over the mountains. "Look how beautiful it is out there."

Griffin stood up and slipped his shoes and coat on before going outside to take in the beautiful sunset. I followed suit. "It's so peaceful up here. These views would never get old."

"Do you like your job, Griffin?"

"I love it. Why do you ask?"

"Just wondering." I let him look out over the sunset before I prodded. "Do you find it hard to date when you work so much?"

He shifted his attention over to me. "I don't work as much as I used to." His eyes fell and he turned away from me. "I was in a relationship for the last year. We broke up not too long ago."

"Oh, I'm sorry. I didn't know, otherwise I wouldn't have brought this up."

"You had no way of knowing. I worked too much and I lost her."

My stomach dropped.

"That's what happens when you work too much and try to have a relationship, I guess."

"What I'm hearing is we're both in the same boat."

"The absolute same boat." Griffin agreed.

We watched in silence as the sun dipped below the mountain peaks and the sky turned a dark blue.

"We should head back inside. It's getting dark." I suggested.

"Are you scared of the dark?" Griffin asked, eyebrow raised.

"No, I'm not. It's just cold out here."

We went back inside and finished off that second bottle of wine. We turned on another movie but spent the entire time talking. Even though it was dark out, we left all the blinds and curtains open. For the first time in a long time, I felt normal. I was having a normal person conversation, not one about a damn folklore.

We had eaten the entire pizza and were snacking again. The wine was flowing once more and I was having trouble keeping all my thoughts in my head and not spilling everything to Griffin. He was just so easy to talk with.

I looked down at my phone and it was after ten. "Can I ask you a silly question?"

"Of course."

"Do you believe in folklores?"

Griffin furrowed his eyebrows, thinking. "I don't know if I one hundred percent believe them, but I do think that they're rooted in some sort of truth. Why do you ask?"

"We're friends now, right? You're not going to judge me for anything?"

"I promise I won't judge." He stuck his pinky out, showing his loyalty.

"Oh, a pinky promise! This is serious now." I joked.

"I take everything you say seriously." He replied. I swooned.

"There was a murder up here not too long ago."

His eyes went wide. "Really?"

I nodded. "Yeah. It was the guest who was supposed to be checking in here. They found his body a few days later out in the woods less than a mile away."

"That's horrible! Do they have any leads?"

"They have one guy in custody that they think is a serial killer. They're convinced that he did it."

"You don't sound so convinced."

"I'm not." I inhaled deeply. "I had some…odd experiences that make me feel like they're not going in the right direction."

"What type of experiences?"

My hands trembled and I couldn't make eye contact.

"Cora, what's wrong?" Griffin grabbed my hands in his, sending an electric shock through my system.

"You're going to think I've lost it. Just forget I've said anything."

"We pinky promised. You can tell me anything. I would never judge you."

I felt safe hearing those words. I could tell that he really wasn't going to judge me.

"Right after Luke, the guy who was murdered, was found, I came up here to check and see if I could find any clues for the detectives. When I was leaving, it was raining. A tree limb fell across the road. I got out to move it, but as I did, something was staring at me—from the tree line. It looked like, like, like… The Beast."

His eyes went wide.

"I've never gotten back in my car and driven home so quickly." That was the mild part. I could leave it there and Griffin would only think I was mildly crazy, or I could continue on and he might leave and take out a restraining order on me.

"I can't even imagine. Do you think it actually was The Beast or do you think it was just another animal?"

"At first, I thought definitely The Beast, but then I told a few people and they thought I was just seeing things. So, I started questioning myself. That is, until last night."

He snuggled in with his blanket even more. "What happened last night? Is it the reasoning behind why you didn't sleep well?"

"Yep, it is." I took a deep breath before continuing. "I went out with Miranda yesterday afternoon. Then last night when I got home, things got weird."

I looked over at Griffin for his signal for me to keep going. "I heard a knocking on the door, but no one was there. Then I thought I saw a shadow of something in a window. I heard something scratching that same window a bit later." I paused there. I opted to leave out the last part about seeing something.

"Cora, that's terrifying. Did you check your security cameras?"

"I did. Nothing was there."

"You should've called the police! There could've been someone out there."

"Or something." I added. I slapped my hand over my mouth. Drunk Cora really liked being Miss Full Disclosure.

"Did you see something?" He asked, ready for more information.

"Yes." I took a long sip from my glass.

"What was it?"

"I…I don't know. After everything happened downstairs, I went to bed. When I was closing the blinds, I saw something in my yard, staring back at me. I don't know what it was, but it backed away slowly and disappeared."

Griffin's mouth hung open, his eyes were wide. "I don't even know what to say to all that."

"I know it's a lot. You're probably wishing that you hadn't had any wine so you could leave."

"Not even close." He wrapped an arm around me. "I believe you. We're going to go outside and sort this out."

My heart started racing. "What do you mean?"

"We're going to get bundled up and head outside. Let's see if we can find it."

"Absolutely not. How is that going to help?" I crossed my arms over my chest.

"Cora, we have to go figure out if what you saw was The Beast or if it was just another animal."

"Have you lost your mind? We could be eaten by a bear!"

"Or maybe by The Beast." A devilish smirk spread across his face.

"You're actually crazy. It's dark—we could get lost!"

Griffin had already tied his shoes and was walking to the closet to get his jacket. "Crazy for you." He handed me my jacket. "Suit up, Cora Grace. We're going exploring."

CHAPTER 21

THE LEAVES CRUNCHED UNDER OUR FEET. I WAS HOLDING onto both Griffin and the flashlight like my life depended on it...well, because it did. I don't know where in his mind he thought that going outside in the middle of the night was a good idea. But here we are. The stillness of, I glanced down at my phone, 12:05 A.M. was maddening. As we walked deeper into the woods, the quieter and more still it got. Who knew silence would be so loud.

The moonlight cast an ominous shadow on the newly barren trees.

We walked for a while, shining our flashlights in every direction. We saw some small animals, but nothing that could qualify as The Beast. Griffin insisted we walk in further as my anxiety built.

"Do we have to go further? This seems unnecessarily dangerous and it's cold."

"There's nothing out here, we can head back. I'm sorry, I was hoping we could get some answers for you to help you feel better when you're home alone or when you're up here. I don't want you to lose sleep anymore." We started back for The Widow's Peak. From my best estimate, it would be a twenty-minute walk back.

We walked in the direction from which we came and ten minutes later, nothing was looking familiar.

"We're lost." I deadpanned.

"We're not lost. We're just…turned around. We'll get back on track and get home in no time."

The leaves behind us were crunching slowly, something was out here.

"Did you hear that?" I whispered, leaning in closer to Griffin.

He nodded in response, wrapping his arm around me in an effort to make me feel more secure, but nothing was going to do that right now.

He pressed his mouth to my ear. "Stay still. Let me listen."

As we stopped, the footsteps behind us did as well. Griffin slowly turned around to look.

"There's nothing there. Let's keep going." We continued on and the footsteps following us had ceased. We found the path we took earlier and I recognized where we were. We continued on, relieved we had stumbled upon the correct trail.

There was a loud thump behind us and as we turned around, we were face-to-face with what could best be described as The Beast.

"Fucking run!" Griffin yelled as he grabbed onto my hand tightly. "Don't let go and don't stop until we're inside the house."

We heard running behind us—this time it sounded like four legs. Whatever that creature was, it was capable of walking on two feet and running on four. It was gaining on us until it stopped, but we kept going until we were back inside the house and the doors and windows were all closed and locked and the blinds were closed.

Once everything was checked, we reconvened on the couch. "What the hell was that?" Griffin finally broke the silence.

"That was the same thing I had seen twice before."

I could see his hands were shaking. "You weren't lying, that's for sure. Do we tell anyone?"

"No, they'll think you've lost your mind, too."

"But that thing is dangerous."

"Trust me, it's not worth it."

"I can back up your story now. That'll help."

"Griffin, trust me. It won't. Let's just drop it."

As terrifying as that was, it felt good to have someone believe me after witnessing the same thing I had before.

We sat in silence, processing everything.

"It's quiet in here. Why don't we put on the television."

I handed over the remote while Griffin chose a movie for us to watch. Neither of us had any intention of watching the movie, but we needed some noise in this very quiet and creaking house.

I couldn't tell you what movie he even put on because I was so lost in my own thoughts.

What had we seen? Did he actually believe me? Was it just another large animal?

I shifted over closer to Griffin and snuggled into his side; I could feel his heart race and he was still trembling. "Your shoulder does make a good pillow." I tried to lighten the mood.

A small smile danced on his lips. "I told you."

My eyelids got heavy and I decided not to fight the sleep. I felt my body get heavier and sink further into Griffin's left side. His arm tightened around me. I drifted off to sleep.

Something woke Griffin up, because he jolted up, startling me. "What's wrong?"

The living room where we both fell asleep was still dark, only illuminated by a television screensaver.

"Shh." Griffin pressed his finger to his lip.

Just then, I heard it. The same noise I had heard the other night at home—a claw being dragged along a window.

"Do you hear that?" The panic was evident in his voice.

"Yeah." I was full body shaking.

"You have security cameras, right?"

I nodded, handing over my phone for Griffin to check the footage. He scrolled through the last few hours. The only thing the cameras caught were us running back in, nothing else.

"That's exactly what it sounded like last night at home."

"Shit. Stay here." Griffin left his place on the couch and went to the kitchen to grab a knife. "I'm going to turn on the lights and go outside to check. Will you be okay in here alone?"

"Yeah, I'll be fine. You don't have to go out there. You won't find anything."

"I need to go check for my own sanity if nothing else. Go lock yourself in the bathroom and I'll let you know when it's all clear."

I wasn't going to argue with him and did as he said. I brought my phone with me so I could call for help if need be. I heard the sliding back door open and close slowly, but then, nothing. I watched the clock. Griffin went outside at 3:30 A.M. and it was now 3:33. I didn't hear anything and started to panic. I had 9-1-1 dialed on my phone, I was just waiting to press the call button.

3:34.

3:35.

3:36.

3:37.

3:38, the door opened again and I heard the deadbolt latch. The footsteps got louder.

"Cora, it's me. It's all clear."

I unlocked the door and opened it slowly, finding Griffin standing there, visibly pale. "Did you see anything?"

He shook his head. "No, but that was unsettling. Whatever it was, it just sounded like it was taunting us."

"I know. That's how I felt last night."

"I understand why you don't come here anymore."

We went to the kitchen. "Do you want to go home?" I asked, hoping he would say yes.

"No, let's stay until morning. I don't feel comfortable being out there if I'm honest."

"We can do that." I poured us two large glasses of water. We needed to hydrate. "Here you go."

"Thanks." Griffin chugged his water in three large gulps. "Let's put the television back on and maybe just stay up and talk?"

"I'd like that." I knew both of us weren't going to be able to sleep and the sunrise was only three hours away. "Only if we can talk about literally anything but what has happened within the last four hours."

"Deal."

We spent the next three hours talking about his family and their holiday traditions. I showed him pictures from James and Lottie's wedding. We talked about what new books were being published this month I was excited about. The conversation was easy and flowed nicely. Neither of us felt awkward around the other, even after what we had experienced earlier.

Around six forty-five, the sun poked over the horizon and the sky weaved us a beautiful sunrise. Right above the mountain peaks, the sky looked like it was on fire—the bright yellow sun glowed. There were ribbons of deep orange and red threaded amongst the lighter blues, creating a beautiful tapestry of color.

"Ready to head home?" I asked, hoping he was.

"Just one more minute." Somehow, over the last three hours, Griffin and I had become a twisted pile of limbs. We cuddled up and talked and it was truly some of the best conversations I've ever had with another human. We even forgot about everything that happened in the woods, as much as we could.

We stayed in our tangled pile and watched the sunrise for a

few more minutes. Once it was high enough in the sky, we gathered our things and headed for the car.

Griffin drove and the majority of the drive was silent. We were about a mile from home when he finally spoke up. "Are we going to talk about last night, or no?"

"We probably should."

"What was that?" Griffin's voice shook a little bit.

"Whatever it was, is the same thing that I saw last night. And that afternoon that I was here when the tree branch fell."

"I've never seen anything like it."

"I know. Now do you understand why I felt so crazy? No one would believe that."

"You're right. I get it."

More silence.

We pulled into the driveway and I breathed a sigh of relief. I was back in my territory again.

We sat there, unsure of how to part ways. How do you say goodbye to someone that you bonded so closely with, so quickly? Then shared a horrifying experience with.

"I guess I'll see you the next time you're in town." I was unsure of how else to break the ice.

More silence.

"I'm not going home."

CHAPTER 22

"What? Why?"

"There's something up there and maybe even down here. it's taunting you and you're not safe alone."

My heart leapt in my chest. "Don't be silly, I'm fine."

Griffin's gaze met mine. "You're a terrible liar. You might be relieved to be home, but there's still a clear and present danger and believe it or not, I care about you and would like to keep you safe."

"There's nothing we can do. No one will believe us, so it's pointless. I'm just going to avoid going up to The Widow's Peak and it should all be okay. You need to get home for work."

Griffin took this as his cue to get out of the car. "Let's walk and get coffee and talk about this."

"While caffeine would be lovely, I haven't showered in twenty-four hours, so I need to do that first. My hair was greasy from all the running we did in the wee hours of the morning."

"Let's do this. You go inside and shower and I'll head back to my grandma's and do the same. Meet you back here in a half hour?"

A smile spread across my face. "Sounds good to me."

I walked up to the front door as Griffin started for Mabel's house. "Would you mind if I came in and just checked the place for you?"

I felt the tension melt in my shoulders. "That would be great." I hadn't realized that subconsciously, I was anxious about going in there. Griffin went in and checked every closet, room, and door. He cleared the house for me to go in.

I was standing on the front porch when he came out. "There's nothing in there. You should be good." He placed a soft kiss to my cheek before disappearing down the street.

I headed inside and breathed in the familiar scent of cashmere and vanilla—my signature home fragrance since I moved in. The house was warm and cozy, despite the cold, windy air outside. I made a beeline for the bathroom because I desperately needed to get the sweat off my body.

I removed my clothes and stepped into the shower, letting the beads of hot water loosen the tense muscles of my neck. I didn't even realize I was crying until a sob shook through my body. Last night had absolutely scared the shit out of me. I don't know what possessed Griffin to want to go outside, but I think we both regret it.

I was able to keep the sobs at bay and eventually calmed myself down, long after the water had run cold. I stepped out of the shower and wrapped a towel around my body, when I heard the front door open slowly.

"Griffin?" I called out from the now-locked bathroom door.

No answer.

"Griff, is that you?"

Again, no response.

My heart sped up and with shaking hands I unlocked the bathroom door and headed to the top of the landing where I could perfectly see the front door. Not only was the door closed, it was locked.

What the hell is going on?

I bolted back into the bathroom and put on clothes, brushed my hair and my teeth, and checked the security footage for the front of my house—nothing. I made my way down the stairs, slowly and quietly. I've lived in this house long enough to know what parts of the stairs and floorboards creaked, so I avoided those areas. I scanned the entirety of the downstairs area and didn't see anything…or anyone. I was hearing things. I'm just being paranoid, even the security cameras didn't see anything.

Maybe therapy would be good for me, even though I would never dare to bring up last night's events to the psychiatrist. How could I? That's a sure way to be checked into a mental institution.

I sat down on the chair in the entryway to wait for Griffin and noticed something on the hallway window. The hallway window. A long scratch was on the bottom windowpane from one side to the other. Something was out there the other night and it wanted me to know it.

My thumbnail went immediately in between my teeth and I chewed until there was no nail left to bite. My knee bounced as I heard footsteps walking up the front steps, then a knock. I peeked out the peephole and saw Griffin's smiling face and my nerves subsided.

I opened the door and saw Griffin standing there, looking much more relaxed than I felt.

"You look refreshed." He said, admiring my freshly washed hair and exfoliated face.

"I wish I felt it." I motioned for him to come in.

"Aren't we getting coffee?" He asked, confused by my change in plans.

"Yeah, but you need to come in here, and see what I found first."

Griffin stepped inside and I closed the door. "What did you—"

I pointed to the window.

"Find." His eyes went wide. "Is that from the other night?"

"I'm assuming so. My best guess is it was from whatever was scratching the window."

"That's only mildly terrifying." Griffin added. "Was there anything else?"

"No, not that I've seen."

"I can go check the backyard, unless you've already done that."

"I haven't. I was too anxious to go out there." My eyes met the floor.

"Stay in here, I'll go check." Griffin went out the back door and walked the perimeter of the backyard. When he got to the back corner, he stopped. I hadn't told him exactly where the creature was that I had seen, so him being over there made me feel like he found something.

I waited by the door, watching his every move until he motioned for me to come outside. I anxiously walked across the large yard, unsure of what I was going to see. I shoved my hands in my pockets to hide both my shaking and to keep them warm.

"Did you find anything?" I asked, almost to where he was standing.

"Nothing too crazy. There are some footprints, though. But to be honest, it could be anything, they look pretty generic."

I closed the gap between us and saw what he was staring at—two large animal footprints, right where I had seen something the other night.

"This is where the creature was."

"I get that, I'm just saying that these could belong to anything."

"Yeah. You're right." I exhaled loudly. "Let's go get some coffee."

We made our way inside and Griffin made sure to latch both locks on the back door before we headed out.

We walked part of the five-minute walk, in silence. I was ruminating on where everything went so wrong for me. One day I was just excited to rent out my damn cabin and the next I'm in the middle of a murder investigation with some creature taunting me.

"Do you think I'm crazy?" I asked, not sure I wanted to hear the answer.

"No, I don't. I'm sure there's probably a logical explanation for everything, but right now, I can't think of one."

I nodded. We walked a few more steps before I opened my mouth, again. "Do you wish we would've just stayed at my house last night?"

"Well that's a loaded question." Griffin pulled his bottom lip between his teeth, thinking about what I had just asked. "No."

I stopped dead in my tracks. "You don't? Did you enjoy running through a freaking forest being chased by an absolutely terrifying creature?"

"The whole going outside part I regret. But not when we were just sitting and talking. I think you have a fascinating story—whether you think so or not."

I smiled at him. I felt like Griffin is the only one who saw me for who I really am. "Can we not talk about it over coffee? I think we could use a sense of normalcy right now."

"Deal." Griffin agreed.

We approached the coffee shop and I could see Miranda inside, bopping around from customer to customer. She loved her job more than anything. She always said she loved nothing more than greeting everyone in the morning and see the smiles on their faces when they left with their drinks of choice and headed off to work.

As we walked through the door and the bell chimed, Miranda looked up and I caught her attention. She practically skipped over to us and my stomach dropped. In a split-second decision, I decided not to tell her any of what had happened last night. She was already so skeptical of everything I was saying, I didn't need to add fuel to the fire.

"Cora!" Miranda sang, wrapping me in a hug. "And you must be Griffin. I've heard so much about you."

He extended his hand, smirking. "Let me guess. From my grandmother."

"She talks about you non-stop when she comes in here. She's very proud of your accomplishments."

I saw a blush creep up his cheeks. I bumped my shoulder into his chest. "Told ya, she talks about you a lot."

Griffin shook his head and laughed.

Miranda headed back behind the register and took our order. Griffin was a gentleman and paid for our drinks and our croissants. We started walking away when Miranda called out for me.

"I'll go grab us a table." Griffin said before heading to the front of the store and sitting down at a two-person table.

"Hey!" I tried to be as perky as possible and not let on, I was chased in the forest last night by some Beast-like creature.

"You didn't tell me about this new development!" Miranda's eyes went wide with surprise.

"It's not a development...yet. We went up to the cabin yesterday and spent the majority of the day talking and getting to know each other."

"And, this morning you're getting coffee together." A smirk formed on her lips. "Cora, did you spend the night with Griffin?"

"Yeah, but not in the way you think. It was innocent, I promise. You know me." I laughed, knowing exactly what she was thinking.

Miranda crossed her arms and pouted. "Well that's disappointing." She brushed a strand of blonde hair out of her face. "How much longer is he in town for?"

"As of this morning, another week."

"Is he staying here because of you?" She couldn't hide her excitement.

"Something like that."

"Will you call me tonight and tell me everything?" Miranda always did love being in the know.

"There's not much to tell. We hit it off at dinner the other night and then hung out again yesterday." My chest was red, a tell-tale sign, I was blushing.

"You're splotchy. You really do like him, don't you?"

I nodded softly.

"Well, go be with him and fill me in on the details tonight!"

As I was walking back to the table, the barista called out both mine and Griffin's names. "Your orders are ready!"

I grabbed the croissants in one hand and Griffin's drink in the other when I felt a warm body behind me, reaching for my drink.

"I'll grab the croissants." He said softly by my ear. A shock of electricity ran down my spine. *I like him a lot.*

With butterflies flying around my stomach, we headed back to the table he had grabbed for us.

"So, how did your grandma take you staying for another week?" I held the coffee cup to my nose, inhaling the aromas.

"Once she put two and two together, she was elated."

"What do you mean?"

"When I told her that you and I had a connection and I was staying for a bit longer, she practically jumped out of her chair."

I smiled. Mrs. Bethel had finally gotten her wish, Griffin and I would go out on a few dates. I don't think she thought that we would form such a connection so quickly…or at all.

"Have you told your firm that you won't be in this week?"

"I haven't; let me do that now. Excuse me for a moment." Griffin stepped outside to presumably call his office and let them know. As he stood there, I realized how lucky I was that not only was he nice to look at, but he believed me and all my nonsense. He really didn't have a choice, though, because he was also being chased last night. I watched as he put his phone back in his pocket and then came back inside.

"How'd that go?" I asked, nervously chewing the inside of my cheek.

"About as well as I had expected. My boss is pissed, but I'm their best architect, so he'll get over it by this afternoon. I never take more than a few days off each year, he can deal with it."

"Are you sure? There's really nothing we can do at this point aside from making sure my doors and windows are triple locked."

"That's what you think. I think we're both very smart individuals and can figure this all out."

"There's nothing to figure out." I lowered my voice. "We were chased last night by something. Something we didn't recognize. Maybe if I stay away from the cabin and just go about my normal routine, it'll get bored and leave me alone."

"I don't know if you noticed or not, but I really like you. And no matter what baggage you think you have, I'm ready to help you work through it and lessen the load."

Those damn butterflies were back, yet again. "I really appreciate that. It means more to me than you know. I still don't want you to lose your job over this. You've known me for not even a week, I'm not worth losing a job over."

"First of all, I decide what's worthy of my time. And, second, they really won't fire me. My boss took me under his wing while I was still in school and he's like a dad to me." Griffin grabbed both of my hands in his. "Cora, I need you to do me a favor and just let me worry about myself and my career. You need to focus on yourself."

I smiled, unable to get the appropriate words of gratitude out. "Enough of this talk. What do you have planned for today?"

Griffin tapped his chin and laughed. "Seeing as I thought I was going home until about an hour ago, I think my day is free. Is there anything you wanted to do?"

"I need to get groceries. But I would really love a day of sitting by the fire at home."

"We can arrange for that." Griffin agreed.

"Once we finish up here, I'll run out and get groceries. I can let you know when I'm back and you could come over."

"I can come with you to the grocery store."

"That's not necessary, Griff. Spend some time with your elderly grandmother." I quipped.

"She's meeting with her knitting club today, so she asked me if I could stay with you." He slapped his forehead.

"Oh, I see." I couldn't contain the laugh. His grandma was more social than both of us. "Then, we'll head to the store after this."

I felt my phone vibrate a few times in my pocket. "Sorry, it's Detective Ambrose, I have to get this."

I cleared my throat. "This is Cora."

"Cora, it's Detective Ambrose. How are ya doin'?"

"I'm doing well, Detective. How are you?"

"Good, good." He paused and I knew he had an update. "We have some updates on Luke Anderson's case."

My blood went cold. "Oh?"

"The suspect that was in custody is being brought here now. He's admitted to killing more than ten hikers over the last five years, so we think we've got him. Once he's here, we'll question him as well. You can start to rest easy now, Cora. I know this was very scary for you."

I stared blankly outside at the sidewalks as I listened to Detective Ambrose. He was trying to make me feel better, but at this point, would anything? I have some sort of creature stalking me, a job I was drowning in, and a gorgeous man here that likes me that's leaving in a week.

"That's great news!" I said excitedly as my eyes were still blank.

"It is. Hopefully we can bring him to the crime scene and he'll confess."

"That would be great. And we can all get on with our lives." I added.

"So true! I hate that this is weighin' on ya."

"I'll be just fine."

"Good. Now you get back to your Sunday, Miss Cora, and we'll talk again real soon."

"Have a good one, Detective."

I put my phone face-down on the table and took a sip of my coffee.

"An update on the case?" Griffin asked, only hearing my side of the conversation.

"Yeah." I didn't elaborate.

"What did he say?"

"Just that they think the guy that's in custody was the one who killed Luke. They're bringing him in for questioning in Byglass now."

"They think it was a serial killer?" Griffin asked, trying to make heads or tails of what I was saying.

I shrugged. "They said that there's evidence to back it up."

"I mean, I don't buy it."

"Neither do I."

"If we take the possibility of the Beast off the table, what are you thinking?"

"That Luke's wife had motive and was sketchy when I met her."

Griffin's eyes went wide. "When did you meet her?"

"The Sunday I went up to the cabin after Luke was found. When I pulled in the driveway, she was already there, staring up at the house."

His face scrunched.

"She told me that Luke was having an affair and that he was likely coming up to the cabin with another woman."

"But was a woman found?"

"No. Which could easily be explained if they were taking two cars."

"Have you mentioned this to the detectives?"

"Yep. They wrote some notes down, but they cleared her pretty quickly. She's not a suspect."

"Have you looked into her at all?" Griffin pried.

"Nope. I was letting the investigators do their job. If they weren't concerned about her, why should I be?"

"I suppose that's fair." Griffin said, taking the last sip of coffee. "All done?" he motioned towards my cup.

"I am. Ready to head out?" I asked, pushing my chair back.

Griffin nodded and we placed our cups in the bin and headed back towards my house to get my car.

"Would you like me to drive?" Griffin asked as we approached my car.

"Sure, if you'd like."

He headed to the driver's side door and got in. "Please don't be afraid to let me know if I'm overstepping."

"Not overstepping. It's nice to have someone help out with things. You're making this trip to the grocery store feel less lonely." I felt a blush creep up my cheeks.

"Well, I'm happy to help you feel less lonely."

I smiled in his direction. I connected my phone to the car's Bluetooth and turned on my favorite country music playlist.

"Are you a fan of country music?" I asked. We had talked about so many deep topics, but never touched likes or dislikes.

"Huge fan. It's really the only music I listen to." That's a tally in the pro column.

"Who's your favorite artist?"

"While I enjoy pretty much everyone's music, I'm partial to Randy Travis and Brad Paisley. How about you?"

"Good answer." I laughed. "I listen to anyone and everyone. I'm one of those people that's a 'mood' listener, so no favorite."

"You're telling me that if someone asked you to name your favorite artist or they would push you off a cliff, you wouldn't be able to choose?" A laugh played on his lips.

143

"That's exactly what I'm saying."

"So that's how Cora goes. Death by indecision."

"Exactly!"

"You're ridiculous sometimes, you know that?"

"I've been told that once or twice." I winked as we pulled into the grocery store parking lot.

I rested my head on the headrest. "Ugh."

Griffin looked over at me. "What?"

"I hate this."

"The grocery store?" He was confused.

I sighed dramatically. "I just get overwhelmed. I can't cook very well, so seeing all the ingredients just stresses me out. I buy a few things that I know I'll need, but my cart usually just consists of snacks."

"Well, good news for you—I can cook pretty well. It's no Michelin star meal, but it resembles a nutritious dinner. Want me to teach you?"

"Good luck. My mom has tried for years and I just don't have the knack for it."

"I find that hard to believe. Have you actually tried?"

"That's a rude assumption that you think I didn't try." I held in a laugh. "Very rude, Griffin Bethel."

"I'm sorry I—"

I cut him off. "I'm kidding. You can relax. I've not given the whole learning thing a real try. Something about my mom teaching me that made me completely zone out."

"If I teach you how to make my signature dish tonight, would you pay attention?" He asked, opening the car door.

"Depends on what it is." Why am I such a smart ass?

"Tomato soup, something super simple. It's my grandma's recipe."

"Oh, so then it'll for sure be delicious. As long as my being in the kitchen doesn't ruin it."

"You being there will only make it taste better." He's flirting and I was a fan.

We walked around the grocery store while Griffin pushed the cart, occasionally throwing in ingredients that he needed for dinner. When he tossed in a French baguette, he had my heart. If it were up to me, I would eat a baguette with butter every day—not caring how unhealthy it is.

"So far we only have what we need for dinner tonight. What did you need to get here?" Griffin asked, placing some fresh basil in the cart.

"Potato chips, French onion dip, and some Tootsie Rolls."

"Are you thirty-two or twelve?" A smirk emerged on Griffin's face.

"Shut up. I like to snack." I shot back.

"We need brain food."

"Why is that?"

"For starters, you still have to work this week. But also because we're going to start looking into the Beast."

I stopped in my tracks. "We are?"

Griffin nodded. "We need to at least try to figure out what that was."

I lowered my voice, "Do you think we'll actually find anything? I've already done as much searching as I could."

"Between the two of us, I'm confident we will."

My heart raced just thinking about what we might stumble upon. When I had looked a few weeks ago, there were a handful of articles that spoke of the Beast, but they were all at least ten years old. I was torn—I wanted answers on what was by my window and what chased us last night, but I was afraid of what we might find.

We finished up at the store and headed back home. I was quiet in the passenger seat, unsure of what to say. Griffin helped me bring in the groceries and while I put them away, he sat at the kitchen island.

"I'm going to pop over and grab my laptop so we can get to work. I'll be right back." He got up and kissed me on the cheek before leaving for Mrs. Bethel's house.

As soon as I heard the front door close, my hand instinctively went to my cheek. I wondered if he even realized what he had done.

Surely, he did, right?

That small peck on the cheek was something couples do, not two people set up by one of those people's relatives.

I finished putting the groceries away as Griffin walked back in with his laptop, charger, and a suitcase in tow. I glanced down at the suitcase and back up at him.

"Staying a while?" I tried to contain my excitement.

"If that's alright? Granny dearest wasn't anticipating me staying for another week and has plans with friends each day. She asked if I could stay here." Griffin sat back down at the kitchen island, this time with his laptop. "I feel like a kid again—nowhere to go."

"Of course, you can stay here," I cleared my throat, "I have a spare room that's already set up and it has a bathroom right next to it."

No sooner the words came out of my mouth, Griffin was getting up off the barstool and coming over where I was in the kitchen. He wrapped his arms around my torso and held me tightly. My head was level with his broad chest, so I snuggled in and enjoyed being held. The longer the hug lasted, the more stress I could feel melting away.

CHAPTER 23

I LISTENED AS THE RAIN PUMMELED THE WINDOWS WHILE Griffin and I watched a movie. I had already gotten my expert's class in making tomato soup and also flirting, so nothing could metaphorically rain on my parade. Mother Nature was, of course, dumping buckets outside. Every cell in my body was thankful that Griffin was kicked out of his grandmother's house and had to stay here for the week.

My stomach growled, ready to inhale that soup, but Griffin insisted that it needed to simmer for three hours. This is why I don't cook. Who has the time?

"Hungry?" Griffin asked, his eyes glued to the television.

"What gave it away? Was it my constant turning around and looking at the stove? Or was it my stomach making noises that sound like the Beast?"

"It was really the noises that sealed the deal." He playfully bumped his shoulder into mine.

"I don't understand why this has to cook for so long. Isn't this the exact reason that they invented the pressure cooker?"

"Just have patience. I promise, it will be worth it. Maybe not as good as what your mom makes, though."

"The smell alone is making me want to override you and go pour myself a bowl."

Griffin paused the movie. "We have seventeen minutes left of this movie. If you can last until then, it'll be ready."

I sighed dramatically in response, grabbing my phone to text Miranda to tell her that I wouldn't be able to call her tonight. Obviously, that text was met with twelve messages from her, asking what was going on. I turned away from Griffin and typed out my response.

> **Cora:** Mrs. Bethel kicked Griff out, so he's staying with me this week.
>
> **Miranda:** Staying with you???
>
> **Miranda:** I love this.
>
> **Miranda:** Why is he staying again?
>
> **Cora:** Long, boring story for another day.
>
> **Miranda:** Please give me more than that, otherwise I'm coming over.
>
> **Cora:** You'll be staying right where you are, thank you. We're just getting to know each other.
>
> **Miranda:** I know you'll tell me the truth sooner or later. Have fun!!

I flipped my phone over on the couch just as the credits rolled.

"Dinner time?" I raised my eyebrows, looking at Griffin for confirmation.

"Dinner time."

I grabbed the bowls and some glasses out of the cabinet while Griffin stirred the soup one last time. I handed over the bowls and he filled them. The kitchen smelled so good the thought of proposing crossed my mind.

We cut up the baguette and headed back over to the couch. I placed my bowl down on the coffee table and sat cross-legged on the floor.

"You're going to sit down there?" Griffin asked, amused.

"Absolutely. It's either I sit here or I end up wearing half the bowl because I've spilled it."

"In that case, let me join you." He sat down on the floor next to me.

I reached for the remote. "What would you like to watch?"

"We don't have to watch anything. We can just talk if you'd like."

"Yeah, I'd like that." I tried to hide the smile that was forming.

"So, what's your favorite color?" Griffin was going to go the rapid-fire question route.

"Purple. You?"

"Green. Favorite season?"

"Summer. Yours?"

"Summer as well. Favorite food?"

"Carbs. What's yours?"

"Cora, carbs are a food group; that doesn't count." He snickered.

"Mr. Negative over here!" I popped a piece of bread in my mouth. "Carbs are life. I love them all, I don't discriminate. Pasta, potatoes, rice—give it all to me."

Griffin held up his hands, "Alright, I'll allow that answer. I love this tomato soup."

I ate my first spoonful and my eyes closed involuntarily, savoring the bite. "I'd like to change my answer. This tomato soup is my new favorite food. This is fantastic, Griff."

A broad smile spread across his face. "Thank you."

"Can you send me the recipe? I feel like I might be able to make this once you leave."

"Using me for my recipes, I see."

"That's not entirely true."

"It's not?"

I shook my head. I inhaled deeply, ready to lay it all out on the table. "Griff?"

"Hm?" He had just shoveled a large spoon of soup in his mouth.

"I…" I reached for my glass of water. My mouth went completely dry. "I like you."

Griffin made eye contact and placed his spoon down. "Is that so?"

I nodded shyly.

"Well, that's really good news because I like you, too. And, I know that you haven't dated anyone seriously before, so I know how much it took for you to say that."

"Thank you for actually taking the time to understand me. I'm sorry if it's too soon or something, I just feel like I needed to let you know. We don't have to feel pressured to date or anything, since we've not known each other very long."

Griffin reached for my hands. "Isn't it funny how it's only been a few days, but it feels like longer?"

"Yeah. Probably because we've spent a fair bit of time together and have spent the majority of that time talking. You're one of the only people who gets me and why I work so much. And as of late, you're the only one that knows all the shit I'm dealing with."

"Does Miranda not know?" he asked, resuming dinner.

"She only knows up to the other night. I didn't tell her about our little escapade in the forest last night."

"Do you think she believes you and everything you've told her about the Beast?"

"I think she believed me in the beginning, but now as my

nightmares have gotten worse, I think she's believing me less and less. She finally sent me her psychiatrist's contact info, so I scheduled an appointment."

"Good, maybe that'll help."

"Until I tell the psychiatrist that a creature in folklore is stalking me and—"

"And then you're shipped off to the nearest mental institution."

"Exactly. So, I think I'll keep it surface-level and talk about my nightmares and that's it."

"Whatever you think is best."

"We'll just see how it goes. The nightmares were happening before any of this, so I think that's the first step."

Griffin nodded in agreement. "I feel like we owe it to ourselves to at least start looking into what we saw last night."

The rain outside intensified as I collected our bowls and put them in the dishwasher. Griffin grabbed his laptop off the counter and sat back down on the couch where I joined him.

"Ready?" he asked, checking to ensure that I was okay with whatever we might uncover.

"As ready as I'll ever be."

Griffin pulled up a fresh Google page and started off with the basic search—The Beast folklore.

"I feel like we should put something lighthearted on while we dig into something so dark." I said, reaching for the remote.

"That's probably a good idea. Maybe *The Office*?" He added.

"Done deal." I pressed play and scooted over closer to Griffin to have a better view of the laptop screen.

I glanced down, seeing the hundreds of pages of results. "Maybe we should narrow the search down a little bit further. How about 'the Beast Appalachian Mountains'?"

"Probably a good call." Griffin edited our search and now there were only one hundred pages of results. If we were honest with ourselves, we knew that the likelihood of us going past page two of the results was nonexistent.

"Have you ever heard the folklore?" I asked, remembering that he didn't grow up in the mountains, so he might be unfamiliar.

"I only know the bits and pieces you've told me. I've never heard the whole story before."

"Before we delve into the search results, let me tell you the story that my friend Kendra told me when I was younger." I started the story off just as Kendra had all those years ago, leaving no detail omitted. The majority of the time, I kept my eyes down, not wanting to see Griffin's reaction. Just as I was finishing up the folklore, I finally looked up to find him slack-jawed and eyes bulging.

"You heard that story when you were young?"

I nodded.

"That's heavy for a kid to hear."

"It is. But, when you live in the mountains and your parents tell you that you can't go outside at night, you inevitably have questions. I just so happened to have my best friend tell me and not my parents."

Griffin shook his head in disbelief. "I'm not so sure I want to look into this anymore. I feel like this is something that we should be leaving alone."

"Then, I'll ask you this—do you think that anything we're going to uncover tonight will be scarier that what we witnessed last night?"

"No, definitely not." He took a long sip of his water. "Let's get back into it."

While I took notes, Griffin read through old blog posts from people who have had encounters with what they're calling The Beast.

"I'd say that what we saw last night matches the description of what others have seen pretty well."

"Yeah, for sure." I squinted at the screen with the search

results. "What's that one?" I pointed to the last result on the second page.

"It looks like it's an interview with Harper Cooper's parents from earlier this year on a blog." He immediately clicked the link.

Harper Cooper's untimely departure from this world was a tragedy that shocked her family and the town of Byglass, North Carolina. Today, I'm sitting down with Harper's parents, Eric and Gina Cooper, for an exclusive interview with The Morbid Blogger (TMB).

"When we first moved to Byglass, Harper kept telling us that she felt like she was being watched. She never slept well, was always unsettled, and wasn't acting like herself. We attributed her strange behavior to the fact that she didn't want to move," Mrs. Cooper shared.

TMB: Can you tell us more about Harper?

Mr. Cooper: Harper was a vibrant and caring person. In New York, she was always with her friends and had a big heart. She volunteered at the local animal shelter on Saturday and Sunday mornings.

Mrs. Cooper: Harper had a bright future ahead of her. She had just decided to pursue veterinary medicine and was looking into potential colleges.

TMB: What brought your family to Byglass, North Carolina?

Gina: I work in tech, and they opened a new facility here, offering me the position of manager. We thought it was an opportunity for our family.

TMB: Harper's disappearance was a tragedy that no family should ever have to face. Do you think her sighting of a creature in the woods was related to her disappearance?

Eric: It's something we think about every day. If only we had listened to her, maybe she would still be here with us today.

Gina: We've done our own investigation and found some evidence that suggests something else might have been going on.

TMB: What kind of evidence?

Gina: I can't disclose that information right now, but we're hopeful that it will lead us to answers and justice for Harper.

The conversation went on to discuss their ongoing investigation, their efforts to keep Harper's memory alive, and their hopes for justice. The Cooper family continues to hold onto hope that one day they will have closure and that Harper's memory will live on.

"I can't believe we found this." I said, breaking the silence.

"I know. I'm not sure why, but I never thought about her parents and family when you told me the story." Griffin rubbed his forehead. "I guess I always thought about the folklore starting with Harper, I have never thought about the original story. Do you know how it even started?"

I shook my head. "I guess that's where we should start first."

Griffin modified the search to target the folklore, which gave us exactly what we were looking for. He clicked on the first result and we both started reading the long history of the Beast. Griffin scanned it quickly while I took in every word, soaking it all in. That summed up our personalities perfectly—I am careful, while he is spontaneous.

The legend of the Beast originated in the mid-1940s, in the town of Byglass, North Carolina. It was a warm summer day, and a group of friends were playing hide and seek outside. One of the young girls went to hide and accidentally ventured further into the forest, becoming separated from the group. As she tried to return to her friends, she heard yelling and ran towards it, but ended up going in the wrong direction.

When she heard a woman's voice, she walked towards it, only to encounter what she described as a creature, the Beast. The creature was huge, with black fur, sharp teeth, and glowing eyes.

Today, the Beast continues to exist in local folklore, with a few sightings reported every year, particularly around Byglass. If you're going to visit, stay inside at night and if you think you see something, no you didn't.

Look away!

"Hey, Griff?" My voice caught in my throat.

"Yeah?"

"I think I know where we can go to get more details of the folklore…"

"Where?"

"The one and only, Mabel Bethel."

"It's late, we can't go over there now." Griffin scratched his arm. "Maybe we can go over tomorrow after work?"

"I think we should."

"Do you think she knows something?" he asked nervously.

CHAPTER 24

WE SAT IN SILENCE FOR A WHILE, GRIFFIN PROCESSING the fact that his grandmother knew something about the Beast. I didn't want to go into detail, it was her story to tell. To ease his concerns, I told him that she lived here around that time and might know something. Not that she was the one where the folklore came from.

He accepted this explanation and continued down the rabbit hole while I pulled myself out of it, focusing on the show that was on the television. I had already spoken to Mrs. Bethel, I wasn't sure why she hadn't told me that she was the initiator.

"Cora, look at this." Griffin turned the screen towards me. "This sighting was from earlier this year…looks like in May someone spotted something near the Widow's Peak."

"What does it say?"

"Just that they were lost in the forest and followed a voice in the hopes of getting back on the trail. When they found it, they were met, face-to-face with a black furry Beast." Griffin skimmed a bit further. "This sounds nearly identical to the story we just read from the young girl."

"Yeah, it does." My knee bounced anxiously. "Why don't we stop our research for today. I'm not trying to dream of the Beast all night."

Griffin nodded. "Want to watch a movie?"

I glanced down at my phone, it was almost midnight. "I have to be up early tomorrow for a call. Do you mind if I call it a night? You're more than welcome to stay and hang out down here."

"I think I might stay down here for a little bit longer and wind down. Unless the television will bother you."

"Nope, you're good. I won't hear a thing upstairs." I started for the stairs. "If you need anything, rummage around. Pretend like this is your house this week."

"Thanks again, Cora. I really do appreciate it."

"Anytime." My steps were heavy going up the stairs. I wanted nothing more than to continue spending time with Griffin, getting to know him more, but I was exhausted—both physically and mentally.

I entered the bathroom to get ready for bed where I caught a glimpse of myself in the mirror. I was not the same Cora from a few weeks ago. I was starting to open up my heart, while being the most stressed I've ever been. I had forgotten about Friday when I laid off some people from my team. I watched as the gravity of the situation washed over my face, my smile falling.

As I headed towards my bedroom, I paused at the top of the stairs and listened. From below, I could hear Griffin's frenzied typing as he watched a cartoon. I chose to settle in bed, and texted him to thank him for an interesting, but good, weekend.

As I lay in bed, I turned on my alarm and stared up at the ceiling, wondering when I would fall asleep and how many times I would wake up during the night. I looked over at the clock on my nightstand—12:05 A.M.

At the sound of my alarm at seven, I was confused. I had actually slept through the night without any nightmares, and for once, I felt well-rested. I quickly wrapped a robe around my body and gently opened my bedroom door.

As expected, Griffin's door was still shut, likely indicating that he was still asleep. Trying not to disturb him, I tiptoed down the stairs, cautiously avoiding any creaky floorboards. Despite the fact that I wasn't sure what time Griffin went to bed, I hadn't heard a sound from him all night.

As I entered the kitchen, I noticed that Griffin was already there, standing by the stove, stirring something in a pan.

"Good morning," I said, my voice still waking up.

"Hey, how did you sleep?" A very tired looking Griffin turned to face me and I was able to get a glimpse of what was in the pan—scrambled eggs.

"Really well. Pretty sure I fell asleep almost immediately."

"Any nightmares?"

I shook my head. "Not one."

'That's great news!" He turned his attention back to the eggs. "Your coffee is in your office. Miranda said to call her today or quote, 'She will beat down the door.'"

"Thank you for getting me coffee. And that sounds like Miranda. I'll give her a call when I have a break in meetings today."

"It was my pleasure. Breakfast will be ready soon…if you have time."

"Let me go login and see what my morning looks like." I grabbed my laptop and coffee and made my way back to the kitchen island. While logging in, I took a sip of my coffee and the combination of sleep and caffeine sent a shock through my normally exhausted body. I examined my calendar and the pre-holiday meeting cancellations had already begun.

"It looks like I have some chunks of free time today, so I'm good for breakfast." I noted.

"Great, because breakfast is ready." Griffin said, sliding a plate of scrambled eggs and toast over before grabbing his own plate and sitting down next to me.

"Did you sleep well?" I asked, shoving a forkful of eggs into my mouth.

"I slept."

"I'm sorry. Were you not comfortable?"

"No, everything was perfect. I just kept doing research after you went to bed and found some disturbing things."

I raised an eyebrow.

"Did you know that over the last eighty years, there have been over fifty sightings of what people are calling the Beast? And that's not counting the other twenty-eight people that have mysteriously died in the woods in Byglass." Griffin drummed his fingers on the counter. "This shit is for real, Cora."

"I know. We'll go talk to your grandmother later this afternoon and then take it from there. I really don't think we can bring this up to authorities. Clearly people have tried for years and failed. We're no different."

"You're right, but I just can't let this one go. People go missing and are then found mauled days later. This...thing needs to be stopped before more innocent people are killed."

"What time did you stay up until last night doing this intense research?"

"It was like four when I went to bed. Once I started, I just couldn't stop. This is all so fascinating."

"It sounds like you read every article that came up."

He scrunched his face, "You're not wrong."

"How about you spend the day reading or watching some

television while I work to keep your mind off it. You have yourself worked up."

"Is it not justified?" Griffin asked, seeming slightly offended.

"It is, I'm just speaking from experience. Take a break from it all." I patted his arm as I got up, placing my dish in the sink. "I have to go get some work done and hope that my team doesn't hate me for having to lay off some of them."

The morning flew by and I was able to talk with each of my employees that were being let go after Human Resources spoke with them. Each of them was upset, but understood. I promised each of them that I would write letters of recommendation, would be their reference, and would help them each find a new role.

"So *this* is working Cora." I turned around to find Griffin leaning against the doorframe, arms crossed.

I smiled, "In all her glory."

"It's weird to see this professional side. It's kinda hot, though." A flush crept up my neck. "I didn't mean to interrupt, I just wanted to check and see if you wanted some lunch. I was debating running to the diner and getting something."

"I'm good but thank you."

"Suit yourself. When I have a delicious smelling sandwich and you're looking longingly at it, I won't be sharing." He laughed, shrugging on his coat. "I'll be back. Text me if you change your mind."

"Will do." As soon as the door closed, I immediately capitalized on the half hour alone I had and called Miranda.

"Why do you hate me?" Miranda asked on the second ring.

"Hello to you, too."

"Hey. Why didn't you tell me about Griffin? Are you trying to keep him a secret? Do you think I'm a crazy overbearing friend?"

Hearing her rambling made me laugh. "You need to chill

out. I'm not keeping secrets. Griffin and I are just hanging out this week. We've bonded over…some things and he decided to stay a bit longer."

"What did you bond over?"

"Do you promise not to judge?"

"Of course, Cora! You're my best friend, I would never."

"You might have a different answer here in a moment." I inhaled deeply before continuing. "Griffin and I were at the cabin Saturday night and made the mistake of going outside."

"Okay…?" Miranda wasn't following.

"We went outside Saturday night in the middle of the night to go check things out and we were chased."

"Oh…my…word. Are you telling me you both were chased by the Beast?"

I nodded, realizing she couldn't see me. "Yeah. Or, something."

"Well that's terrifying." Her tone changed, "Does Griffin believe it, too?"

"He does. He was up until like four digging into it."

"How have your nightmares been?"

"I didn't have any last night. Slept through the night for the first time in months. It feels like having someone who believes me has eased my mind, allowing me to get some good rest." I was met with silence. As soon as the words came out, I wanted to shove them back in.

"I didn't mean it like that, Miranda. I just…he was there. He saw the same thing I did. It's different."

"No, I understand what you're saying. You said you made a therapy appointment?"

"Yes. Next week."

"Good. Make sure you go. I feel like you have a lot to talk through."

"I'm looking forward to going. I think it'll be good for me."

"I think so, too. I have to get back to work, the owner is staring at me. We'll talk later!"

The line went dead.

"Cora! Are you ready to go?" Griffin beckoned from the couch, anxiously waiting on me to finish up work so we could head over to Mrs. Bethel's house.

"Yep! Just hitting send on this last email and then I'll be done." I glanced down at the clock and it was barely after five. Maybe Griffin being part of my life was a good thing—I would log off at a normal hour and have my evenings back. Closing my laptop, I grabbed our coats out of the closet and tossed it at Griffin, who was lounging on the couch.

"Not going to lie, it's weird having someone else in this house with me." I smiled softly, not wanting to come across as needy.

"I'd offer to leave, but I have nowhere else to go…"

"Not what I meant. I don't think it's a coincidence that you were here last night and I didn't have any nightmares. Now, it's barely five and I've already logged off for the day. Are you domesticating me, Griffin Bethel?" I let out the broad smile I had been holding in.

"You caught me." He winked, getting up and putting on his coat. "Let's go see granny dearest and see what insight she pretends to have. I don't think that woman has ever done anything reckless in her life."

"You'd be surprised," I said under my breath.

"Did you say something?" Griffin asked.

Shit. "Nope."

I locked the door behind us and we started down the street, Griffin grabbing my hand about half-way there. He glanced down at our interlocked fingers and then back up at me and smiled; I wasn't pulling away. We strolled up to the door and Mrs. Bethel welcomed us inside.

"I wasn't expecting you two today. I figured you'd be off having a romantic dinner somewhere." The blush creeped up Griffin's cheeks.

We hung our coats in the closet and then made our way to the living room to have a seat.

"Can I get you kids anything to drink? Maybe some tea?" Mrs. Bethel asked, going into full grandma mode.

"No, thank you." Griffin and I said in unison.

"So what brings you both over?" Mrs. Bethel asked, her hands folded in her lap.

I nudged Griffin, "Go ahead."

"We have some questions that we think you might have some insight on."

"Spit it out, G." She was getting impatient.

"The Beast. What do you know about it?"

Mrs. Bethel's knuckles went white and she wrung her hands, glancing at me. "Why do you think I know something about it?"

"Well, you lived here when the first instance was reported, so we wondered if you knew anything."

She looked over at me, silently thanking me for not telling Griffin before looking back over at him. "I'm familiar with that story, yes."

"Did you know the girl that had the encounter?"

Mrs. Bethel's eyes fell. "Griffin, I think it's time that I let you in on a secret." She recounted the story in excruciating detail, more than she had told me, highlighting how terrifying it was.

It took some time for Griffin to process everything. "So you're where the folklore started."

"I am. When I told my parents, they thought I was crazy. When I told my friends, they somewhat believed me. For months after it happened, I would hear a woman outside wailing at all hours of the night. Then, I would see shadows walk by my window. Once those instances stopped, I constantly felt like I was being watched."

"When did it stop?" I asked, selfishly curious.

"It never has."

My eyes went wide. "Never?"

She shook her head. "Sometimes, when I head upstairs at night, I feel like I'm being watched from the glass in the front door. I've never had the guts to look back."

"Did you tell anyone else about it as you got older?" He asked, fully invested in his grandmother's story.

"Anytime I would bring it up, I was always told it was probably just a regular animal, it had just mutated. I never believed it." She took a sip of her water, "Why are you asking so many questions all of a sudden?"

Griffin remained quiet, so I took this as my cue to talk. "I had another encounter. Well, *we* had an encounter the other night."

Her face went pale and she looked at me. "Did you?"

"Yes. The same thing as last time. This time, it chased us."

"Did you tell anyone?"

We shook our heads.

"Good. Don't tell anyone, there's no point. It's not like they would believe you."

"What do we do now? Leave it alone?" Griffin spoke up.

"That's your best bet. Try to forget that it happened. It'll be hard, but it'll get easier over time."

She clearly didn't want to talk about it anymore because she quickly changed the subject to what we had done all day yesterday. We had a good visit with her, but we were getting hungry and she was kicking us out. We said our goodbyes and started towards my house. As we stopped at my front gate, I looked at Griffin.

"Do you want to get dinner out?"

"I thought you'd never ask." He laughed.

We headed into the diner and we sat at a booth towards the front.

Griffin sat with his head in his hands. "What do we do now?"

"I don't know."

CHAPTER 25

HAVING GRIFFIN AROUND WAS WORKING WONDERS FOR me. Not only did he cook for me and treat me well, but, subconsciously, I think him believing everything I've mentioned about the Beast has helped me calm down, because my nightmares have completely stopped. I'm getting a solid eight hours of sleep each night. When I wake up in the morning, I feel rejuvenated and ready to tackle the day.

Crazy what sleep will do for you.

Griffin is only staying with me for two more days. I half-joked last night that I didn't want him to go, but he didn't say anything, so that was probably too much. We've spent so much time together since we met that it feels like we've known each other for years.

While I've been working, he has been looking more into the Beast and the different sightings. At this point, he's driven himself into a state of obsession and he won't rest until we have answers.

I crept down the stairs, listening carefully for Griffin in the kitchen. I was up earlier than normal, but he was nowhere in sight. I checked all the rooms downstairs and he wasn't there, his jacket still in the closet.

He must still be asleep.

Grabbing my laptop, I headed to the couch—it's Friday and I only have two meetings today, a rarity—so I planned on working from the coziness of my living room. Grabbing a blanket off the back of the couch, I snuggled in and turned the fireplace on, answering emails.

Around six-thirty, I heard movement upstairs and froze. I had been so lost in Email Land I had forgotten Griffin was upstairs and it wasn't some creature that was going to kill me. Soft footsteps padded down the wooden planks, somehow managing to hit every squeaky bit of the stairs.

"Shit," I heard Griffin say softly, hitting the last stair.

"They're noisy!" I called out from the living room.

Griffin came into view. His plaid pajama pants hung low on his hips and his white t-shirt was all wrinkled.

"How did you sleep?" I asked, more awake than he was.

"Like crap. I could've sworn I had heard something outside around three. How about you?"

"I didn't hear anything, at least in the back of the house. I slept well...again."

He sat down next to me on the couch and put his head on my shoulder, closing his eyes. Over the last five days, we've talked about the potential for a relationship. Both of us really enjoy each other's company and get along perfectly, we just have the whole long-distance thing to work out. We agreed to take things slow, just enjoying the time we spend together without putting a label on it. There have been stolen kisses and cuddling up during movies, but that's it and it's been ideal.

"I did some thinking last night, so feel free to say no."

I cocked an eyebrow, "About?"

"Gina and Eric. Harper's parents. I think we should try to reach out to them and see if they know anything."

Chewing on the inside of my cheek, I thought about it. There were worse ideas…like going exploring outside in the middle of the night. "What do you hope to accomplish?"

"Maybe just some more answers around what made them change their minds? They were so set that it was another animal and now they're saying they agree that it might have been something supernatural, like the Beast."

"I think it's a good idea. Only problem is you leave on Sunday, so we need to try to reach out to them as soon as possible. Just set your expectations that they won't respond."

Griffin sat up and looked down at his folded hands.

"You already contacted them, didn't you?"

He nodded.

"Why does that not surprise me? What did they say?"

He cleared his throat. "That they're free next Friday night and were more than happy to talk with us."

"But you're leaving Sunday. Are you planning on coming back?"

"I was planning on it. If that's okay with you."

"Of course."

The rest of our weekend together was spent at The Higher Ground drinking coffee and not talking about the Beast. We got to know each other on a deeper level. We talked more about our hopes and dreams of what life could look like. We also spent an exorbitant amount of time talking through long-distance relationship logistics. It was only a two-hour car ride, so it wasn't the hardest to navigate.

What was going to be hard? The good-bye.

Here we are, sitting silently on the couch, Griffin's suitcase staring at us, reminding us that all good things must come to an end.

"I should get home before it gets late." Griffin finally spoke up.

"Yeah, you should."

We made our way to the front door without a word. Griffin turned to look at me and wrapped me in a hug. I felt safe. "I'll drive back Friday early afternoon and leave Sunday, that way we have some more time to spend together."

"That sounds good."

He pressed a kiss to the top of my head. "I've really enjoyed the time we've spent together. Thanks for being you, Cora Grace."

I stood outside as the snow fell and watched Griffin get in his car and drive away. Stepping back into the house, it suddenly felt empty and lifeless.

I was already on-edge, again.

CHAPTER 26

THE WEEK DRAGS WHEN YOU'RE HOME ALONE, YOUR terrifying nightmares come back, and you're dreading your first therapy session. Monday through Wednesday were exhausting, except at night when Griffin and I would spend an hour on the phone talking about our day. The lack of meetings I had last week were made up this week. I was working from seven in the morning until nine or ten at night since we had lost headcount. I was more than ready for Griffin to come back since he seemed to be the key to getting a good night of sleep.

This morning, when I woke up, it was Thursday. My stomach sank and my palms were sweaty. I wasn't sure what was going to come up in therapy, but I was scared to find out. The day flew by and my work calendar sent me a reminder I had to leave for my appointment in a few minutes.

I finished up what I was doing and got ready to head out the door. Reaching for my phone to toss it in my purse, there were two texts, one from Griffin and one from Kendra.

Despite being the one who finally talked me into therapy, Miranda wasn't thrilled with me because she was hurt that I hadn't told her about Griffin sooner, so I wasn't going to hear from her for a bit. We've been through this before, I knew how to treat the situation.

The drive to the psychiatrist's office was silent because the anxiety inside bubbled up. I pulled into a parking space right in front of the building and sat there as my thoughts raced.

Why are you doing this?

They won't be able to help you.

Nothing is actually wrong.

As the clock struck six, I got out of my car and went inside the building. It gave off doctor's office vibes. When you walked into the building, there were doors lining the perimeter. I looked at the map and found Dr. Ophelia Ray. Her office was located in the far-left corner. I walked up to the door and before I had the chance to either knock or run away, the door opened and a gruff man walked out.

"I'll see you next week, Steve!" The curly redhead said, waving him off before meeting my eyes. "And you must be Cora. Miranda speaks very highly of you. Please, come in." She stepped aside and motioned for me to come in.

I stepped through the door and took in the space. It wasn't a big office, but it wasn't too small that I felt claustrophobic. The walls were painted a pale blue, likely because shades of blue calm people down. The floors were laminate vinyl and there was a large, patterned rug covering it that pulled out the blue in the walls perfectly. Since it was a corner office, there were two large windows that were covered by both blinds and curtains.

She takes her patient confidentiality seriously.

There were a variety of seating options and me being me, I was anxious that I would sit in Dr. Ray's seat.

"Please have a seat and make yourself at home."

I looked at the couch that was across from a chair that had a notepad on it. There was a tissue box sitting next to the couch, so I took that as my seat. I felt my shoulders tense and my guard go up.

"Would you like a water or something to drink before we get started?" Dr. Ray asked as the click of the door lock echoed in my ears.

I'm trapped now.

"A water would be great, thank you." I turned my phone off, something I never do. I didn't need to be spilling my metaphorical purse out to this psychiatrist and have it accidentally call my mom or something. My mom doesn't need to know all of this.

She grabbed two water bottles from the refrigerator and sat down in the chair that I had guessed was hers. I observed as she performed her ritual—sit down, adjust in the chair, reach for the notepad, open up to a new page, grab her pen, take a sip of water, and start the timer on her phone before flipping it upside down on the table next to her.

"So, Cora, why are you here today?"

We were getting right into it. Here I was thinking that today was going to be a "get to know Cora" situation and I wouldn't have to answer this question.

"Miranda has been trying to get me to come for a while. Probably for the better part of this year, honestly. I think she thinks I have some deep-seeded issue I need to work through."

"But why do you think she tried to have you schedule an appointment?"

"Aside from her thinking I have some deep-seeded issues, I'm not sure." I paused, examining her kind face, "I've had bad experiences in therapy before, so I was hesitant to try again."

Dr. Ray's face immediately softened and she leaned forward, "Cora, I'm so sorry to hear about that. What happened, if you don't mind me asking?"

"My last therapist shared what I told him with a family member, who confronted me about it."

Her jaw dropped, "That's not okay. That's against our legal code of ethics. We can go ahead and start filing a complaint and—"

I cut her off. "No, it's fine. I'd just like to move forward and forget the past. I can tell that you're a trustworthy person and won't go blabbing everything I say to the world."

"You have my word. I would never do something like that."

I nodded, there's no beating around it. "Well, Dr. Ray, I've been having nightmares pretty regularly for the last six or so months and it's really been affecting my sleep schedule. I'm up anywhere between two to five times per night."

Dr. Ray was scribbling notes down before she looked up at me. "First, please call me Ophelia. These nightmares, do you remember when they started?"

"I think it was around the time of my promotion, so March."

"And they happen nightly?"

I nodded, "Well, they did. I had a friend stay with me last week and they stopped. As soon as he left, they started back up."

More writing. "So the nightmares started around the time you got your new job?"

"Yes."

"Can you tell me what happens in your nightmares? Is it the same every time or is it a central theme and they vary?"

"It's the same every single time. High-level, it starts with me in the woods, looking for something. Then I stumble upon a dead body. When I call for help, they wrongly accuse me of murdering him, when I was just the one to call it in to the police."

"That's very interesting." Ophelia rubbed her cheek. "Usually dreams like that are due to stress. Did you want your promotion?"

"Yes, I did. It's my dream job."

"But is it worth it?" She asked.

I sat back further into the couch, my eyes growing wide. "Excuse me?"

"Is your job worth this much stress? Your nightmares are

likely caused by external stressors. Usually, it's family, friends, or work that's the culprit."

As silly as it was, I had never assumed that my job was the cause of all this. "I love my job. I worked so hard to get here. Do you really think that's it?"

"I can't be sure, but that's my preliminary thought. Why don't you tell me more about who stayed with you last week that seemed to be the magic fix."

An involuntary smile spread across my lips. "His name is Griffin. Funny enough, his grandmother is one of my neighbors and has been trying to get me to meet him for years. I finally caved right before Thanksgiving and we were inseparable. He even stayed an extra week."

Careful, Cora. Don't say too much.

"That's great." More note taking. "How does he compare to past relationships you've had?"

"Griffin is the first guy I've seriously considered dating. I've always put a focus on my career and getting that all settled."

"I see. So this would be your first real relationship. If you don't mind me asking, why did you focus so much on work?"

"I'm not sure. I'm one of those people who when I set my mind to something, I have to see it all the way through. I guess I thought if I dated someone and fell in love, then I wouldn't have as much time to dedicate to my job and I wouldn't be where I am now."

Ophelia nodded, not saying a word. I filled the void. "I didn't want anyone to stand in my way."

"That's more common than you realize. When he was with you, why do you think the nightmares stopped?"

"If I had to guess, it was because I felt like someone was actually taking care of me. We ate breakfast every morning, he would come say hi during the day when I wasn't on a call, he also made sure I logged off no later than six every night so I had time to decompress."

"So it sounds like he helped fix your lifestyle."

"Yeah."

"Have you talked about the future and what that could look like?"

"Yes. We're taking things slowly, though."

"Good. That's great, actually." She tapped her pen on her notepad. "Let's dive a little deeper. Tell me about your childhood."

"It was pretty average, nothing for me to complain about."

"How was your relationship with your parents?"

"Fine. My mom worked a lot and my dad was home sometimes."

"So who raised you?"

I gave her a questioning look.

"If your parents weren't home, who raised you?"

"My parents hired a nanny to manage us. Her name was Elyna. They hired her right from France…so, I guess she was more of an au pair. She was wonderful."

"Did you view her as a mother figure?"

Nosey. "No, she was always just the woman that took care of us. My mother was always home on the weekends—when it mattered."

"Gotcha. And how is your relationship with your mother now?"

"It's fine. I mean, we're not best friends, but we manage. Obviously, I would have loved her to have been more involved with my life when I was younger, but the past is the past. We've talked about it and are handling it in the best way we can."

"So it does bother you?"

"I mean, only when I think about it. She loved her job, I was an accident. I was six months old when she moved to New York for a year."

Ophelia's eyes went wide. "Wow. She didn't live at home?"

I shook my head. "Not really. While I lived at home, bounced between New York, Los Angeles, and then, back to Byglass every other week. It was normal for us. She was a hot shot chef, people wanted her all over the country to train their chefs, to open their restaurants, or visit and leave a good review."

Ophelia nodded. "When you said you were an accident, what do you mean?"

I pulled my lips into a straight line. "I meant exactly what I said. My parents had decided that after they had my brother that they were done. I was a drunk night after a Christmas party."

"I see. And how does that make you feel?"

Is she for real? "I mean, not great. But, I had loving parents, even if they weren't around a whole lot."

"Surely it has bothered you more than you had thought." She paused, "If you had to diagnose yourself, what do you think the root cause of you working so much is?"

"I'm not clear on that…part of the reason I'm here."

"I was curious to know if you had picked up on it based on our conversation."

I stared blankly at her.

"I'll take that as a no." Ophelia observed, putting her pen and notepad on the table. "Let me bring you up to speed. First off, I believe there are two causes at play. The first is that you were trying to prove your worth. In your mind, since you were an 'accident,' you had to do everything possible to show your parents that you weren't a mistake."

I took her words in and let them marinate. She was good at her job. "I had never realized that."

"Most people in situations like yours don't see it. They don't know where it comes from, so they flounder until someone pushes them to come see me."

"Is there anything we can do to fix me?"

"You don't need fixing, Cora. You just need to acknowledge the problem and make the change. Set some stricter work boundaries."

I nodded, it made sense now that someone was telling me what the problem was. "And the second cause?"

"That one is a bit easier. You saw your parents both working so hard growing up, so it was normal for you. I hope you know, both of these are very common causes and can be addressed very easily."

"So you're saying that my nightmares will stop again if I set strict work hours for myself?"

"That's exactly right. I think your nightmares are stemming from overworking yourself. If you slow down a bit, I think you'll feel good as new."

The alarm on her phone went off, signaling the end of our first session. "Cora, it's been wonderful getting to know you. After conducting this preliminary evaluation today, I don't feel that there's anything wrong with you. I think your body is in desperate need of a break from work. My best suggestion would be to take a few days off and clear your mind."

"That works perfectly because I'm heading up to Pittsburgh next week to spend some time with one of my best friends."

"How lovely! I think that'll work wonders for you." Ophelia stood up and I took that as my cue to also get up and walk towards the door.

I extended my hand and said my goodbyes, exiting the building. Sitting down in my car, a million thoughts raced through my mind. For starters, not feeling completely insane. I think it was helpful to get Dr. Ray's opinion on how I grew up and how it shapes my life today.

Pulling into the driveway, I thought back to that day that shaped who I am today. I distinctly recalled a conversation I had with my mom years ago.

I was maybe ten or eleven and had just gotten in from school. I had received a perfect score on my math test and was so excited to show my parents so they would be proud. It was one of the rare times my mom was home during the week and she was working away in the kitchen. The house smelled like roasted tomatoes and apple pie.

"Hey, mom! Guess what!" I exclaimed, bounding into the kitchen with my backpack hanging off my shoulder.

She didn't even look up from the pan in front of her. "What, Cora?"

My heart sank, she wasn't in a good mood. "I got a perfect score on my math test! I was the only one in my class to do that."

"Good. Now keep working this hard. You have to maintain these grades to get into a good college." My mom turned to look at me, solely because she had to wash her hands and the sink was in front of me. "You want a good career, right? One where you'll make a lot of money so you can afford anything you want." She patted me on the head.

"Yes, ma'am. I've been thinking about what I might like to do." I was wise beyond my years and spent most of my time in the school library with Kendra, reading books on different careers.

"And, that is?" My mother's back was turned towards me again, the sarcasm dripping from her voice.

"I've done a lot of reading about marketing and I think I might enjoy it."

"Keep thinking on that. You still have some time."

I sulked up to my room and latched the door. Since my mom was in a bad mood, I should hide out tonight and read, only going downstairs for dinner. I sat down at my desk and diligently worked on my homework until I heard a soft knock on my door.

"Come in." I called from my desk.

The door creaked open slowly. "Cora?" A quiet voice called out.

"Hey, James."

"What's up?" My brother came in and closed the door behind him, sitting on my bed.

"Just finishing up some homework."

"Cool. Listen, I overheard what mom said earlier and I just wanted to tell you how cool it is that you might have found something you're interested in. I know she means well, but she has a terrible way of showing it. Some advice? Leave mom out of any decisions you make. Do what will make you happy."

I snapped back into reality, palms sweaty in the driveway of the home that I owned. My mother could never say that I didn't chase my career goals and then crush them. At freshly thirty, I was the Director of Marketing at Alliteration and owned two homes. I could take some time and slow down with work. I can handle everything life is throwing at me.

Right?

CHAPTER 27

I SPENT THE ENTIRETY OF LAST NIGHT SOBBING, FEELING like I had let what my mom wanted for me dictate my life. I enjoy working with my colleagues and my job. The last time I looked at the clock, it was well after three.

Last night I only woke up from the nightmare twice. An improvement, but still not ideal. When my feet touched the floor this morning, I made it until two o'clock and Griffin would be pulling into the driveway, so when his car pulled up a bit before. The stress left my body and headed towards the front door.

Still in his car, I could see a wide smile spread across Griffin's face. Not caring about the rain-soaked ground, I bounded towards him, in need of a hug. I not-so-patiently bounced on the balls of my feet, waiting on his to grab his duffel bag and get out of the car.

As soon as he did, I was scooped up in a bear hug. "It feels good to be back."

"You've been missed."

"Let's go inside and we can catch up." Griffin urged, "It's at least twenty degrees colder here than it was when I left home."

Heading inside, the house felt full of life again. Who knew

that a guy would be just what I needed to get through this tough season of life. He took off his jacket and met me on the couch.

"I crashed early last night, so we didn't have a chance to talk. How did therapy go?"

"I don't want to talk about it." I muttered.

"It couldn't have been *that* bad."

"She asked me how I felt about things! I thought that shit was made up for the movies."

Griffin stifled a laugh, "How did it make you feel?"

"You're an ass. Why are you back here?" I scooted closer and laid my head on his shoulder.

"Because we need to solve this mystery of what we saw last week."

I rolled my eyes. "I know why, I was just trying to be funny."

He winked at me. "So was I."

"I think the therapy session helped a little bit. The only thing that she brought to light is that I have spent my life trying to live up to my mother's expectations of me. Hence why I work myself to death."

"Well, that's good that you were able to get to the bottom of it. Did the nightmares stop?"

"Nope. My guess is that it might take some time. I'm just hoping I can kick them before I leave for Pittsburgh next week. I'd love to have a restful trip."

"That's right. I forgot you were heading up there to see your friend Kendra, right?"

"Yeah. She has a packed agenda for us, so it'll be a good time. We've not seen each other in a few years, so I'm really looking forward to it. maybe seeing her will bring about a sense of peace."

"I've only been to Pittsburgh once for work, but it was beautiful."

I smiled in response. "So, what are we hoping to accomplish this afternoon when we go visit the Coopers?"

"I've spent the last week doing some more digging, so I have questions planned."

"Did you find anything else?" I wondered.

"Not really. I just think her parents know more than they're letting on. Obviously, I'm going to be extremely polite, but I would love some answers."

"We can't just go into these people's home and accuse them of withholding information, G."

Griffin stiffened, "I'm aware. I just want to hear their story of what happened. See if it's any different than what they said in that interview or all those years ago. Something just isn't adding up."

"I'll let you lead the conversation. What time did you want to leave?"

"It looks like it will take us just under an hour to get there. Want to leave around three?"

"Sure! Can we stop for a coffee first?" I batted my eyelashes. "I need some more caffeine."

Griffin smiled, "Of course we can."

We walked over and caught up over coffee before heading out.

"I'm nervous," I admitted shyly.

"About going to meet Harper's parents?"

I shrugged.

"How come?"

"I don't know. I don't like barging in on people's lives and this just seems like such a touchy subject. It might be uncomfortable."

"I can tell you spent your entire life not ruffling feathers." Griffin grabbed my hand before turning his attention back to the road. We were already almost there and I was chickening out.

"Cora, it will be okay, I promise. When I spoke with them on the phone, they sounded very nice and willing to talk. I made it well-known that we weren't coming to visit to invade their peace, that we just were curious because we both have had some odd incidents."

"And they were okay with us coming on such short notice?"

"It's been a week! I promise, it's okay." He squeezed my hand tighter.

I looked out the window and took in the familiar scenery, "I didn't realize their house wasn't all that far away from The Widow's Peak."

"Nope, just another fifteen minutes up the road. We should be there soon."

The trees were barren. The once beautiful hues of orange and yellow were now long-gone, only to be replaced with a blanket of gray. My stomach turned and I felt the anxiety bubbling up.

We pulled up a long driveway, a commonality in the mountains, and up to a large, cozy-looking brick house. The front door faced the mountains and the rest of the house was surrounded by trees.

I inhaled sharply before getting out of the car. Griffin grabbed my hand and interlocked our fingers as we walked up to the Cooper's front door. My hand shook as I rang the doorbell. A couple in their mid-seventies opened the door and greeted us.

"Good afternoon, y'all! You must be Cora," The woman hugged me. My body tensed, I hated being touched. "And you must be Griffin." She extended out her hand. "It's so nice to meet you both."

"Come on in, kids," Eric called from behind his wife.

The four of us entered the house and I was taken aback by how modern and beautiful the inside was. Griffin and I sat down on the couch while the Coopers sat on armchairs across from us.

"Can I get you both anything to drink? We have soda, wine, beer, tea, coffee, lemonade—" Gina started.

"Two waters would be great, thank you." I piped up, stopping the laundry list of beverages they had.

She nodded and presumably headed for the kitchen, returning only a moment later.

"You have a beautiful home."

"Oh thank you, dear. We renovated it two years ago. It was so out-of-date, it was in desperate need of a makeover."

"So, what brings you both all the way up here?" Eric asked. He had such a calm demeanor, not at all what I was expecting.

"Funny enough, I own a cabin about fifteen minutes down the road, so this isn't that far out of the way." I took a sip of water and cleared my throat. "Have you heard of the case of Luke Anderson?"

Both of the Coopers nodded. "It's just so sad. I hope they catch whoever did that to him. Just terrible."

My cell phone started vibrating in my bag, but now was not the time. I reached in and silenced the phone without diverting my attention from the conversation.

"The police have someone in custody and are questioning him. They're hoping to have answers soon." I thought about it, "Luke was supposed to be staying at my house, which I renovated and turned it into a rental. He was my first guest, never checked in, and then was found dead a few days later."

Griffin finally spoke up, "And Cora and I have reason to believe that it might have been something…"

"Non-human." I finished his sentence.

I could see the expressions change on both of their faces. Eric crossed his arms, tucking his hands under his armpits, a universal sign that he was protecting himself. "I'm guessing you wanted to talk about what happened thirty years ago?"

Griffin nodded. "I also had some questions for you both. Why don't you tell us what you know."

"It's been so long, we've not discussed it very much. We were shocked when that blog asked us to do an interview. But when you reached out, Griffin, we were even more surprised." He took in a deep breath before continuing on, "That was the darkest time in our lives. We never fully recovered…I mean, how could you?"

"I can't imagine the pain you all felt and continue to feel."

Gina reached for my hand, visibly uncomfortable. "While they talk, would you like to go upstairs and look at some photo albums?"

"Of course," I gave her a sad smile.

As we climbed the stairs, I took note of the lack of pictures of Harper. There were family photos from throughout the years, but not one of Harper. Weird, but maybe seeing her face around is a constant reminder of their immense pain. I'm nosey and craned my neck to see what other rooms were on the second floor, but all the doors were closed.

For whatever reason, alarms were going off in my mind. I didn't feel like we should be there, I had gotten a weird vibe from Eric, and now all the doors are closed.

Who closes doors to unoccupied rooms in their home?

Gina was ahead of me, reaching for the handle of the only door in the house that wasn't white. As the handle turned and the room opened up, the old, brown wooden door made sense. My eyes went wide as we stepped into Harper's room, a portal into the mid-nineties.

The walls were painted a bright magenta, the little of it I could see. Posters of celebrities, boybands, and Harper's friends covered the walls. The wooden floors appeared to be original, not matching the refinished ones in the rest of the home.

My eyes moved to the center of the room, and although I was younger at the time, I recognized so many things. The bedding was a hideous green and pink floral pattern…one my mom insisted I also have on my bed.

On the bedside table, there was a lava lamp that was still plugged in and was on. Glancing around, everything was still plugged in. There were door beads instead of a closet door, dream-catchers galore tied on her headboard, piles of CDs, and magazines strewn across the desk.

That's when I noticed my own personal version of hell—a Furby on top of a dresser. I shuddered.

The day Harper walked out that door was the last time her room had been touched.

"This is Harper's room." Gina began, stepping further inside the room. I reached for the desk chair.

"Oh. Please, don't touch anything. We'll stand in here."

A shiver ran down my spine and my hand froze above the back of the chair. "How come?"

She was silent for at least a minute before starting back up, "No one else is allowed to touch Harper's things. Just…just her father and I."

I shot her a 'what the fuck' look. I'm not sure if this is sweet or creepy. "May I stand here?" I pointed down.

"Yes, of course. Don't be silly!"

"What did you want to show me?" I was desperate for conversation now because the silence between us was maddening. She stared at me, not saying a word. I wasn't even sure she was blinking behind her thick-rimmed glasses. I started counting the seconds.

Ten. Forty. Eighty. One minute. Two minutes. I was starting to believe she died in front of my eyes.

"Gina…?"

"Yes, dear?" She shot right back.

I pulled my arms close to my chest, my eyes wide. "What did you want to show me up here?"

"Oh, right!" She moves effortlessly across the room towards the nightstand, softly opening the second drawer. A pink and purple furry diary appeared in her sun-spotted hands as she approached me. My heart sped up involuntarily. I'm not sure if it was because she was coming near me or because of what the diary might reveal.

"Look, don't touch." She made stern eye contact with me before flipping open the front cover.

I nodded, holding her stare. The first page, in high school bubbly handwriting said *Property of Harper Cooper.* "You can flip the pages to what you'd like me to see."

Gina flipped to the next few pages, showing me some diary entries from around the time when she was killed.

Dear diary,

Ugh, what a terrible day. My algebra test today kicked my butt. I studied, but clearly the two hours last night didn't help at all. It's not my fault that I heard someone screaming outside last night and couldn't focus.

My mom and dad still don't believe me. I swear that something was following me while I was walking home today. Every time I took a step, I could swear that I saw something in the tree line that was keeping pace with me. I don't know what to do anymore. Even my friends are starting to think that I'm making this all up. I'm scared. No one believes me. I have no one to turn to until this all stops.

Until tomorrow,

Harper

I understand how Harper felt. She felt like she was becoming crazy and like she had no one. The only difference between us being that I had Griffin in my corner. I wasn't sure what to say. Gina flipped a few pages to another diary entry and my eyes caught the date—April 18th, the day that she went missing.

Dear diary,

Another morning of running to school. As I ran down the driveaway, late for school, I heard a rustling in the trees. I glanced in that direction, but there was nothing there. Why does this shit have to keep happening to me? I just want to be left alone.

Right now, I'm sitting on a bench outside of the school gate, enjoying the spring air before my classes start for the day. The trees have started blooming and the flowers have popped out of the formerly frozen ground. For me, this is the best time of the year. Despite everything going on, I felt like today is a fresh start. I'm going to push this all out of my mind and move on.

There's the bell. I don't want to go in. I want to go back home to New York. I love my friends here, but this isn't my home. Every morning I sit here and wonder if I could just run away. Would anyone aside from my parents notice? I doubt it. Screw it, I'm skipping today. I'll go get myself a coffee down the street and then figure it out from there.

Until later,

Harper

My eyes went wide. "Was that the day Harper went missing?" This is news to me.

"Yes, it was." Gina sat down on Harper's bed. I knew better than to move from my standing spot near the desk.

"So, she purposefully skipped school that day. Do you know anything else about what happened after?"

Her eyes fell, looking back down at the diary in her hands. "We know that she went to the coffee shop down the street from her school and was there until around noon, and then she was never seen again."

"Is there any surveillance footage that has caught her going anywhere else?"

"It was the mid-nineties, there weren't many cameras around, especially in this town. I mean, let's be honest, there aren't even many surveillance cameras around town today."

I thought about it, "Yeah, I guess you're right. I'm assuming you found out about Harper going missing because school called?"

Gina nodded sadly. "That was a phone call no parent should ever receive."

"I can't even imagine. I'm so sorry again for your loss."

"It's okay. There's nothing we can do about it." She looked out the window. "Well, there's nothing we can do about it now, huh?"

"Yeah, I suppose." *That was an odd thing to say.* "Was there anything else you wanted to show me while we were up here?"

"Hmm. I don't think so. Just her diary entries."

I didn't respond. I looked around the room and my eyes fell on a notepad on the desk. The date on the top page was from April 19th. I started to read it but stopped when I felt Gina move closer. Looking up, she was six inches away from me and I could see the rage in her eyes.

"I think it's time for us to go back downstairs." Her voice was stern, yet flat.

I wanted to speak up and probe. The handwriting wasn't the same that was in the diary she had just shown me.

Whose was it? The only thing I was able to read was the date and then the top of the page that said, "Death: April 18th Time: 4:32 P.M."

I did some quick recalling and Harper was killed on April 18th but wasn't found until the 21st. Whoever wrote this knew that Harper was dead before anyone else did.

What the hell? A knot formed in my stomach, and I knew that I needed to get out of that room, and we needed to leave.

Gina escorted me back downstairs where Mr. Cooper and Griffin were engaging in a tense conversation.

"The Beast is real. How many times do I have to tell you that?" Eric's voice boomed from the living room.

I heard Griffin speak up, "Sir, you've said that, and I believe you, but I'm just asking what the investigators found at the crime scene that led them to a dead end. And why you believe that it was the Beast and not someone wielding a knife."

Eric's voice went up an octave. "I think you should leave now."

"I just asked a simple question." Griffin shot back.

"We trusted the investigators and they didn't find any evidence. The case went cold. A few months after Harper died, we started having similar experiences as she did. We heard screaming in the woods behind the house, felt like someone was watching us, and then one night we saw something outside our bedroom window. That's when we realized that Harper had been telling us the truth the entire time." Eric's voice was robotic.

Griffin opened his mouth to probe further, but I cut him off. "I think it's time for us to leave."

"We were just getting to the helpful information." Griffin hissed in my direction. I hadn't seen him like this before. He seemed suspicious. "How long did the investigators search for?"

"You best stop asking questions. Now!" Eric's face went red, and a vein bulged out of his forehead.

"It would probably be for the best if you left now." Gina looked at me and my heart sped up. I was starting to connect some dots and it wasn't painting the Coopers in a good light. While it was weird that they kept her room the same, I couldn't stop thinking about that note that had Harper's time of death. No one would know that if she was missing.

Did the Coopers kill their own daughter?

My eyes darted between the husband and wife, examining their faces. His fists were balled up and her brows were furrowed. I could tell they were losing their patience with us.

"Griff, let's go." I turned back to the pair. "Thank you for your time today."

I started for the door, completely forgetting about my jacket. I turned back around and saw Eric standing chest-to-chest with Griffin.

"What did you say, boy?" Eric's thick southern accent had come out. He was furious.

Griffin puffed out his chest. "I said that you both didn't seem to care very much when she went missing. Most parents would have pressed for them to keep looking."

Gina was standing behind me, arms crossed, blocking the front door. Panic immediately set in.

"I don't think y'all understand. You've disrespected both me and my wife. You ain't leavin'."

"Sir, I'm sorry this is how our visit has come across. We didn't mean anything by it. We were just trying to gather some information because I've been having some weird things happen lately after Luke Anderson was killed."

The Coopers looked at me, daggers in their eyes. "I said, you disrespected me and my wife. You ain't leaving." Eric pulled a large knife from his waistband and in a swift motion pinned it against his neck.

I sucked in a breath and my blood ran cold. We shouldn't have come here. This was a bad idea. We could be in the home of people who killed their daughter in cold blood.

Gina stepped closer to me, a scarf in her hands.

They're going to kill us, too.

CHAPTER 28

RIFFIN STOOD THERE FROZEN, STARING AT ME WITH anxious eyes. I felt the scarf pulled tightly around my neck as it got harder to breathe. I knew I only had a few seconds before the world would go dark.

Think quickly, Cora!

I remembered a safety video my dad had made me watch years ago on how to get out if someone was strangling you with something. I somehow managed to slip a finger under the scarf and move it slightly away from my throbbing neck. I gasped for air before threading another finger under the scarf. I had a few pounds on Gina, so if I used all the remaining strength I had, I might be able to pull it off me. I knew I had one shot to get this right.

In one smooth motion, I slid my fingers under the scarf and pulled. I fell to the floor face first, hitting my head. Gina fell on top of me, still loosely holding the scarf.

"Get off me!" I yelled hoarsely, still struggling to catch my breath.

"Gina, just kill her already!" Eric screamed at his wife.

I somehow managed to slide out from under her with the

scarf still around my neck. I pulled it from her hands, inhaling as much oxygen as I could and as I tried to stand up, but she grabbed onto my foot.

"We told you already many times, you're not leavin.'" Eric uttered, looking directly at me. "You came into my house and caused mayhem, now you'll pay. I've done this before, I ain't afraid to do it again."

Did he just admit that he killed his daughter? And possibly Luke? What motive did they have either time? I shook myself out of my questions—*focus, Cora, you need to get both of you out of here.*

"You're going to kill us like you killed your daughter?" I shot back, still lying down. Griffin's eyes were wide, and he wasn't saying a word. The knife was pressed further into his neck now and I wasn't sure how we were going to make it out of there.

"Don't you ever talk about my daughter again, ya hear?"

I nodded to placate him, thinking maybe he would let us go. Gina was still holding tightly onto my right foot, so I used as much force as I could and kicked her in the face, causing her to become unconscious. As her grip loosened, I stood on my shaky legs and made eye contact with Griffin. Right now, I wish that telepathy was real. I wanted to tell him that I was going to do whatever I could to get us out of this hell.

My plan was to lunge at Eric as carefully as I could to ensure that Griffin's throat wouldn't be sliced, and I wouldn't be stabbed in the process. Both minor details. I knew I had to make a split-second decision and figure out how to execute. If I aimed for his upper body, he could kill Griffin on his way down. If I went for his lower half, he could also kill Griffin on his way down.

Eric looked at me in the eye and mouthed "you're dead." I gulped.

How did this easy conversation turn into us potentially dying? They seemed like such kind, loving people and now I had to kick a woman in the face because she was trying to strangle me.

The silence in the room was maddening. Seconds felt like minutes. Eric released the non-knife wielding arm and reached down towards the table they were standing next to. He was reaching for a gun. I knew this was my window of opportunity and ran towards him, knocking him backwards.

"You stupid bitch!" Eric yelled, hitting his head on the table on the way down, rendering him unconscious.

Griffin fell to the side, throat still intact. "Nice job!"

"Are you hurt?" I asked, crawling over to where he landed.

"Hurt? No. Terrified of these people? Yes. Let's get out of here before they wake up."

"I need to go upstairs and grab something." I said, heading towards the stairs.

"Are you crazy, Cora? These people just tried to kill us for asking questions about the murder of their child thirty years ago, I don't doubt that they would try again if they had the chance."

"Listen, I think they killed her. There's a notepad upstairs with something that might be helpful, I need to get it. I'll be right down, just stand by the front door and hold the knife in case either of them wakes up."

I bounded up the stairs and into Harper's room. Looking around the room, the notepad was nowhere in sight. I ruffled through the desk drawers to find it, but no luck. It was like a lightbulb went off in my head—the notepad was small enough to fit in a pocket, Gina probably grabbed it and put it in the pocket of her jeans.

Running back down the stairs, I saw the Coopers both passed out and took this as my opportunity to reach in Gina's back pocket, sure enough, pulling out the notepad. We sprinted towards the door, not bothering to close it. Throwing ourselves in the car, we sped away.

The entire thirty-minute car ride was quiet. Both of us still processing the trauma we had just been through. We walked through the front door of my house and that's when I realized that my body was still shaking. Making our way to the kitchen, I got us some waters and we sat down at the island.

"What in the world was that?" Griffin asked, gulping down the glass of water. I took note of the red line where the knife was pressed.

"I...I don't know. That was horrifying. What were you talking about that made him snap like that?" I put my forehead on the cold marble countertop to ground myself back in reality because that felt like a sick game.

"I was asking basic questions. I wasn't even prying. He just took it the wrong way, I suppose." Griffin stared out the window, looking out at the night sky for a minute before continuing, "What did y'all talk about upstairs?"

I shook my head, "For starters, they never re-did Harper's room. It looks the exact same as the day she walked out for the last time. It was like walking back into the nineties. I wasn't allowed to sit anywhere or touch anything, but Gina did show me show diary entries from the day Harper disappeared. They basically said that she wanted to run away and go back to New York."

"Is that what you went back for?"

I silently got up and got the notepad from my bag.

"This is what I wanted to take." I handed the notepad over to him.

"What does this have anything to do with why we were there?" He raised an eyebrow.

"I think that there's a highly likely possibility that they killed Harper. I don't know how or why, but they seemed suspicious. Logical people would ask people to nicely leave their home, murderers will try to kill you instead."

The words hung in the air between us, both of us considering the likelihood.

"Again, what makes you think that?"

"Griff, look closely at the paper. Look at the date and then look at what the paper actually says."

Griffin examined the paper, putting two and two together. "Oh shit. No one knew the actual time of death."

"Exactly."

"Should we call the police?" He asked, uncertainly.

"I really don't know. Part of me wants to report them for trying to kill us, but then we have to tell authorities that we're trying to find answers about a damn creature in folklore. Who's in the wrong there, then?"

"But they tried to kill us!"

"I am painfully aware," I rubbed my bruised shoulder. "But we have to try to keep this under wraps until we get more answers about Luke Anderson."

"Maybe we should throw in the towel on this whole investigation."

"At this point, for our own safety, I think that's a good idea." I downed the rest of my water. "I think I'm going to go shower and wash this horrible day off my body. You can shower in the bathroom down here if you'd like."

He shook his head. "You go shower. I don't trust those people. I'll keep an eye out."

"They don't know where we are, so I think you'll be okay to shower."

"Cora, just go shower and let me collect my thoughts. I had a knife to my throat an hour ago."

I went upstairs and soaked my body in the hottest water that would come out of the faucet. I washed, scrubbed, and exfoliated before feeling enough like myself to get out of the steamy shower. Making my way down the stairs and back into the kitchen, I heard soft weeping.

I poked my head around the corner and saw Griffin sitting

in the same spot he was, head in his hands, crying. Do I go in and comfort him? After all, I am the reason he's in this situation.

Walking over softly, I sat down on the barstool next to him and put my hand on his back, rubbing slightly. "I'm so sorry I got you into all this mess. This whole situation is my fault."

At that, he removed his head from his hands and sat up straight. "No, Cora. Please don't think like that. I was the one who became obsessed and had us go over there. I put you in danger and I don't know if I can forgive myself for that."

"It was a combination of a lot of things. Let's just try to move passed it."

"Want to go to the diner and get some dinner?" I asked, trying to change the subject.

Griffin nodded somberly. "I'll go shower quickly and then we can walk over."

I moved to the couch and turned on the television. I needed some noise to keep me company. If I was alone with my own thoughts, I'd go mad right now. I reached for the notepad that I had brought to the couch with me and flipped through the other pages.

The next page was blank, but then the third page had numbers written on it. I'm in marketing and not a numbers whiz, so I took a picture and sent it to Kendra. She knows all the things, so she might be able to help.

> Cora: Do you know what these numbers could mean?
>
> Kendra: Those look like map coordinates. Where did you get that from?
>
> Cora: Long story I'll tell you when I'm there next week. Can I put these in a map app and see where it is?
>
> Kendra: Yep, should be able to, but, me being the best friend in the world, I already did that for you.
>
> Cora: You're the best! I owe you a cocktail next week!

Kendra: I'd never say no!

I clicked on the screenshot of the map Kendra had sent over and my mouth fell open. That was pretty damn close to where Luke was found. My heart thumped in my chest.

My phone buzzed on the couch next to me.

Kendra: What's with the date above the coordinates?

I looked at the paper again and hadn't even noticed that there was a date in the top righthand corner. November 12th. I quickly did the math and that was the date Luke was supposed to be staying at The Widow's Peak.

Did they kill Luke?

The shower turned off, so I knew I had a few minutes to collect myself before Griffin came back down. I took some deep breaths and my attention back on the show, ignoring her message. I would text her back tonight after I went to bed.

"Ready to get dinner?" I didn't hear Griffin come down the stairs, he must be learning where to walk to avoid the squeaky boards.

"Yep, let me put my shoes on and I'll be ready. I'm starving."

We locked up and started down the street for the diner. I was going to keep this new finding to myself until I could figure out why they had it written down. I felt Griffin weave his fingers through mine; this was the first time and my heart fluttered. Dinner came and went, and the conversation was kept to a minimum, neither of us sure of what to talk about.

We settled back in at my house and turned on a movie.

"Hey, Cora?" Griffin spoke, just barely above a whisper.

I lowered the movie, "Yeah?"

"I'm happy that if I have to have a near-death experience, it was with you."

My heart melted. "I am, too, Griff." I paused, rubbing my neck,

"When I was trying to escape from Gina, all I could think about was how I could save you."

Griffin scooted next to me and wrapped me in a hug, rubbing my back. I finally let myself relax and the tears started flowing. I fell into him as the sobs shook through my body.

"It'll all be okay. I will do everything in my power to keep you safe, okay?"

I nodded. Griffin held me for a while until the tears were long dry and my eyelids were heavy.

"Do you want to head up to bed?" Griffin asked, his voice tired.

"Yeah. I can't keep my eyes open anymore."

In one swift motion, Griffin scooped me up in his arms and carried me up the stairs.

I erupted in a fit of giggles, "This was extraordinarily unnecessary."

"You said you were tired; I was trying to be accommodating." He laughed.

"Too accommodating." He dropped me on my bed, and I snuggled in under the blankets. Griffin walked towards the door, hand on the light switch. "Hey, Griff?"

He raised his eyes in a questioning manner.

"Will...never mind."

"Do you need something?"

"I feel weird asking this."

"Just spit it out."

"Will you stay with me tonight?" I asked shyly.

"Of course!" He was happy to oblige. I breathed a sigh of relief—either he was going to be more than willing, or he was going to run screaming from the house.

Griffin flipped off the light switch and settled in beside me. We both laid awkwardly there for a moment, flat on our backs, unsure of what to do.

Finally, I broke the silence. "Thank you for staying with me. After this afternoon, I don't really want to be alone."

"Anything for you, Cora."

I flipped on the television and put on *The Office* for background sleeping noise. "Is this okay?"

"It's my favorite show, so more than fine with me." Griffin rolled over to face me. "What are we doing here?"

"Is this some kind of philosophical question about the meaning of life?"

I rolled on my side. "I more meant between us. We've not known each other for all that long, but it feels like we've been lifelong friends. Everything between us feels so natural."

"I agree. Aside from my group of friends, you're the only person I've opened up to. Hell, you know more about me than some of them do."

"Really?"

"Yep. I mean no one else knows about the shit we've dealt with, so…"

"I guess you can't really tell any of your friends, right?"

"Miranda already thinks I'm going crazy. I think Kendra would believe me, though."

"That's the one who told you about the Beast originally?"

"Yep. She's been my best friend since I was little. I haven't seen her in a few years, but we always pick right up where we left off."

"Are you going to tell her?"

"She knows some of it. I'll probably test out the waters and start telling her, then see how she's reacting." I had to text her back.

I felt for my phone in my pocket, "I forgot to take off my makeup, I'll be right back."

I hopped out of bed and went into the connected bathroom, turning on the faucet as soon as the door closed behind me. I needed an excuse to get out of bed so I could let Kendra know that I would explain everything in a few days.

> Kendra: Those coordinates are close to the Widow's Peak…
>
> Kendra: Wait, isn't that the date that the guy went missing?
>
> Kendra: You're not answering me! Are you alive?
>
> Kendra: Cora Grace Lincoln. If you don't text me back soon, I'm calling the police to do a welfare check on you. Don't send me this shit and then ghost me!
>
> Kendra: I'll cancel your reservation to my spare bedroom if you don't answer within the next 10 minutes.
>
> Kendra: Just kidding, I love you too much to do that.

I laughed. The last text message only came through a few minutes ago. I sent back laughing face emojis and then started typing.

> Cora: You really need to chill with the million texts. What if I was asleep? Lol.
>
> Cora: I promise that I'll tell you everything when I'm up there next week.
>
> Kendra: You better! I can't believe I get to see you in two days!
>
> Cora: I can't wait!

I turned off the faucet and went back into the bedroom. Griffin was sitting up, scrolling on his phone when I got back into bed. This is the first time I've had someone else in my bed with me and it was strange. With an extra body, my Queen-sized bed felt incredibly small. I scooted closer to the edge to give Griffin some room.

"You don't have to move away; I have plenty of room." He said, not looking up from his phone.

I moved back over.

"Do you want to continue the conversation from a few minutes ago?"

"About what we're doing?"

Griffin nodded. "I really like you and, correct me if I'm wrong, but I think the feeling is mutual."

"It is. We've spent the last few weeks getting to know each other on a different level. I mean, you shared your hot air balloon story and that was pretty bad, so I feel like we can talk about our situation. Especially because we're currently in a bed together."

"First, thank you for staying with me. I hope that you know I really appreciate it. I'm hopeful that you being here will help keep the nightmares away." I paused, "I mean, if I were to date anyone right now, it would be you in a heartbeat. I feel like we have so many similar interests. How would we do long-distance though?"

"It's only two hours, that's an easy drive for me to make."

I took his words in for a moment. "Wanna try this?"

"I absolutely do. We can take things slow; we don't have to rush."

"I'd really like that." Almost on cue, a yawn escaped my mouth.

"Why don't you get some rest? I'm going to keep watching TV if that won't keep you up."

"Go for it. I fall asleep with the TV on every night. I like the background noise."

"Good night, G. Thank you again for staying with me tonight."

"Absolutely." He pressed a light kiss to my forehead. "Good night."

Griffin and I had an amazing weekend of getting to know each other more and talking about logistics of our blooming relationship. I was anxiously awaiting my trip to go see Kendra, despite knowing that my nightmares might return since he was gone, and I was traveling.

As soon as Griffin pulled out of the driveway this afternoon, I sprinted inside and grabbed my suitcase out of my closet, along with the piles of clothes I had planned on packing. Rolling the suitcase towards the front door, I saw the scratch on the window once again and shuddered. I would get that fixed once I returned from my trip.

All I could think was 'if these walls could talk…' what would they say?

I fully intended on having a relaxing night at home, but Detective Ambrose interceded. I stared at my phone as it was ringing on the table next to me, Detective Ambrose's name on the screen. I debated answering for three rings but knew I should.

"Hello?"

"Cora! It's Ambrose, how are ya doin'?"

"I'm doing well, Detective. How are you?"

"I've been better, but that's why I've been calling. Ya know the guy we brought in for questioning?"

"The serial killer?"

"Yes. We did everything we could. We did DNA testing, extensive questioning, we checked into his alibi many times—absolutely nothing. Now we're back to square one." He sighed dramatically, before continuing. "We're at a loss right now. No tips have come in."

"None at all?" I asked, surprised. Usually with these types of cases, there were anonymous tips coming in, even if the people were making it all up.

"No, ma'am. We're going to bring Cathleen, Luke's wife, in again, but that's our last hope."

"I mean, in most cases, isn't it the spouse that does the killing? She had motive since he was cheating on her."

"Everything checked out last time we spoke with her, and

we didn't have any reason to believe she was the murderer, but we think it's worth a shot. We'll bring her in and will have a body language expert observing the interrogation to pick up on any nuances that we might miss."

"Hopefully, if nothing else, maybe she'll be able to provide clarity around the situation."

"That's our hope. The only reason I was calling was just to tell you to be careful if you come back up this direction. Whoever did this is still out there."

"I appreciate the update. I'm heading out of town tomorrow for a few days to clear my mind before the holidays."

"Good idea. Anywhere fun?" he asked.

"To Pittsburgh."

"What will you be doing up there?"

"My best friend lives up there, so we'll be doing some sightseeing."

"That'll be a fun time for y'all."

"Yeah…" I responded, unsure of what else to say.

"Well, Miss Cora, I'll let you go. I know it's late. Have a great trip and hopefully I'll have some good news when you get home."

"Thank you! Talk soon." The line went dead.

I snuggled in bed, waiting patiently for sleep to overtake me. I felt my eyelids get heavy and my body sunk into the bed.

Finally, sweet, sweet sleep.

CHAPTER 29

WHEN MY ALARM BLARED AT FIVE THIS MORNING, I wanted nothing more than to roll over and pull the blankets over my head, hiding from the world. I was up all night after having the most intense nightmare yet.

I'd classify this one as a night terror because I was *terrified*.

This one started off like all the rest. It was dusk and I was being chased in the woods and ran until my legs were on fire. In my haste to escape, I kept looking behind me and missed the massive fallen tree. Tripping over it, I tumbled to the ground and felt a snap. I let out a wail as tears clouded my vision. Blinding pain radiated from my left leg. The sound of crunching leaves got closer, and I knew I needed to move before I was caught.

I glanced down to see where the excruciating pain was coming from—my leg was broken, and I had a shard of bone sticking out of my calf. There was blood pouring down my leg, pooling in my shoe. In that moment, I knew my only hope was to try and wedge myself inside the hollowed-out tree. I tried, but the pain was too much.

The footsteps were in sight now and there my hunter was.

Cathleen. She sauntered over to my hiding spot behind the tree, a sharp object in her hand.

"Hello, Cora," Her voice was jovial. "How are you doing today?"

I tried to speak, but nothing came out.

"That's what I thought. You're so pretty. It's such a shame that you have to die like this. But, after all, it's only fair."

In a swift motion, she pulled the knife up above her head with both her hands. As the last beams of sun hit the blade—that was the knife that James had found in the Widow's Peak under the bed. Unable to move and losing consciousness from the amount of blood I had lost from my leg; the knife was plunged into my abdomen.

"Checkmate." That was the last thing I heard before the world went black.

They say if you die in a dream, you die in real life. I don't know if that's even remotely true, but I didn't want to find out. It's safe to say, I shot up in bed immediately, drenched from head to toe in sweat. I got up to take a shower and then went right back to my spot in bed, flicking on the television. Which brings us to now, sitting at the gate for my early-as-shit flight up to Pittsburgh.

I watched the other passengers. My early Monday morning flight was filled with road warriors—those people that travel for work all the time. Each of them had a laptop on their lap, typing away furiously on the keyboard, headphones wedged in their ears. Some were already on calls, which, I also understand. Most of the people surrounding me looked like they wanted nothing more than to be home. I thought back to my work laptop that is sitting on my desk at home—should I have brought it in case of an emergency? No.

"Now boarding Flight 1205 for Pittsburgh." The female gate agent said over the PA system.

I got up and walked towards the gate since I had an early boarding group thanks to my frequent work trips.

"Boarding group two." The same voice called.

I try to exclusively travel with a carry-on suitcase. I've had way too many horrible missing luggage experiences to take such a risk for such a short visit. I rolled my suitcase over to the line and waited my turn. As I approached the desk, my boarding pass was scanned, and I was on my way to the airplane.

I found my seat, sat down with my book, and texted Kendra, letting her know that I was on my way to her. The engines roared to life, and I popped my noise-cancelling headphones in my ears to block it out.

As I flipped to the last page in the book, the plane's wheels touched down. The entire flight, I occasionally glanced up at the screen in front of me to see where on our path we were. I knew I was excited to see Kendra, but I hadn't realized just how excited.

Once the flight attendants gave the passengers the green light to use their phones, I turned mine on and immediately texted Kendra to let her know that she should start heading to the airport.

Thirty minutes later, a red SUV with the window down was pulling up to me at Arrivals. I could hear her screaming out the window.

"Cora!"

A wide smile spread across my face as I approached the car. "I'm here!"

"You are and I'm so excited!"

I threw my suitcase in the trunk and hopped in, ready to start out on whatever adventures she had planned for us. I reached over the center console and gave her a quick hug before we were off.

"I was thinking maybe we could drop your bag off at my place and then head out and get some lunch?" Kendra asked, eyes locked on the road.

"That works! I feel like you should know—I didn't bring my work laptop with me."

Kendra's jaw dropped, "You're kidding! Cora Lincoln is without a laptop. This day should go down in history!"

"You're an ass."

"You've kept me around for this long," she laughed.

"You make things interesting." I joined in the laughter. We pulled into her driveway and I ran inside to drop off my suitcase before we were on our way to sustenance.

Once we were seated at our table, we spent the time catching up, even though we talk a few times per week. I was doing everything in my power to keep the conversation away from myself.

"So, what did you want to tell me the other night?"

"About…?" I pulled my eyebrows together.

"The map coordinates. You left me on the edge of my seat."

"Now's not really a great time. It's more of an at-home conversation."

Kendra looked around. "It's 11:30 and even the older people aren't here having lunch yet. There's no one around. Just tell me already." She teased.

"I…fine. Promise not to say anything until I'm finished. It's going to be a long one."

"Double pinky promise." Kendra stuck both of her pinky fingers out. I interlocked mine with hers.

"Ready?"

She nodded eagerly.

"Alright, after Luke was found, I started having some weird experiences. I felt like I was being watched and followed and I saw something…a creature…staring at me in the woods up by the cabin." I watched as Kendra's eyes went wide, putting the pieces together of what I was saying. "Then, when I was at home, something was staring at me through one of the downstairs windows and scratched it. When I went upstairs, there was something in the backyard, still staring."

"What—" I could see the questions all over her face.

I cut her off, "There's still more. Griffin and I went up to the Widow's Peak last weekend to hang out and I told him everything. He insisted that we go on a middle-of-the-night exploration to find the creature I thought I saw and well, we found it."

"What was it?" I let her ask her top question.

"The Beast."

She nodded, "Continue."

"It was terrifying. It chased us until we were almost back to the cabin. That led Griffin to believe me, which had resulted in him doing tremendous amounts of research. He reached out to Harper Cooper's parents, and we went there on Friday. What a fucking nightmare."

"What happened?" Kendra was sitting on the literal edge of her seat, rocking back and forth. I was so happy that she seemed to believe me.

"It started off normally—they seemed friendly; it was great. Griffin stayed downstairs with the husband while I went upstairs with the wife. When we got to Harper's room, they hadn't changed it at all, which I get might be part of the grieving process, but I wasn't allowed to sit or touch anything."

"That's so strange." Kendra added.

"Isn't it? The wife was either ignoring me or just genuinely didn't hear me, because there were a few times that she just stared at me. We started off looking at some diary entries that were a little strange and before we went downstairs, I found that notepad. As soon as I saw it, the wife got super weird and insisted we go downstairs. Once we got down there, all hell broke loose. Long story short, they tried to kill us."

"What!" Kendra exclaimed, unable to show restraint. "You're making all this up!"

"No. But we got out of there once I knocked them both out. I ran back up to grab that notepad. As soon as I saw that second page, that's when I sent it to you."

"This is just too much. I thought you were going to tell me that they were true crime fans or something like that. I wasn't accurately prepared for this." She showed me her hands and they were shaking. "What are you going to do? Are you going to press charges?" Her mind was racing a million miles per hour, trying to make heads or tails of what I was saying.

"I don't think so. At this point, I just want them to be out of my life."

"That's totally fair." Kendra took a long sip of her water. "I don't even have the right words. I have so many questions."

"And I'd be happy to answer them all, just not here."

"You can't seriously make me wait. That's just plain cruel." She shot back.

"There are people sitting in the booth behind you now. Get me drunk tonight and I'll spill all the details." I laughed.

"How can you laugh in a time like this?"

"Because I'm numb to all of this." We stood up and put our jackets on, heading out into the cold once again. "The last month of my life has been hell. Even therapy didn't really help."

"You went?" Kendra stopped in her tracks.

"I did. She helped a bit, but the nightmares are still happening. She thought once I stopped focusing so much on work that they would stop. It seems like the only time I'm able to get a solid night of sleep is when Griffin is around."

"Ohh that's the new boy toy! Do you have a picture?" Kendra wagged her eyebrows, getting in the car.

I pulled out my phone and went to his Instagram profile before handing it over.

"Cora Lincoln! He's a hottie…" She scrolled to a picture of him shirtless this summer at the beach, "With a body! My word."

Kendra pretended to fan herself. "Does he treat you well?"

"Very much so."

"Good. Otherwise, I'd have to kill him." She slapped a hand to her mouth. "Poor choice of words."

"It's okay. We might be together."

"Might, what do you mean, 'might'?"

I knew I had to explain. "We talked the other night about what we were. We both really like each other, but both want to take it slow, so that's what we're going to do."

She gripped my hand, looking me in the eyes. "I'm happy for you. Obviously, I hate that you're dealing with so much shit, but I can see that under all that, you're happy."

"Stressed, but happy." I desperately wanted to change the subject, "So, where are we off to?"

"To make candles." We drove to a cute boutique candle shop in Market Square. Over the course of two hours, we learned how to make our own candles.

"That took way longer than I thought it would." Kendra admitted, adjusting the wool hat on her head as we left the store.

"It was fun, though. I feel like we learned something new."

"She could've just told us to pour the wax in. She didn't have to go into so much detail." Kendra snickered.

"I think that was the point of the class. Did you not read how long it was?"

"Clearly not!"

We returned to Kendra's house after a few more stops, having no intentions of going back out. Between being up so early this morning and absolutely no restful sleep, I wanted nothing more than to stay in, relax, and catch up.

While Kendra ordered some pizza and grabbed two bottles

of wine—one for each of us—I found a new rom-com for us to watch. The more engrossed we were in the movie, the quicker the wine disappeared. We were both almost done with the bottles when Kendra looked at me.

"We're not out anymore, how have your nightmares been?" She slurred.

It was the alcohol because I was ready to spill everything. "They just keep getting worse. The one I had last night was horrible. I never went back to sleep."

"Is it still the same one? Just over and over?"

"It was for a while, now it's changing. It seems like they just keep getting more and more scary and real. In this one, Luke's wife killed me."

"That's crazy! I wonder why she was in your dream."

"The detective working the case called last night and told me that the serial killer guy that they thought was responsible isn't," I thought about it, "They're bringing in Cathleen, Luke's wife, again for more questioning."

"Shit. That's the woman that was at the cabin when you showed up, right?"

"Yep. I don't know what they'll find."

"You seem like you have other thoughts." Kendra observed.

I shrugged.

"You can tell me. I'll never judge you…like the others."

I knew she was hinting at Miranda, who still hasn't talked to me. She was still upset I didn't call her. I involuntarily rolled my eyes.

"I haven't even told Griffin this…" I paused, unsure if I should continue. "I think Harper's parents killed her, and potentially Luke."

Kendra did a spit-take and red wine went all over her couch. "Shit." She got up to grab paper towels to clean up the mess. "What makes you think that?"

"Obviously, I don't have really anything to go on, but I think that notepad was a huge clue. The first page was dated the day after Harper disappeared with her date and time of death. Then the second page had the date of Luke's disappearance and the co-ordinates of where his body was found. I'm no detective, but…"

"That's suspicious as hell." She pulled her hand up to her chin and tapped on it, clearly thinking. "You know," she hiccupped, "You know what we should do? We should dig into the cases to see what's similar. What if they killed Harper and have been killing people the same way all these years?" Kendra's drunken eyes were glassy.

"That's what I was thinking. It could happen, right?" I was looking for drunken approval.

"Oh, for sure."

Kendra got up, threw away the paper towels, and disappeared into another room.

"I figured I should get this…for research purposes. We're going to get to the bottom of this. We need to know if the Coopers did this, or it really was the Beast." Her eyes went wide. "What if they're shapeshifters? What if that's why the wife kept staring at you? What if they're actually the Beast?"

Blame it on the alcohol, but I didn't think Kendra was too far off base. "I think these are valid questions and you should bring that laptop over here so we can start looking!"

Kendra sat down next to me and we dove in, hoping for some clarity and answers.

CHAPTER 30

Two hours into searching and sobering up, Kendra asked the question on both of our minds, "Why do you think they did it?"

"*If* they did it." I emphasized the first word. We had to assume that they weren't guilty otherwise we were going to start finding things coincidentally.

"Fine. Why do you have suspicions that they killed Harper?" She rephrased her question.

"When I was reading the diary entries, the first one Mrs. Cooper showed me was one from the night before Harper disappeared. She really felt like she was alone and like everyone thought she was making things up."

"Hmm."

"But then the next one I saw was from the day Harper went missing. It turns out that she skipped school on purpose because she wanted to run away and go back to New York. She ended up at the coffee shop by her school and that was the last time she was ever seen."

"Well, that's an interesting tidbit of information. Do you think that was a reason for the Coopers to kill her?" Kendra questioned.

"I don't know. Who kills their child because she wanted to move back home?"

She shook her head, "There are some sick people in this world."

"I know. I doubt they did it, I was probably just hoping to find answers."

"No, I think you might actually be onto something. I don't know how we're going to figure it out, but we will do our best. You said she got weird when you saw the notepad?"

"Yeah. She insisted we head back downstairs. As we were leaving the room, she stuck it in her back pocket. Which, now that I think about it, was a weird move. Why grab it if we were going downstairs?"

"That makes it even more suspect. Whatever that notepad means, she didn't want you to see it."

"That was evident. I should've grabbed the diary while I had the chance."

"No, because then that would've been too obvious. The notepad can be played off that it fell out of her pocket when you knocked her lights out. The diary being gone points directly to you."

"What stuck out to you initially about what you saw?"

"The date and time of the death of Harper. Authorities were never able to pinpoint an exact day or time. They just had a general idea."

"Yeah, that's damning for sure. That would surely be something that the police would be interested in knowing. I think you should talk to the detective that you've been working with."

"He already thinks I'm weird for bringing up the Beast. I can't throw this on his plate, too. He'll have questions as to why I'm looking into a thirty-year-old cold case."

"That's a fair point. If we could somehow connect Harper's case to Luke's, then you'd be well within your rights to bring it up."

She had a good point.

"Wait a second." Kendra paused, lunging for her phone. "My mom knew the Coopers when they lived in Byglass. I wonder if my mom could give us any other information about them."

"It's late, don't call your mom now."

"She's in Los Angeles for a work trip. It's still early for her. Besides, she hates her coworkers, so she's either eating dinner alone or she's hiding in her hotel room."

Kendra pressed a few buttons before putting the call on speaker. It rang a few times and then a very relaxed Mrs. Knox answered.

"Hey, mom. Do you have a minute?"

"Of course! What's up? Are you and Cora having a good time? Tell her I said hello!"

"Tell her yourself. You're on speaker."

"Cora! How are you?"

"I'm good, Mrs. Knox. I hope you are, too!"

"Currently hiding out in my room from my co-workers, but all good. What can I help you girls with?"

"Mom, what can you tell us about the Coopers?"

The other side of the line was silent.

"You still there?"

"Yes, sorry. Gina and Eric Cooper?"

"Yeah." Kendra replied.

"I'm not sure I understand the question."

"You can be honest with us. We just want to know what they were like—both before Harper and after."

"Before, they seemed like a lovely family. Your brother was two years younger than Harper, so we were somewhat close. Your father and I had dinner with them on more than one occasion." Mrs. Knox paused, "Right before Harper went missing, they started acting strange. They pulled out of all school events, didn't reach out at all, no one ever really saw them out. We all thought it was strange but didn't want to pry in case they just decided one day that they hated the entire town. Your brother had said that Harper wasn't acting weird in school—she was still just as friendly. So, when she went missing, the entire town was surprised."

"And then what happened?" I probed.

"After she was found, Eric and Gina did everything in their power to squash the case. The investigators urged them to offer a reward for information that led to the capture of the murderer, but they declined. They were never out there helping the police. It was just such a strange situation. It was at that point that we felt that something was off and distanced ourselves completely."

I shot Kendra a look before asking, "How did they act after the case went cold?"

"At first, the same. They didn't want to associate with anyone except for a select few. Then, one day, they started showing up at events and hanging out with us all again. That's when we knew something was up. The pair would act strange anytime someone would try to give them their condolences."

"What did they do?" Kendra asked.

"They just kind of shrugged it off, or they would say 'it's okay, these things happen.'"

"Who says that after their child was brutally murdered?" I wondered.

"That's exactly how the rest of us felt. We always thought that the Coopers knew something they didn't want everyone else to find out. Obviously, I would never assume anything, but I always had a hunch that maybe they did it."

"What?" Kendra and I asked in unison.

"I shouldn't say. I'm purely speculating." Mrs. Knox defended.

"Spit it out, mom. That's exactly what we wanted to know."

"I feel so bad even saying this, but here it goes." Mrs. Knox inhaled sharply before continuing. "I understand that everyone grieves differently, but they never showed an ounce of emotion. Anytime they were interviewed on television, they were always very stoic, sometimes laughing here and there. And then after when they would say that these things happen, that's just not something a parent in distress would say. I never told anyone about that because I'm sure the investigators had done extensive looking into them, but something in my gut says that they were to blame."

We sat there in silence, alternating our staring between the phone and each other.

"Why do you ask?" Mrs. Knox asked.

"I also had some suspicions that might pertain to a new case, is all."

"Got it! Well, I hope you both enjoy some quality time together. Make good decisions!"

"Thanks, mom."

"Thanks, Mrs. Knox."

"You're welcome, girls. Talk soon."

Kendra turned to me, "So they totally killed Harper."

"We have literally zero proof except for a sheet of paper; and even that doesn't prove anything."

"It gives us something. We just need to think about why they would do that."

"I can't think of a reason." I racked my brain.

"Since when have the tables turned? I'm the true crime junkie now and you're not." Kendra remarked. "Here's what I'm thinking. Harper wanted to go back to New York, maybe threatened to leave, and her parents got sick of it and...ya know."

I chewed my lip, shaking my head as Kendra was talking. "No. I don't think that's it. She had to have known something or maybe..." I stopped mid-sentence, pieces of information connecting in my tired brain. "Harper fully believed in the Beast, right?"

Kendra nodded.

"Okay, hear me out. Harper kept bringing it up and more and more people were hearing about it. What if the Coopers were getting embarrassed by or annoyed with her? If Harper was talking about this fictional being, it could've been embarrassing for them to garner such attention. Especially since they had just moved, and they were trying to make a name for themselves."

"See? This is why you're the crime junkie, not me. That would make way more sense."

We spent the rest of the night reading every. Single. Article. About Harper and the Cooper family. We found out that Mr. Cooper was involved in the hit and run of a pedestrian, Mrs. Cooper was accused of threatening the woman doing her nails at the salon, and Harper's older brother, Baron, was kicked out of three schools because he constantly started fights—all before they moved.

With their violent checkered past, it would make sense that they wouldn't want Harper to go back home. They moved to Byglass to run away, none of them could ever go back to New York.

"Hey, Kendra?" I spoke up after a few minutes of silent reading.

"Hm?"

"I have something to tell you that I think might help with the case."

She immediately slammed her laptop shut and I had her full attention. "Go on."

"When James and Lottie were home for Thanksgiving, we went up to the Widow's Peak. James found a knife under the bed upstairs."

Her eyes went wide, "Excuse me? Was it one of yours?"

"That's the thing, I don't know. I don't recognize it."

"Cora, what if it's the murder weapon?"

"How the hell did it get in my house then?"

Kendra sat forward in her chair, "Hear me out. What if the Coopers killed Luke and then broke in and hid the knife?"

"Why would they hide it in my house though? That's what doesn't make sense."

"Was there any blood on it?"

"Nope, it was clean." I remembered holding the knife in my hand for the first time. It was heavy; whatever it was used for took some strength.

"I still think it's a possibility. I wish there was a way that we could find out how similar the wounds Luke had were to Harper's."

"Unless I straight up ask Detective Ambrose, we'll never know."

"And you're sure that it's not yours?"

I shook my head. "I've never seen it before."

After the research-heavy evening we had last night, we spent today doing all the touristy things. We went to the zoo and aquarium, hopped around a few bottle shops, and now we were heading to a Pittsburgh Penguins hockey game. Admittedly, I don't know a whole bunch about hockey, so I was there for the experience, not to understand what was going on.

Before we left, Kendra forced me into one of her Penguins jerseys stating that I "will stand out like a sore thumb". Stepping into the arena, I understood what she was talking about—everyone was dressed in white, black, and gold. We got some snacks and drinks and headed to our seats.

The arena roared to life when the players hit the ice and for the first time in a long time, I had a blast. I fed off the crowd's energy and felt ready for anything life was going to throw at me.

"Are you having a good time?!" Kendra yelled over the buzzer.

I nodded in response. "This is a blast!"

"Goo—NO!" Kendra screamed at the ice.

I might be enjoying myself, but I had no idea what was going on. I just knew that we wanted the team with the penguins on their jerseys to win. The more I shoveled the nachos in my mouth, the more I realized that this is what I should be doing with my time rather than working. I should be out with friends. Out on dates with Griffin. Enjoying my life and not sitting at my desk working for twelve hours each day.

The Penguins won by a hair and the arena cheered so loudly, I was convinced that I was going to lose my hearing permanently. Genuinely, one of the best days of my life. I had my best friend, I was away from the mess at home, I had a wonderful potential boyfriend, and it was such a fun day getting to explore and experience some of Kendra's favorite things.

Nothing could go wrong or rain on my parade.

CHAPTER 31

M Y PHONE RANG EARLY THIS MORNING, PULLING ME OUT of my deep slumber. Both nights I've been here have been without nightmares—a huge relief. Without even looking at the screen, I answered. "Hello?"

"Cora, sorry to call you so early." Detective Ambrose's southern drawl echoed through the phone, cutting through my hangover headache. "Something has happened. I know you're on your trip and don't want you to be alarmed, but I think you should come home."

I rolled onto my back, throwing my arm over my eyes, "What happened?"

Surely nothing could be so dire that I had to leave only a few hours before my flight.

"There was a break-in at the Widow's Peak."

I shot up in bed, "Say that again."

"There was a break-in at the cabin. We just received an anonymous tip. I'm heading over there now to investigate. What time can you be home?"

"I…uh…my flight is supposed to get in around four. I can check and see if there's an earlier flight out." My heart raced.

"That won't be necessary. Just get home safely. I'll call you back with any details as soon as I know."

My throat was dry, "Thank you."

I got up and walked like a zombie over to Kendra's room, not bothering to knock. Since we were kids, we had no concept of personal space and even at thirty, nothing had changed. I opened the door quietly and climbed into bed with her, just lay there until my presence woke her up.

"Why are you in my bed?" Kendra mumbled, throwing the covers over her head.

"The detective just called. Someone broke into the cabin."

She was awake now, "Who? How do they know?"

"Apparently it was reported anonymously. I don't know what the hell is going on." Tears streamed down my face.

Kendra wrapped me in a hug. "It'll be okay, I promise. Why would someone want to break-into the cabin?"

My blood ran cold and I sat up, looking Kendra in the eyes. She met my gaze, her eyes wide.

"You don't think…" My voice trailed off.

"I mean, I think it's possible." Times like these made me so thankful for a friend that always knew what I was thinking.

"Do you think the Coopers broke in looking for the notepad?" I picked at my cuticles. All I wanted to do was call Griffin and tell him what happened. I wanted that reassurance that everything was going to be okay—except for the fact that I hadn't told him about what was on the second page of the pad.

"It would make the most sense. Are there a lot of break-ins up there?"

I shrugged, "I'm not sure."

"Don't stress until you know what happened. Maybe it was just random."

"After all the crap I've told you, do you honestly believe that?" I asked, unsure of how she was going to respond.

"No, I definitely think they had motive to do such a thing. They knew where you lived, right?"

"Yeah. When I mentioned it, they seemed to know exactly what house it was." I paused, "What if they were afraid that I was going to go to the police with the pad?"

"If they had nothing to hide, then they wouldn't care if the paper was missing. What are the odds that they knew the exact time of Harper's death but not the police?" Kendra wondered. "If you want my opinion, I think you should talk to Ambrose about what went down when you and Griffin went there last week. With their sketchy pasts in New York, they're dangerous people. Who knows what they're capable of."

I shot up, completely disregarding what Kendra had just said. "What about the brother?"

"What about him?"

"What ever happened to him? In our hours of research, we never looked into him."

"I did while you were watching the movie. He's a realtor down in Florida. Has a wife and kids. Doesn't seem like a sketchy dude."

"Well, that answers that question." My phone rang again—Detective Ambrose. I answered and put it on speaker.

"Cora, it's Ambrose again. Do you have a minute?"

"Yes, of course. What's up?"

"We just got to the cabin, and it's completely ransacked. We're going to start combing through everything now. Do you have any ideas of who might have done this?"

My mouth was dry, no words would come out.

"Cora, are you still there?" Ambrose was concerned.

"Hi, this is Kendra, Cora's friend. She's currently just sitting here, processing everything. Would you mind if she just spoke with you when she got home this afternoon?"

"Yes, of course. Take care of her. This is a lot to take in." His drawl carried on.

"I will. Have a good day, Detective."

Kendra turned towards me, "You're going to need to tell them at some point. These people have already tried to kill you and now they might have broken into your cabin. What more will it take? If nothing else, you have to at least tell Ambrose about the strangling and knife-wielding."

I thought about it for a minute, "You're right. But there's still a massive question mark around what the damn creature was outside my window that was watching me."

Kendra's eyes went wide again. "Shit, I forgot about that. Maybe it was just a creepy bear or something."

"Emphasis on the 'or something'. I wish that night I wouldn't have been frozen in fear because I would have taken a picture."

She nodded slowly. "And you said Griffin also experienced it?"

"Yep, when we were out on his midnight exploration."

"That was a terrible idea," she laughed, "I think the best thing you can do is just go home and try to relax. I know that's way easier said than done, but you need to try. I also don't think it would be the worst idea to go back to therapy for one more session."

I marinated on what she had just said. I knew she was right. I knew therapy wasn't just a one-time visit and you're cured. After the events of the last week, going back was probably the best decision. I reached for my phone and texted Ophelia.

"I just texted the psychiatrist, so let's hope she can get me in."

"It must really be bad if you caved so easily. I hope she can help. I hate seeing you like this."

I was on my flight home when the tears made their way back. How did I get to this point in my life—a house broken into, almost killed, and having experiences with a being out of folklore. At least I was focusing on other things aside from work…begrudgingly.

It felt like no sooner we took off, we were landing. This was the one time you would find me wishing a flight was longer. Unsure of what I was going to find when I got to the Widow's Peak, my stomach bubbled with nerves. I got in my car and drove the hour from the airport to the house. I pulled up the winding driveway to find three police cars and two unmarked ones—likely some Crime Scene Investigators. I took in a shaky breath and got out, heading into shit show.

When Detective Ambrose said that the house was ransacked, I certainly wasn't expecting to see this. The door was ripped off the hinges and the security cameras were smashed, hanging by a thin wire. I stepped over the broken glass and found a sight so much worse than I thought.

There was stuff everywhere. The drawers were all pulled out and the cabinets were opened in the kitchen. The knife James found was still in the drawer, untouched. I moved through the house, taking in all the damage I was going to have to repair. It looked like whoever did this was looking for something and when they didn't find it, they took a sledgehammer to the wall.

"Cora, I'm so glad you're here." Detective Ambrose came out from one of the bedrooms and wrapped an arm around my shoulders. "We've gathered evidence, but the forensics team is diligently searching for fingerprints or any sort of DNA."

He motioned over to a team of people around my age, dusting for fingerprints on light switches, furniture, and any hard surface that might hold the key to this mystery.

"Right now, we don't have anything to go on. Whoever did this was very familiar with how not to get caught. We checked the security footage and there weren't any cars in the driveway and then it stopped recording around five this morning. Our best guess is that's when the security cameras were broken." He looked me in the eyes, "We're going to find out who did this, Cora. I promise. You've not had an easy go of it lately and we just want to help."

A lone tear cascaded down my cheek and Detective Ambrose handed over his handkerchief. "Unfortunately, I'm going to have to ask you to come down to the station with me and answer a few standard questions."

"I figured." I looked around once again, "Do you mind if I look around once more?"

"Of course not, go right ahead. Call one of us over if something is missing."

I nodded, circling the house again. From the looks of it, nothing was missing. I headed back downstairs and told Ambrose I was ready to go. We each got in our respective cars and went down to the police station.

"Can I get you anything?" Detective Ambrose asked, grabbing a coffee for himself.

"No, thank you." While he fixed his coffee, I texted Griffin to let him know what happened, conveniently leaving out the part where it could have potentially been the Coopers. I placed my phone back in my bag and heard the constant vibration, Griffin was either calling or he was sending a million messages.

Ambrose sat down at his desk and faced me, "Why do you have the worst luck?"

I half-laughed, "I wish I knew. I had good luck until about a month and a half ago."

He shook his head, "Hopefully, we can figure it all out and you can rest easy." He twirled his mustache. "Before I forget, we did a more extensive questioning with Luke's wife Cathleen. Her story changed a bit, which set off some alarms for us, but we called in a body language expert as well as did a polygraph and everything checked out. We asked her why she changed her story, and she said that all the stress had her forgetting details when it first happened. Unfortunately, now we're at a dead end again."

I opened my mouth to say something but shut it.

"We'll get to the bottom of the murder, but right now, we need to focus on what happened at the Widow's Peak. To do so, I have to ask you some questions first. Can you think of anyone who would have the motive to do what they did? Form my years of experience, this looks targeted. It also looked like whoever did this was looking for something."

My eyes fell to my clasped hands in my lap. It's now or never. Tell him or don't. "I think I might have an idea."

"Oh!" His bushy white eyebrows shot up, "Please, tell me everything. No detail is too small."

"Do...do you know the Coopers? They live up a bit further up the mountain."

"Yes, I've met them a few times. Their daughter was killed in the nineties. The case was cold within a few weeks."

I nodded slowly. "I feel like I shouldn't be telling you what I'm about to, but I need to get it off my chest." I started to hyperventilate. My breath sped up and my heart raced.

"Cora, please, take some breaths. Would you feel more comfortable if we went into a room?"

"Yes," Was all I was able to get out.

We got up and headed into an interrogation room, grabbing a water along the way. I sat down in the same chilly metal chair as when I was here initially, my back tensing as the cold went through my sweater.

"Are you feeling up to talking yet? If not, take all the time you need."

"Yes, I think so. I don't know how to say this without it coming back on me, though."

"It won't, I promise. Just tell me what you know."

I took in a deep breath. "It all started a few weeks ago. Griffin, my neighbor's grandson, and I had an experience in the woods up here. Something was chasing us."

"Mable Bethel's grandson, right?" Ambrose interrupted. I forgot everyone knows Mrs. Bethel.

"That's correct. He became obsessed with figuring out what the creature was and started digging into the folklore of the Beast. He reached out to the Coopers to see if they would talk with us. He just wanted to know if they had seen or heard anything around the time Harper was killed. We went over there Friday night, just to have a relaxed conversation and things went south."

"How so?"

"I went upstairs with Mrs. Cooper while Griffin stayed downstairs with Mr. Cooper. Everything was status quo until Mrs. Cooper showed me Harper's diary." I finally raised my eyes, "I found it strange that Harper was planning on running away the day she was killed."

"What?"

"She wrote about how she just wanted to go back home to New York. That raised a red flag for me, but I tried to see through it. It could've just been an awful coincidence. I noticed a piece of paper on Harper's desk and it had some interesting information written down on it."

I pulled the notepad out of my bag. I had brought it with me to show Kendra, but mainly because I didn't want it out of my sight. I slid it across the table towards Detective Ambrose. His eyes fell on the first page with Harper's date and time of death.

"How in the world..." he trailed off.

"Flip to the next page."

He did as I said, and he saw the coordinates. "That's near here, isn't it?"

I nodded, "It's where Luke was found."

I could see the wheels turning. "Before you think I just up and stole that from their home, there was one other thing that happened."

"I don't know if I can handle much more of this. This is damning enough."

"After I saw the paper, Mrs. Cooper got weird and immediately wanted to go back downstairs. I'm not sure what all happened while we were upstairs, but Mr. Cooper went from a friendly older gentleman to enraged in a matter of minutes. When we re-entered the room, Mr. Cooper accused Griffin of asking horrible questions and pulled a knife to his throat. That's when Mrs. Cooper took a scarf and wrapped it around my neck, trying to strangle me."

Ambrose was slack-jawed, "Cora, I'm so sorry that happened. How did y'all get away?" He was furiously scribbling on his own notepad.

"I somehow wiggled out of her grasp and then body checked Mr. Cooper to help Griffin get away. They were both unconscious when we left. Am I going to be charged with assault?"

"First of all, that was incredibly brave of you. Second, absolutely not. They were trying to kill you both, you were defending yourself. I hope you know that we are most certainly going to have to bring them in for questioning—both for the deaths of Harper and Luke, as well as for attempted murder."

"No, I don't want to press charges for that. We were probably in the wrong for being there."

"Cora," his voice was stern, "Stop being so accommodating. What they did was against the law. If it wasn't for your fast thinking, both you and Griffin would either have shown up dead or I'd be searching for you both because you'd be missing. Despite what you might think, you're the hero here."

"It just feels like I've caused chaos."

"Not at all. I'm going to keep this notepad and we'll bring in the Coopers in as soon as we can. Why don't you go home and get some rest. We'll handle everything, I promise."

"There's one more thing."

"I don't know if I could handle much more thrown at me right now." He half-smiled, "What is it?"

"When I was on my trip, my friend Kendra, the one you spoke with earlier today, and I researched the Coopers. It looks like they have a history of violence."

"My word. Okay, thank you for being so thorough…even though it's not your job. Head home, I'll keep you up-to-date with any information."

"I'll be home the rest of the evening if you need to get ahold of me." I stood up and slipped my jacket back on, exiting the building.

I got back in my car and sat there for a moment, processing everything that happened. I felt like a fifty-pound weight had been lifted off my shoulders. Reaching in my bag, I pulled out my phone to find six missed calls from Griffin, fourteen texts from him, and one text from Ophelia confirming my appointment for next Monday night.

I pulled out of the parking lot and headed home for the first time in three days. Walking into my house, as soon as I locked the front door, I felt the relief wash over my tired body. Being one of those people that unpacked as soon as I get home from a trip, I dumped my suitcase in the washing machine and headed upstairs to take a much-needed shower.

Now that my achy body was relaxed, I called Griffin back.

"Cora! Are you okay?" Griffin's panicked voice echoed over the phone. "You never texted back. I was worried."

"I'm fine. I was in with Detective Ambrose."

"How did that go?"

"Interesting…"

"Why interesting?" Griffin asked, completely confused now.

"He asked if I had any idea of who would have motive to break into the Widow's Peak and the conversation went from there."

"Do you have an idea?"

"I do. I think it was the Coopers." I almost whispered.

"You think they were trying to finish what they started the other night when we were there?"

"I don't think so…" I trailed off. "I think they wanted the notepad."

"Why would they want that? Didn't it just have Harper's time of death on it?"

"That was just the first page. There was more after that?"

"What? Why didn't you tell me? Do you not trust me?"

"No! It was nothing like that, I promise. It was the coordinates of where Luke's body was found."

"Really?"

I nodded like he could see me. "Yeah. Detective Ambrose is going to bring them both in for questioning this week."

"Shit. Did you tell him the whole 'they tried to kill us' part?"

"I did. He's going to cover that with them, as well. I don't know what's going to come from all this, but I just want it to all be over."

"You should take some time off from work." Griffin suggested.

"That's my only distraction at the moment."

"Why don't you come down here to Charlotte? Get away for a little bit?"

"I have to stay close in case they need me to come in."

"I understand. Just take it easy for the next few days."

"That's my plan. I have a therapy appointment on Monday, so I think that will be helpful as well."

"Good. It's late, why don't you try to get some sleep?"

"Yeah, I think that's a good idea. Here's to hoping I can get a good night of sleep."

"Good night, Cora. Rest well." I could almost hear the hurt in his voice. He wanted me to be safe and under his care, but I knew it just wasn't feasible now. I could take a few more days off towards the end of the year and go down to him and visit.

I fixed myself a quick dinner, a can of soup would have to suffice. I choked it down like I hadn't eaten in forty years, went upstairs to lay in bed and watch some TV, hoping to get a full eight hours of sleep tonight.

CHAPTER 32

I FELL ASLEEP WITH THE TELEVISION ON, MY NIGHTMARE waking me up like clockwork. I shot up in bed, glancing at the clock; it was only 3:20. Of course, as soon as I'm back home, the nightmares start up again. I reached for the remote to turn the volume up on the television to help expedite falling back to sleep.

I always feel unsettled when I have these nightmares, but tonight was different. Tonight, I felt like I was being watched. Hand on the remote, I heard the floorboards creaking downstairs. I sat still, barely breathing.

Was someone in my house? Did the Coopers figure out where I live?

I grabbed my phone off my nightstand and checked the security camera footage—there was no one there. This is an old house, maybe it was just settling. I heard the stairs start to creak with what sounded like heavy footsteps that got closer and closer to my bedroom door until they stopped.

I held my breath and laid there as still as can be, clenching my phone in my hand. If I needed to run, I could either lock myself in my bathroom or jump out the window onto the porch roof. Game plans ready to go, I waited. And waited. And waited. I didn't hear another thing.

Naturally, I didn't go back to sleep, so I was awake to see the most stunning North Carolina sunrise. The pinks and oranges painted the sky, little white clouds becoming visible like a Bob Ross painting. Needing to go downstairs and start working, I dreaded opening that door. Surely if someone or something was there to kill me, it would have by now, right?

I garnered all my courage and slowly turned the door-knob—nothing in sight. I made my way to my office and sat down, breathing a sigh of relief. I logged into my laptop and started playing catch-up from the last three days.

Early afternoon, my phone rang. As I had assumed, it was Detective Ambrose again.

"Cora, I hope you rested well last night. I'm calling to say that we're bringing in the Coopers, did you want to come in as well?"

"I…I don't want to see them."

"You'll never see them; they won't even know you're here—you'll be watching through the two-way mirror. We need you to confirm what they're saying is true or not."

"I'm just now getting ready to hop on a work call." I lied, I needed to get changed, "Can I come in a bit?"

"Absolutely, whenever you are able."

"I'll be in around three."

"See you then."

I wanted nothing more than to call Griffin and tell him that he should come, too, but it's a Thursday in the middle of the day and he needs to get work done. He's already taken enough time off to be with my needy self.

Fighting my better judgment, I called, and he picked up on the second ring.

"Hey, beautiful. How's your day going?"

"Kinda sucks, not going to lie. I'm heading up to the police station here shortly. Apparently, they have the Coopers, and they want me there validating information."

"Do you need me to be there? I can be." He was so accommodating.

"Don't be silly. You have work, I can step away for a few hours."

"Will you call me back tonight and let me know how it goes?"

"Of course. How's your week been?" I asked, wanting to change the subject.

"It's been fine. Missed talking with you, though. I'm happy you had a good trip with Kendra."

"It was nice to get away for a bit and clear my head. I got some clarity that I needed."

"Oh?" He sounded surprised.

"With work. I'm going to take a massive step back in the New Year so I can focus on us." I couldn't hide the smile in my voice.

"Wait…really?" I could hear the surprise in his voice.

"Absolutely. I enjoy spending time with you more than anything else. I loved our slow mornings at home, our late evening chats, and your awesome cooking."

"You know, I'm so happy to hear you say that. Spending time with you feels like I'm with my other half. I know that's crazy to say, but I'm just throwing it out there. How about you come down to Charlotte this weekend? I can show you all the sights."

"You act like I've never been there before," I laughed. "I should be good to do that. I can leave around noon tomorrow."

"That would be perfect. I'll plan a nice dinner for us out at my favorite restaurant."

"I can't wait!" I paused, "I guess I should go get ready and head out."

I stood there, visibly shaking, as I watched the Coopers sit down at the same cold table I was at the other day. Detective Ambrose was in there with them and started the questioning while I stood behind the wall with a young detective.

"Would you like some water?" he asked kindly.

"I have a water bottle with me. Thank you, though." I tapped my bag.

I focused my attention back on the couple in front of me. Just seeing them again made me want to run for the hills. Were they the ones who broke in and destroyed my beautiful cabin?

"So, Mr. and Mrs. Cooper, do you know why you're here today?" Detective Ambrose spoke up.

"Please, call us Eric and Gina." Mrs. Cooper replied.

"I'd rather not." Ambrose deadpanned, garnering a laugh from me.

"No, we don't. When you showed up at our house, it was quite the surprise. Imagine our embarrassment since we had a group of friends over." Eric quipped.

"I apologize for not letting y'all know that we were coming." Detective Ambrose was sarcastic.

"Why are we here?" Gina asked.

"We wanted to talk to you today about the murder of Luke Anderson."

"Who?" Eric asked.

"Luke Anderson. He was missing for a few days and then he was found in the woods near your home."

"Doesn't ring a bell!" Gina piped up a little too eagerly.

"So, you're saying you have no knowledge of this murder investigation at all?"

"None at all." Eric lied through his teeth.

"I understand. I've heard that Luke was also killed in a very similar fashion to that of your daughter, Harper. How did she pass?"

The Coopers visibly stiffened. "It was some kind of animal attack." Eric spoke, his words terse.

"I see. Did you know that's how Luke passed away, too?"

"We did not." Gina replied.

"Interesting, because this," I watched as Detective Ambrose pulled the small notepad from his front pocket and slid it across the table. "Was found in your home. This is the date of death and coordinates of where his body was found."

The Coopers' eyes went wide, and they shared a look between them.

"Where did you get that?" Eric was on high alert.

"It doesn't matter."

"Was it that Cora woman?"

"Again, that's not relevant right now. Can you explain to me why you just said you didn't know him, but this paper here says you do. Or maybe you'd care to explain why on the first page, the time of your daughter's death was written. The police didn't even know that."

They were silent. Either they were about to spill all the details, or they were going to shut down. My money was on the latter. I watched the clock as the two of them sat there—Eric nervously bouncing his knee, Gina unable to sit still, neither saying a word.

Eric finally sat back in his chair and crossed his arms. A body language expert I watched on YouTube once said that crossing your arms is a visible representation of shutting down and blocking others out. "That paper proves nothing."

"Is that so? Because to a detective, this certainly looks like you have information that we don't have. I'm going to be blunt here. Did you murder your daughter?"

Gina spoke up, "Oh gosh no! We would never!" She wiped a stray tear away, the first genuine emotion I had seen out of her.

"Then y'all better start answering my questions." Ambrose snapped back.

Eric rolled his eyes, "We didn't kill Harper or Luke. We…" he trailed off.

The Coopers shared another look.

"We were keeping track of the murders that happened nearby. It was helping the grieving process."

"Excuse me?" Detective Ambrose was confused.

I looked at the young detective standing beside me, "How does that even make sense?"

"Sure beats me. Murderers will usually try almost anything to run police in circles." He responded.

We focused our attention on the shit show happening in front of our eyes.

"We think that there's a copycat killer out there. Harper was likely killed by an animal, but was Luke? How did his wounds compare to Harper's?" Gina asked.

"I didn't think this was my interrogation." Ambrose's eyebrow went up slightly, mildly intrigued by what she had just said.

"Just answer the question for us, Detective. We're grieving parents that just want answers about their daughter that was taken from them way too soon."

"In reviewing the case files, it does appear that Harper's wounds were, in fact, from an animal, whereas Luke's looked like they were from a knife." He replied, "But how do you know what his wounds looked like?"

Eric's eyes dropped, "We heard the commotion when Luke's body was found and headed over. We saw everything."

Why was hearing that, so chilling? Also, a copycat killer?

Why didn't they tell Griffin and I that? Why did they insist on trying to kill us?

Ambrose glanced towards the mirror. "We will continue that conversation later. For now, I would like to talk about Cora Lincoln and Griffin Bethel. How do you know the couple?"

Couple. My stomach flipped.

"Those assholes showed up at our house unannounced and started harassing us with questions." Eric spoke up.

"That's not true at all! Griffin has the emails to prove it." I was furious.

"Ambrose knows that. He's just trying to get them to tell the truth. If they won't, they're just working themselves in a web of lies." The detective standing next to me tried to comfort. "Just let him do his job. He's very good at it."

We turned our attention back to the room in front of us.

"What kind of questions were they asking?" Detective Ambrose asked, trying to pull more information out of them.

"They were asking questions about the Beast and Harper's disappearance." Gina said.

"I see. And is it true that you, Mrs. Cooper, tried to strangle Cora with a scarf? And, that you, Mr. Cooper, had the blade of a knife pressed up to Griffin's jugular vein?"

"That's absurd!" Eric exclaimed.

"Is it? I have a written statement from Cora Lincoln that all of this happened, with time and date stamps. Why would she lie about this?"

"Because...because...she's unreliable." Gina stated plainly.

"That makes absolutely no sense. I am going to need you to elaborate, please." It was crazy, Detective Ambrose's southern accent has almost completely disappeared while he's been interrogating them.

The two stared back at Ambrose, showing no emotion

whatsoever. The silence was maddening and lasted for what felt like forever. You could cut the tension in the air with a butter knife.

"Are y'all going to say anything else, or no?" He finally asked after two solid minutes of silent staring. I'm not even sure they blinked. "Listen, you can either admit to it right now and this process will go a lot quicker or, you can just keep sitting here and I'll just keep getting angrier."

Another minute of silence.

"I can't stand it anymore!" Gina broke the silence. "It's true. We did try to kill them. We had told them things that have happened with us and what we think is the Beast and we were afraid that they were going to go out and tell the whole town about it."

The relief washed over Detective Ambrose's face; he had gotten a confession.

"You do realize that I have to arrest you both for attempted murder, correct?"

"What? No!" Gina broke down into sobs. Eric was stoic.

"Did you really think you could get away with what you did?" Ambrose shook his head at them, staring into each of their eyes. "Eric and Gina Cooper, you're both under arrest for the attempted murder of Cora Lincoln and Griffin Bethel."

My eyes went wide, and my mouth hung open, I didn't expect that to happen.

Immediately, they were handcuffed, and I was ushered away from the interrogation room for my own safety while they were brought out and booked.

Detective Ambrose gathered his papers and met me at his desk.

"Do people usually admit to their crimes that quickly?" I asked. "From all the shows I've seen on television, it always seems like it's an arduous process. This was so quick."

"It really depends on the people. I could tell the moment they sat down that Mrs. Cooper was going to be the one to break first." He patted my shoulder. "We'll get to the bottom of the break-in. I genuinely don't believe that they were the ones that killed Luke, although I think her point about a copycat killer was very interesting."

Ambrose stroked his white mustache. "It's really an avenue I hadn't thought of. Someone committed this murder thinking that they could mask it as an animal attack..." he trailed off, getting lost in his thoughts.

"Do you need me for anything else? Otherwise, I'm going to head home and try to get the insurance all sorted out for the break-in."

"You're good to go, dear. Thank you for coming this afternoon."

"Of course. I was planning on going down to Charlotte this weekend to visit Griffin, are there any issues with that?"

"No, none at all. I'm off tomorrow through Monday, so you won't hear from me until Tuesday at the earliest."

I nodded. "Thank you again, Detective, for all you've done to help keep me safe. It means so much."

His southern drawl returned, "Anythin' for you!"

With that, I threw my jacket back on and headed home with a peace of mind. As soon as I was inside and the doors were locked, I called Kendra to tell her the news.

"They arrested them?" She asked, surprised.

"Oh yeah, right then and there."

"That's crazy! How do you feel about that?"

"Relieved." I paused. "So relieved, you have no idea."

"Good, now maybe you'll be able to relax."

CHAPTER 33

MY NIGHT LAST NIGHT WAS ANYTHING BUT ORDINARY.
Here I was thinking that having the Coopers behind bars
would help my nightmares. It only made them worse.

No sooner I shut my eyes, the nightmare rolled in like a storm
on a balmy southern summer afternoon—fast and intense.

It started off like all the others. I was running in the forest,
being chased, but this time, instead of one person—or thing—
chasing me, it was three. Cathleen, Eric, and Gina.

I tripped and fell, breaking my leg again, the blood pouring
out. I was in and out of consciousness while being dragged to a
location I had never seen before. It looked like the woods where
Luke was found.

I was brought into a shed-like structure. My wrists were
bound, and my limbs were rendered useless.

"Suits you right." Eric said, kicking me and spitting in my face
before the three of them locked the door and left. It was dark and
my eyes took a while to adjust. After my moments of initial panic,
a smell wafted up my nostrils. The most horrific scent I had ever
encountered. A smell so foul it turned my stomach. Between my

loss of blood and the smell, I got sick multiple times in the corner over the course of the night.

Somehow, I was able to put enough pressure on my leg that the bleeding stopped, despite the excruciating amount of pain. Completely disoriented, I sat there and prayed for the sun to come up so I could figure out a way out. As the moon gave way for a new day, the first rays of light shone through the small window, revealing my new reality.

I was two feet away from a dead and quickly decaying body. It was a woman, around my age and it looked like she had sustained injuries just like Luke. The slices were clean, definitely from a knife and not from an animal. My stomach turned.

Her face was familiar, but I couldn't place it until I could— she was the "dead" woman from my nightmare a few weeks ago that choked me.

I needed to get out of there. With every ounce of strength I had, I used my one good leg to scoot myself towards the door. Freedom was getting closer and closer. My back was pressed up against the door when it unlocked from the outside.

Shit.

"Where do you think you're going?" Gina and Cathleen stood there.

My mouth was dry. No words came out.

"That's what I thought," Cathleen said. "Are you ready to die, Cora?"

I shot up in bed, gasping for air. I flicked the light on immediately and have been sitting here shaking, still in bed, for the last five hours. I didn't attempt to go back to sleep.

Why would I?

I already had my bags packed to leave for Griffin's house this afternoon. The last two nights of sleep have been pitiful, so I was hopeful that I might get some more rest while not at home.

Logging into work, I did the absolute bare minimum until

noon when I left for Griffin's. it was an easy drive, an audiobook keeping me company. I pulled into his driveway to find a house much bigger than I expected.

I knew architects made money, but *damn, Griffin.*

I grabbed my small suitcase and tote bag out of the car and made my way to the front door, immediately greeted by Griffin's smiling face. He wrapped me in a hug and held me for a few moments.

"Come in, it's cold out." Griffin placed his hand on the small of my back, ushering me inside before grabbing my suitcase.

I slipped off my shoes and coat and made my way further into the house. It was immaculate.

So, clean you could eat off the floors.

"Are you hungry?" Griffin asked, heading towards what I presumed was the kitchen.

My stomach growled on cue. "Starving."

Stepping into the kitchen, I marveled at how beautiful it was. The cabinets were a deep gray color, which perfectly contrasted with the white marble countertops, stainless steel appliances, and navy-blue walls. Someone creative definitely lived here.

"I made some baked potato soup last night; would you like some of that? Or we could go out if you prefer."

"That sounds delicious. I'll have a big bowl of that, please."

Griffin moved effortlessly around the kitchen while I sat and watched. I knew I was more useful just staying out of his way than attempting to help. A few minutes later, the soup had been warmed and he was pouring two bowls for us.

The first spoonful hit my soul. "This is fantastic! If you ever lose your job, might I recommend going to culinary school."

"Funny you should mention that. Culinary school was actually my Plan B if architecture didn't work out."

"Is it too late to pursue that?" I laughed.

"Not too late, but I'm already in massive amounts of college debt." He smirked.

We chatted about what our plans were for the weekend. I had insisted we just hang out, but Griffin had other plans.

"I booked us a nice dinner tomorrow."

"Is it a fancy restaurant?" I asked, knowing I didn't pack anything except sweatshirts.

"It's nicer than a McDonald's," he laughed.

"Only one small hiccup in that plan."

"What's that?" He cocked his head.

"The only attire I brought was my finest sweatshirts."

"That's okay! We can run out either later or tomorrow if you'd like."

"Yeah, that'd be great." I was surprisingly looking forward to getting dressed up and going out. Maybe that would make me feel human again.

There was something about being around Griffin that felt natural. He made the rest of the world quiet down and helped me find peace amongst my chaos.

"So, what ended up happening yesterday at the station?" He asked, changing the subject.

I had completely forgotten I hadn't told him the details. "Well, the Coopers have been arrested."

His eyes nearly bugged out of his head. "Excuse me? Going to need you to backpedal a bit there, champ."

A smirk danced on my lips; he had a funny way of showing affection. "They came in and denied absolutely everything. Ambrose whipped out the notepad and that's when shit got real. They said that they wanted to kill us because they had told us about their encounters with the Beast."

"Well, that's a bullshit reason. We went to see them because they had answers about it."

"I know. They are under arrest for attempted murder," I sighed.

246

"Good. Serves them right. What about Luke, or the break-in?"

"Interestingly enough, they brought up the fact that whoever killed Luke was human and not the Beast. They said that the wounds were clean, unlike something an animal could do. No news on the break-in. Detective Ambrose was going to try and get them to talk more."

"Huh…" Griffin sat back in his chair. "So, not a creature, but a human being did that."

I nodded slightly.

"I guess I had been so set in my thoughts that it was the Beast that I hadn't really entertained the thought that the killer was still out there. Do they have any leads?"

"None. They already thought it was that serial killer, but that didn't pan out. They looked into Luke's wife and that didn't either. It sounds like they're back to square one."

"Shit. So, there's still a killer on the loose. Stay away from the Widow's Peak until everything is sorted out, please." He kissed the side of my head as he stood up, collecting our empty bowls, placing them in the sink.

"Absolutely. I have no desire to go up there anytime soon."

"You can pick out anything you'd like. My treat!" Griffin held my hand in his as we entered the mall. I opted to spend last night just hanging out at home and for the first time in a while, I got a solid night of sleep, cuddled up in Griffin's side. When we got up this morning, went for breakfast, and headed to the mall to get me something pretty to wear tonight to dinner.

"Don't be silly. I can pay for my own clothes." I squeezed his hand, which, felt strange. It felt like I was home, though.

"I just want to treat you to something special. Please?" He pushed his lip out like a child asking for ice cream.

"If you insist!"

We weaved in and out of nearly all the clothing stores in the mall. I tried on no less than thirty dresses and was about ready to throw on a burlap potato sack until Griffin pulled a little number off the rack. It was a stunning, long green wrap dress that hugged all my curves. It complimented my skin tone perfectly. I came out of the dressing room and Griffin's jaw dropped.

"Wow…just…wow."

I pulled my hair up in a faux updo. "Does it look okay?"

"You look amazing." He got up and snaked his arms around my waist, whispering in my ear, "You're amazing."

A blush crept up my chest to my cheeks. "Thank you."

I went and got changed back into my regular clothes, feeling very plain after that dress. Griffin paid, as promised, and we finished our shopping and headed back home to get ready.

Griffin's master bathroom had a double sink, so we got ready side-by-side. On more than one occasion, I caught him staring at me in the mirror.

"What are you looking at?"

"You."

"I'm nothing special to look at."

"I beg to differ."

I playfully rolled my eyes, putting the finishing touches on my makeup.

We drove to the restaurant, and I already knew what I was going to order. Call me crazy, but I always checked out the menu at a restaurant before we even left the house.

We arrived at the time of our reservation and were seated immediately in a quiet booth in the corner. As we made our way through dinner, the food just kept getting better. I wasn't sure anything could top the filet mignon and garlic mashed potatoes. If I was ever on death row, I would want that to be my last meal.

We laughed until we cried. We shared sweet kisses. Everything was utter perfection. I wanted to stay in this moment forever.

"Can I just stay here a little bit longer?" A tear fell down my cheek as I held on to Griffin in the driveway. "I'm not ready to go home yet. I feel so much better when I'm with you."

"You have your therapy appointment tomorrow."

"I can reschedule!"

"Cora…"

"Fine." I let go of him and crossed my arms. "I'll go, but can I come back next weekend?"

"Absolutely. I think it's supposed to snow, so we can just have a snow-cation."

I stood on my tippy toes and planted a kiss on his lips, "I can't wait."

"You better get on the road now before it gets too late. I know you don't like driving in the dark. Text me when you get home?"

"Will do!" I got in my car and rolled my window down.

"Hey Cora, I love you!"

My heart thumped in my chest and a smile spread across my face. "I love you too, Griffin Bethel!"

I watched as his fist-pumped the air, laughing. This is the life I wanted.

CHAPTER 34

I'VE HAD WORSE NIGHTS OF SLEEP, THAT'S FOR SURE. FOR whatever reason last night, I just couldn't fall asleep. Maybe I was still wired from Griffin's 'I love you' because I haven't stopped smiling since. Whatever the reason, I was happy that I only had a few more days of work before Christmas and I could spend more time with Griffin, just relaxing.

I took advantage of my early morning and threw on leggings and walked up to the coffee shop. I was hoping that Miranda was there so we could talk through things.

Entering the building, the coffee smell was rich and velvety and made me crave it even more than I already was. As I approached the cash register, I scanned the shop to see if Miranda was in.

"Is Miranda here today?" I asked the barista, who I hadn't seen before.

"Who?" She looked at me with big doe eyes.

"Miranda. Shorter woman, blonde hair, really sarcastic."

She looked to a barista I had seen many times before. "Miranda?"

"Miranda quit a few days ago. I thought y'all were friends, I assumed you knew."

I had been a terrible friend to her. Once she got mad for me not telling her about Griffin, I never really made an effort to make things better. I made a silent vow to myself I would call her tomorrow after work and see if she wanted to get dinner.

"Oh. Thanks for the update." I was thrown off. "Can I please have a chocolate chip muffin warmed up and a large hot latte?"

"$8.21 please."

I swiped my card and headed to a small table by the window. The world looked different today. Despite getting no sleep, the sun was shining and I felt reinvigorated. Is this what love felt like? Being mushy and happy all the time? Because if so, I was even more excited to be in love.

The barista brought my muffin and coffee over and I inhaled it. I skipped dinner last night since we had a big lunch and my blood sugar was paying for it this morning. I enjoyed a leisurely hour, scrolling on social media, before heading home and getting my workday started.

It went off without a hitch—my calls ended early, I finished up a PowerPoint deck I was working on, and it was good to feel like I had accomplished something. Safe to say, I was feeling good heading into my therapy appointment.

When the alarm on my phone went off around five, reminding me to leave, I was up and out the door immediately. I was hoping to maybe get to the bottom of these evolving nightmares. I had taken Ophelia's advice and had scaled back my hours at work, which, had helped my mental state with not feeling as overwhelmed, but I just couldn't stand not sleeping anymore. I was constantly running on fumes, and it wasn't sustainable.

I pulled into a front parking space and entered the building, knowing where to go this time. Walking over to the door, I hesitated, a little anxious, but knocked anyway before taking a step back in case a patient was already in there.

The door opened, Ophelia greeting me, "Cora! I'm so happy you came back. Please, come in."

I felt more relaxed than the last time, mainly because I now knew where I was supposed to sit.

"How have things been?" she asked. My knee bounced nervously.

"I mean, I've definitely been better."

"Want to talk about it?"

I nodded. "So, my um…boyfriend and I were almost killed last week."

Her eyes bugged out of her head.

I continued on before she could ask any questions. "Obviously, we're fine and the people responsible were arrested, but that was not a fun time. And, on top of all that, my nightmares haven't stopped. In fact, they've gotten worse—or, should I say, evolved."

"I see we have a lot to unpack today. I have my next hour free after this, so we can run over if we need to."

"We definitely might need to." I laughed nervously.

"Where would you like to start?"

I thought about it for a moment, wondering if I really needed to talk through the whole almost dying thing or if I was more scared of my nightmares. "The nightmares. I think I'm at peace since the assholes were arrested."

"Perfect. Why don't you start with the details of your last one. When was it?"

"The other night. Thursday, I believe. I don't sleep well at all anymore unless I'm with Griffin."

"And, Griffin is?"

"My…boyfriend?" It came out more like a question than a statement.

"You seem unsure." She observed.

"I don't think I am. I think it's weirder for me to say."

"After not dating someone for a long time, I understand that. Those are valid feelings to have."

"So, tell me about the dream."

"It felt more…sinister than the rest. When they first started, they were simple. I almost long for them, as silly as that is to say." I hadn't admitted that even to myself yet. "I would be chased in the woods and then stumble upon a dead body. I'd call the cops and then I'd be arrested for the murder, even though I didn't do it."

Ophelia was scribbling frantically, trying to keep up with what I was saying. When I saw her pen stop and she looked up, I knew that was my cue to continue.

"The other night was way worse. I didn't go back to sleep. I was in the woods, which, looked like the ones by my cabin. I was being chased by three people, fell and broke my leg, then was locked up in a shed next to a rotting corpse. I woke up when they came back to finish what they had started."

Her mouth hung open. "I…I don't know where to start. This is a pretty severe case." She got up and paced for a minute before heading over to a bookcase, grabbing a thick book on the shelf.

She sat back down in her chair and opened up the book, reading a few pages. "I have something I'd like to try if you're open to it. I think it might help."

"I'm willing to try anything at this point."

"Perfect. It's called IRT, Imagery Rehearsal Therapy. It's a cognitive-behavioral treatment that can help reduce the number and intensity of your nightmares."

"That works for me. What do we have to do?" I asked, ready to try anything so I could be fixed.

"It's actually pretty simple. In IRT treatment, you're reimagining your nightmares with different, less scary outcomes. What we hope to accomplish is reprograming your brain to find the nightmares to be less terrifying if they happen again."

"That sounds easy enough! Should we get started?" I asked.

"Let's get to it! Why don't you put a pillow on the arm of the couch and lie down. That'll help your body relax while you're focusing."

I grabbed the pillow that was behind my back and placed it on the couch, laying down. My back sank into the couch and my eyelids got heavy. "I might just fall asleep here and now."

"Don't do that. We need to talk through everything so you can get a good night of sleep!"

"Are you comfortable?"

"I am." I shimmed further into the couch.

"Alright, let's get started. Close your eyes and just let everything leave your mind." Ophelia's voice was soothing, comfortable. "Now. I need you to bring yourself back to Thursday's nightmare. Picture it, just like when you were in it. Tell me when you're there."

I took a deep breath, hoping that this would help. "I'm there."

"Great. Now I need you to do your best to remember what happened and start telling me what you see out loud. Can you do that?"

"So, just replay it to you?" This sounded too easy.

"Exactly. Start whenever you're ready."

"I'm in a forest, it looks like the one near my cabin. It's nighttime."

"Good, keep going."

"I hear footsteps behind me, three sets of them. They're charging me. I'm looking back and I recognize all three of them. There's Cathleen, the wife of my murdered tenant. The Coopers are also there." I opened one eye. "Those are the people that tried to kill me."

She nodded. "Close your eyes, stay in the dream."

"I'm running now. Running away from them. I trip on a fallen tree. My leg is broken. There's a bone popping out of my calf and now blood is pouring out of my leg. I can feel myself going in and out of consciousness as Mr. Cooper drags me to a shed. It's run-down and dirty. I don't know where I am, but it looks like the area where Luke was found."

I took in a deep breath. "They brought me into the shed-like structure and both Mrs. Cooper and Cathleen hold me down and bind my wrists. I'm sitting on the floor by the smallest window imaginable. I know it's not going to be easy to escape. Mr. Cooper is just standing above me, then he kicked me in the side and spit in my face. They locked the door and left."

I stopped. "I don't want to continue," I said, my eyes still closed. In my mind, I was still in the nightmare.

"Cora, you have to push through. I know this is hard, but just do your best."

"I…okay. I'm panicking. There's a weird smell. It's very strong. I've never smelled anything like it before."

"What is the smell, Cora?"

"It's foul. My stomach turned and I got sick. I just got sick, again. I know this might be a lost cause at this point, so I close my eyes, praying that the sun would rise soon. It doesn't feel like very long before the sun is poking through the tiny window. I look around to see what is causing that horrific scent—a dead body. It's a woman. Her face is familiar…"

I shot up on the couch, unable to breathe. My blood ran cold and I broke out in a cold sweat. I was in a full panic attack. My limbs were heavy, the world felt like it was caving in on me. I looked around the room and Ophelia was staring at me, on the edge of her seat.

"Cora? Cora, are you okay?"

My ears were ringing. My mouth was dry. I needed to get out of there. I grabbed my bag, leaving my coat behind, and sprinted out to my car, tears threatening to fall.

"Cora, wait! Come back!" Ophelia called from the doorway.

I sped home, shaking the entire way, my mind racing a million miles per hour.

I remember everything.

I pulled into the driveway and sprinted into my house, closing the door behind me. Back pressed up against it, I slid down, collapsing on the floor in a fit of sobs.

"What did I do?" I muttered.

I reached for my phone, dialing Griffin.

"Griff, I need you to come here. *Now.*"

"Cora, are you okay?"

I hung up.

CHAPTER 35

TWO HOURS LATER, I SAW HEADLIGHTS PULL INTO MY driveway. The door was already unlocked when Griffin burst through the door.

"Cora?" He called out breathlessly.

"Living room."

"Are you alright?" He jogged into where I was seated, his eyes falling on the table in front of me. "What's that?"

I just stared at the knife sitting on the table in front of me. "A knife."

"No shit! Are you okay? You sounded terrified on the phone."

I shook my head. "No, I'm not."

Griffin sat down next to me; his eyes worried. "Cora, please, tell me what's going on. I can't help if I don't know what the problem is."

I couldn't bring myself to stop staring at the shiny blade in front of me. "It's nothing you can help with. I just…have some answers."

"In regard to?"

"Luke Anderson."

Griffin cocked his head. "What answers? Did you find something?"

I shrugged my shoulders. "Not necessarily."

"You're scaring me now. Are you okay?"

I couldn't bring myself to get the words out. I kept opening my mouth and then shutting it.

"Cora, please."

"Griffin, I know who killed Luke."

He was visibly taken aback. "That's fantastic news!"

"No, it's not."

"What? Why?!"

"I went to therapy tonight."

He smiled, trying to take my hand in his but I wouldn't give it to him, because I held the knife tight. "I know," he said, "How did that go?"

"Good or bad, depends on how you look at it," I replied, unsure I'd want to spill the beans.

"That doesn't make any sense."

"I killed Luke." I raised my eyes to meet his.

"What? No. Stop it! This isn't funny."

"Griff, I'm not trying to be funny. Dr. Ray had me do what she called IRT. Imagery Rehearsal Therapy. I was supposed to walk through the nightmare I had the other night. It was going well until I got to the part where I was in the shed with the dead woman."

"Excuse me?" I hadn't told Griffin about this particular nightmare because I didn't want to re-live it over the weekend.

"I had a nightmare Thursday night that I was locked in a shed by Cathleen, Gina, and Eric and there was a dead woman next to me. I was recounting it and as I was, everything came flooding back to me. I killed Luke and the woman that was with me."

"Cora, you're sleep deprived, you're imagining things." Griffin's knee bounced nervously as he wrung his hands in his lap.

I shook my head again. "No, I remember it all. It came flooding back to me like a tsunami wave crashing on a beach. I came home and knew I needed to go to the Widow's Peak and look at the knife my brother found under the bed. This is what I used to kill them both."

His eyes were wide, his mouth hung open. "I—"

"You don't have to say anything. I need you to promise me that you'll make sure this house is sold. I need you to call Kendra and Miranda and tell them everything. I need you to remember me not as a monster, but as a loving girlfriend. I love you, Griffin. I'm so sorry."

"You're talking crazy! You can't even be sure of any of this. Maybe it's just another nightmare you had!" The tears were pouring out of his eyes.

"Please don't try to rationalize it. I'm going to turn myself in first thing in the morning when Detective Ambrose is back from his vacation."

"How can you be so calm about this?"

"As odd as it sounds, knowing the truth has brought me peace."

"This is crazy! Please, you can't turn yourself in. Can we at least have one more night together?"

"That's why I called you."

I snuggled into his side, resting my head on his comfortable shoulder for as long as I could. At some point during the night, we both fell asleep. The sun poked through the window and woke us up. I went upstairs and took one final shower in my beautiful, tiled shower stall. I got dressed in my favorite jeans and my hoodie that Kendra had given me all those years ago when she moved away.

"Cora, you don't have to do this."

"I know it's the truth. I took two lives; I need to pay the price."

Griffin drove to the police station; we didn't say anything. We exchanged some wordless glances in the car, saying everything we needed to. We pulled up and parked, I got out of the car immediately, the knife in a plastic bag, in my bag.

The receptionist greeted us warmly. "How can I help you today?"

I threw on the fakest smile I could, "I'm here to see Detective Ambrose."

"Oh! He just got back; he should be at his desk. You can head on over there."

"Thank you." We walked over to Ambrose's desk.

"Cora! What a surprise! I wasn't expecting to see you today."

"I wasn't anticipating being here."

"I was going to call you today. The Coopers didn't kill Harper, but they did break-in to your home, so, they'll be charged with that, too."

"Okay."

"We're still working on Luke's case though. I'm hoping we will get a lead soon."

"It was me." I dropped the knife down on his desk.

He looked up at me skeptically. "What?"

"Can we head into a private room?" I asked, motioning towards the interrogation room I had become well-acquainted with, except this time, I was the one being questioned for a crime I committed.

"Of course." He followed me to the room, closing the door. Griffin waited outside, listening through the two-way mirror.

I sat down and asked for a water. Ambrose obliged, handing it over. I took a large sip and began my confession.

"Are you recording?" I asked, ready to get this over with.

He nodded, "Cora, are you sure this is the truth?"

"Yes, it is. May I continue?"

"Whenever you're ready." His eyes were sad.

I took a deep breath and began my recorded confession. "I believe I killed them both in a stress-induced hallucination. I didn't remember any of it until I was in therapy last night working through some nightmares I've been having for a while."

"Both of them?" His head shot up, looking at me.

"Luke and Samantha Katz, the woman he was having an affair with. I vaguely remember standing out in the road on the way up to the house. I flagged down a car and asked them to help me. I told them that my daughter's foot was stuck in a rock, and she couldn't get out. I told them that I didn't have a cell phone and couldn't call for help. They pulled over to the side of the road and got out to 'help' me."

I shook my head, needing a minute before I continued.

"Take your time, Cora." Ambrose comforted. I was surprised he wasn't throwing me in handcuffs then and there.

"I had them follow me out to the middle of nowhere and that's when it happened. I stabbed Luke in the chest and then pulled the knife down, slicing him open. It mimicked how an animal would kill someone…just like Mrs. Cooper said. I took Samantha out to a shed and bound her hands and then stabbed her as well, leaving her there to die. The guy I had been seeing in my dreams was Luke. The woman in my dreams was his mistress," I said, took a deep breath and continued, "I verified on Facebook. After it happened, I used Luke's phone to message myself, covering my tracks, then went home and cleaned up, then drove back to the Widow's Peak and must have hid the knife under the bed. That last part I don't remember, but I can only deduce."

Detective Ambrose sat there and stared at me. "I can't tell if you're making this up or not. We didn't see a missing person's report for the woman."

I shrugged, "I'm not sure about that. Maybe she didn't have family or she was a flight-risk. I don't know. I can take you out to where she is. I think I could figure it out."

He swallowed hard. "Yeah, I think you should do that. We can go now. I have to handcuff you, though."

"I understand. You have my full cooperation." I shook my head. "I don't know how this happened. How did my life go from so great to so horrific so quickly?"

"I don't know. Stress will make people do crazy things. Sadly, believe it or not, this is more common than you'd think. I know I shouldn't be saying this, but it takes a lot of courage to come in here and confess all this."

"I've ruined so many people's lives over the course of the last few months. I would never be able to live with myself if I didn't."

Ambrose stood up, pulling the handcuffs off his hip, his voice shook. "Cora Lincoln, you are under arrest for the murders of Luke Anderson and Samantha Katz."

Just like that, my hands were pulled behind my back and the handcuffs were shackled to my wrists. Justice was served for those two innocent lives I took. I could've blamed the Beast until I was blue in the face, but I knew that while I was definitely seeing an animal, it wasn't the Beast. I don't know if Griffin was humoring me or not, but it was just a manifestation of everything in my own head.

The law doesn't care if you were in a stress-induced hallucination or not. I killed two people in cold blood and that was it.

I deserve whatever is to come for me.

EPILOGUE

FOLLOWING MY ARREST, I WAS REQUIRED TO LEAD THE authorities to the location where Samantha's body was hidden. We searched the woods for what felt like an eternity until we came across the trail that led us to the shed. To my surprise, it was the exact same shed that had haunted me in my nightmares, as if my subconscious had been warning me of the truth all along.

I stood outside with Ambrose as the Crime Scene Investigators went inside.

"I really screwed up, didn't I?" I asked, turning towards him, tears streaming down my face.

"I hate to say it, but yes. You took on too much and overwhelmed yourself."

"Have you called Cathleen and told her?"

"Yes, she's aware." Ambrose stared straight ahead. "When I called to tell her, she actually asked if she could come and visit you. Is that something you would consider?"

"Sure. I don't think she could say anything worse than I haven't already thought about myself."

"I'll give her a call when we get back to the station and let her know."

A few minutes later, a white body bag was being carried out of the shed. "It's exactly as Miss Lincoln had described." One of the investigators said, walking by us. "We'll continue gathering everything here. You can take her back to the station now."

They escorted me back to the police car. Detective Ambrose and I rode back almost the entire way in silence. When we were about a mile or so away, he finally spoke. "Cora?"

My mindless staring out the window was interrupted. "Yes?"

"This is me speaking to you as a person and not a detective. Stress manifests in very strange ways. I don't for a second believe that you would do this if you were in your normal lucid state of mind."

"Thank you for saying that."

We pulled back into the station's parking lot. Ambrose helped me get out and get situated in a holding cell. "Your lawyer should be here shortly. I'll come back and get you once they are."

I nodded, unsure who my lawyer was, assuming I was assigned one. Shortly after, a young woman strode in, her red-bottomed high heels clanking against the hard floor. She held her head high, perhaps because she had never committed murder. Approaching the bars of my cell, she made eye contact with me. "Cora Lincoln?"

"Yes?"

"I'm Mia Elrod. I'm your attorney." She turned her attention to the guards. "Please let her out. We need to have a conversation."

We were escorted by the guards to a room with no windows which was colder compared to the interrogation rooms I had been in before. I took a seat at the table opposite to hers.

"Were you assigned to me?"

"No. Your boyfriend, Griffin, hired me. He reached out as soon as you were arrested. He told me to tell you that he's paying for my services, so you don't need to worry about anything. I'm based out of Charlotte and am one of the best criminal attorneys in the state."

"Thanks, I guess."

She smiled. "Cora, please walk me through everything that's happened." She was all business. No cordiality.

As Mia scribbled, I recounted the story from the beginning. My nightmares before that fateful day had almost been a warning something bad was going to happen if I didn't slow down. She nodded as I finished speaking. "Thank you for filling me in. You said you thought you saw a Beast?" One of her black eyebrows raised.

"Yes, that's correct."

"Understood," she said, tapping her pen on the table while gazing at the legal pad covered in notes. "I believe the next course of action would be to conduct a psych evaluation. I can arrange for someone to meet with you tomorrow."

"What will that prove?"

"That you were in a state of stress-induced psychosis when the murders took place."

"Which means?"

"There might be an opportunity to possibly have some sort of insanity plea."

"An insanity plea?"

"Yes, there are a few different types. We can delve further into that once the evaluation has been done."

"I'm still going to jail, though, right?"

"Depending on the insanity plea. It may help you get out sooner. Based on what you just told me, you didn't have any intention on killing them. During the incident, you couldn't distinguish between reality and your nightmares," she explained, while packing her belongings. "I'll return in a few days to discuss this further."

"Thank you, Mia."

"Of course," she said and nodded in response. "Griffin is here to see you. I'll have them send him in."

My heart raced, my leg bouncing under the table. I couldn't wait to see him. He practically pulled the door off its hinges coming in.

"Cora!" he wrapped me in a hug. "I never imagined we'd end up like this."

Tears streamed from both of our faces.

"I know. This isn't exactly how I planned my life would go." I wiped the tears away with my handcuffed hands. I watched as Griffin's eyes trailed towards the handcuffs, making him cry harder. "They're going to have me undergo a psychological evaluation to see if that will lessen my time here."

"You weren't aware of what you were doing. I think that's a prime candidate for it."

I shrugged, "I don't know. I understand the whole under psychosis thing, but I ruined people's lives. I killed two people, Griff! This doesn't go away. I deserve to be here for the rest of my life."

"Don't say that! You didn't know!"

"That's not an excuse." I deadpanned.

"What does this mean for us?" Griff asked, as his head glanced at the floor.

I raised his face, and let his eyes meet mine. "Do you really want to put the rest of your life on hold because your girlfriend is in prison for killing people?"

He thought about it for a moment. "For you, absolutely. I know the real you, Cora. I'll wait forever for you."

"I love you to the ends of the universe, but I need you to be happy. You need your happily ever after." My heart shattered into a billion pieces.

"You're my happily ever after. Stop talking like this." His voice was stern.

"Let me ask you this, are you okay if this is how our entire relationship goes? Visits once per week? No warm, cozy home.

No kids running around. Everything we talked about is off the table now."

"You're my person, Cora Lincoln. I will do whatever I need to in order to spend my life with you, even if it means supervised visits once per week."

I was sobbing now, unable to form words.

The door opened, the same guard who brought me in here was summoning me now. "Time's up. Cora, time to head back."

Griffin got up and gave me a long kiss on the top of the head. "I love you."

"I love you, too." He started for the door. "Griffin! I have one last question."

He turned to face me. "Shoot?"

"Why did you play along when I was convinced what we saw was the Beast?" I asked with concern in my voice.

He stood quiet for a few seconds, then, he spoke, "To be honest, whatever it was, which in my opinion was something," he said and continued, "It didn't look like anything I had ever seen before. It was an animal that hadn't been discovered before."

"Or was it, though—" I said, trying to convince myself.

The following day, they ushered me into the same room where Cathleen already sat with her hands folded on the table. I braced myself for whatever verbal assault she had in store for me.

"Hello, Cora."

As I sat across from her, a small smirk danced on Cathleen's lips. "Hi, Cathleen. Listen, I'm so sorry. I don't have any excuses for—"

She cut me off, before I could finish, "Shh. Let me talk first. The only reason I'm here today is because I wanted to thank you."

"Thank me? For what?"

"I wanted to thank you for doing my dirty work for me."

"I'm confused."

She smirked. "I know, isn't that the beauty of life?"

"What?"

"Cora. Cora. Cora, you have no idea how free I feel."

"Again, what—"

"Well, being of my status, you wouldn't understand where I was coming from. Coming off as the loving and doting wife, whom I thought, I had a loving husband. But when I heard he was killed, my prayers were answered, in the most, not subtle way of course, but you get what I am saying, don't you?"

"I'm not following…"

"Okay," she said, and looked towards the door. "Do you know if there are any recording devices in here?" She looked around the room.

I shrugged while shaking my head. "I don't know. I have no idea."

"Hmm." She got up and circled the room, searching for something, then sat back down. "Anyway, thank you for killing Luke and Samantha."

"What?!" My eyes went wide. "Come again?"

"No matter how many times I brought it up, to Luke, he'd always deny any affair. I was actually coming up to the cabin to catch them in the act. I wasn't sure how it was going to go, but I was ready to slit their throats."

I blinked at her in confusion. "So, you're what? Thanking me… for killing your husband and his mistress…?"

"Yep!" She said gleefully. "Like I said, you did the dirty work for me."

I stared at her with wide eyes. "I'm not sure how to respond to all this."

"No response needed. I just wanted to stop by and ease your conscience."

"You didn't do that. You've confused me even more. I think you should leave now."

"As you wish." Cathleen stood up, pushing her chair in. "For what it's worth, I hope you don't die in here. You seem like a nice person."

Her stilettos clicked on the tile as she walked out of the room, leaving the door wide open.

What the actual fuck?

BONUS CHAPTER

Griffin

I T MIGHT NOT HAVE BEEN A LONG RELATIONSHIP, BUT MY dedication to Cora has been unwavering ever since her trial. She was sentenced to prison, as well as state-mandated psychiatric evaluations.

When she was on trial and had to testify, she was finally able to string all the pieces together. The knife her brother James found wasn't one of Cora's but was identified by Cathleen as the one Luke carried with him when he went out of town.

While that raised some red flags, ultimately Cora remembered the entire event and how it played out that Saturday of Luke's arrival. She had left her house and hadn't remembered anything after that—she only remembers pulling back into her driveway.

Sitting in the courtroom as Cora sat up there and recalled the most traumatic experience of her life, I couldn't help but look over at Cathleen. She was happy both Luke and his mistress were gone, and someone had done the dirty work for her.

No one understands why I've stayed with Cora, but the truth

is, I really do care for her and often think about the life we could have had together. That's why I go to visit her as much as I can. I even moved into Cora's house to be closer to her, making the occasional trip to Charlotte for work.

After Cora was arrested, I reached out to her family and friends to let them know what had happened. Kendra flew out immediately to support her friend as best as she could, in the process, also helped me through the trenches.

After stopping by The Higher Ground to talk to Miranda, they told me she no longer worked there. The staff were kind enough to provide the address of her new workplace. It was a library located down the street.

She didn't want to talk to me, when I showed up to her new workplace. It was because she claimed Cora had abandoned her as soon as I came into the picture, but after stopping in two times per day for a week, she finally agreed to talk with me.

I told her about Cora's situation and her face stayed cold. She didn't care. I pressed for answers until she told me she had a feeling something was wrong. Since, she was slowly stating to make a name for herself in Byglass County, she didn't want it spoiled by Cora and her "episodes" as she called it.

Miranda told me she had been trying to get Cora to seek help, just to talk through her stress, but since Cora didn't feel it was necessary, Miranda gave up. After I entered the picture, that was Miranda's prime time to create some distance.

A shitty thing to do, if you ask me (what friend does that).

When people ask me about the night, I spent exploring the forest with Cora, I struggle to find the right words at what we encountered. It was unlike anything known to man; a massive creature, roughly the size of a bear, towered before us on two legs.

Its black skin was completely covered in fur, and its eyes were a bright white, completely devoid of pupils. When the creature looked directly at us, it saw straight into my soul.

In that moment, fear consumed me as I had no idea what kind of harm it could do to us. Without any other explanation, I attributed the creature to the Beast.

Looking back now, the creature we encountered in the forest was most likely just a large breed of bear I had never seen before. However, there were still so many unanswered questions. What was responsible for the deep scratch marks on Cora's hallway window? The Coopers were not responsible for the deaths of Harper and Luke. How were they able to easily overpower us? What truth was the small town of Byglass hiding?

Unfortunately, I'll never have the answers I need to find peace with this situation. It doesn't mean I haven't been doing my research. I am convinced something out there exists, concealed within the shadows of the night. I spend one night per week up at The Widow's Peak hoping to catch a glimpse of whatever it was we saw.

Maybe the Beast isn't real.

Maybe it's just a manifestation of our fears.

Maybe we're all the Beast.

ABOUT THE AUTHOR

 Ashley has always loved to write, it didn't matter what it was. It could be a short story, full-length book, or to-do list, as long as words are coming out of her brain and onto paper, she loves it.

Working as an IT Project Manager by day, Ashley uses any free time in the evenings to write. She lives in South Carolina with her husband, Ross, and her two dogs - Teddy and Lilly. Ashley's favorite genres to both read and write are romance and thrillers.

When her nose isn't in a book, you can find her watching true crime documentaries or wishing she was at the beach.

Connect with Ashley:

Instagram: www.instagram.com/the_shelf_love
Facebook: www.facebook.com/groups/ashleymcconnell

OTHER BOOKS

No Proof

Made in the USA
Monee, IL
30 March 2023

30875652R00155